CURSED

NIGHTWIND PACK, BOOK 3

LAURANN DOHNER

KELE MOON

Editor: Kelli Collins

Cover Artist: Dar Albert

Ebook ISBN: 978-1-7342109-2-7

Paperback ISBN: 978-1-7342109-3-4

1

---

*S*hawna Paltner never thought she'd return to Hollow Mountain.

She'd fled sixteen years before and swore to herself that she would never come back.

Never say never.

She climbed out of the Jeep slowly and reached behind the seat. It only took her moments to prepare herself. She released the safeties of all four weapons and shoved each one back into the holsters strapped to her body. Next, she removed her loose trench coat from the Jeep, put it on, and pulled out her long red ponytail so it hung down her back.

Shawna slammed the driver's-side door before she could change her mind and hightail it out of there. She wasn't the sweet, naive girl she once was. Not that she'd ever been, really. Life had thrown her a pile full of bullshit since the start, but these days she gave it back tenfold. She slipped on her sunglasses last, and then observed the bar with apprehension.

The Barn.

The bar had been around for as long as she could remember. Her parents, the ones who'd adopted her after her birth parents had died in a car accident, had frequented this place.

It was a local hangout for werewolves.

She knew things in Hollow Mountain didn't change much. Time had brought in new homes and more people, but it was still werewolf territory.

Rosa and Henry Markum had taken her in when she was nine years old. They had two teenage boys, but no daughters. Ralph and Morgan had been thirteen and fourteen years old, respectively, when Shawna came to live with them. She had instant hero worship for her new older brothers, and they looked after her. She adored both boys, but she knew within the first week that her adoptive family was different. Two teenage werewolves were an impossible secret to keep from the human child living in their home. They weren't old enough to hide it like their parents did.

Maybe it had been her young age, but she'd taken the existence of shifters as a reality easily. So much so, she had actually fallen in love with a werewolf in her teens...but she refused to let her mind focus on that.

That girl who'd fallen in love with the tall, blond wolf with beautiful blue eyes and an easy laugh had died a lifetime ago. She'd perished in a small corner of the vast woods that surrounded Hollow Mountain one summer afternoon at the young and tender age of fifteen.

Shawna took a deep breath and blew it out. Then she rolled her shoulders and marched toward the bar. She called home rarely, since they all agreed it was safer, but four days before she'd talked to her adopted parents for the first time in over a year.

That's when she'd learned about Ralph.

Pain stabbed through her as she remembered her adoptive mother telling her, through tears, that he'd been dead and buried for a long nine months. Ralph had been her family. She'd loved him as if they'd been blood. His life had been wrongly taken and she was about to be avenged.

She pushed open the door to the bar and stopped inside as it swung shut behind her. Shawna's vision adjusted to the dim room easily with her specially tinted sunglasses to help her see in darker places. The lightened lenses had reflective capabilities with mirrored interiors. They were expensive, but worth every penny. Her gaze slowly roamed the bar from left to right.

The inside of the bar hadn't changed much, with the pool tables sitting deep in the back. A dance floor area was dead center along the back wall and the long, curved bar sat to the left. Tables filled the space between on all sides. She knew the place would be packed on a Friday night. The sun hadn't gone down yet, so it wasn't standing room only, but the seats were filled.

She ticked off a headcount of men. There were at least forty-six of them in the room. She searched out women next, only finding twelve. Some things never changed. The men outnumbered the women by far.

She scanned the room once more and spotted her target. He was from the same pack that her adoptive family used to belong to, but he'd been a teenager the last time she'd seen him. It didn't matter. He still looked like the same thick, dumb werewolf, only taller and buffer.

Shawna ignored the soft sniffing she heard around her. She saw heads popping up and turning her way. She clenched her teeth. Her fingers itched to reach inside her coat, but she kept her hands calmly at her sides. Her body was tense, but she outwardly hid that fact. She commanded her hammering heart to slow. She knew predatory wolves like the one she was hunting loved the smell of fear and female. They were sick that way. It turned most of them on.

Her target lifted his head fully and grinned.

Shawna wanted to wipe that smile off his face. She stopped about six feet from the table, keeping the heavy wood surface between her and her target. Weres had the ability to move inhumanly fast. They were amazingly strong too. She knew a lot about fighting shifters these days.

She smiled in earnest. *Hell*, she thought, *this should be fun*.

He'd never been her favorite werewolf, even before he killed her brother.

"Hello, Merl," she drawled loudly. "How are you today?"

Merl's grin faded. "Do I know you?"

She'd anticipated him not recognizing her, planned on it, actually. Everything from her body shape, to hair color, to her eyes were different than what he would remember.

"No, but I've heard things. I came a long way to say hi to you, baby."

He blinked, looking unsure, but then he smirked again. Merl hefted up his large frame until he was on his feet. He looked and dressed like a biker, and it took genuine effort for Shawna not to roll her eyes. It seemed that a lot of the wannabe badass shifters thought the biker look was in. Her gaze flew over his leather jacket, the t-shirt that was tucked into a tight pair of jeans, and his black leather boots.

"Tell me what you heard." His voice dropped into a soft growl. "Was I that good?"

She wanted to flinch, but she got in his face instead. "Not by a long shot. Actually, I heard you were about the worst damn lay a woman ever had. Kind of pathetic, to be frank with you, Merl. It was just sad and sorry to hear. You put all your kind to shame. I'd tuck that sorry excuse of a dick you have between your legs and go hide somewhere if I *were* you." She drew out the word *were*, pronouncing it like *ware*, implying werewolf instead.

He snarled and showed teeth. His beefy hands clenched at his side and a low growl tore from his throat. "Who the fuck are you? That's the stupidest thing anyone has ever said to me."

Shawna saw movement and her gaze darted to the side for a fraction of a second. A few of the men had stood. They didn't move for her though. If they did, she'd react. As a warning, she decided to say something to try to dissuade his pack mates from coming to his rescue.

"My fight isn't with anyone but Merl here. Back off, please."

The male bartender was frowning. "What's going on?"

"Merl and I have something to settle," Shawna said loudly, and moved her jacket, showing off her weapons. "I'd clear the bar if I were you. Emphasis on the *were* and who needs to be cleared."

"Clear them out," the bartender called out after a few stunned seconds. "Now. Move it!"

Yeah, it's still a were bar.

She saw most people leaving, being ushered out by some of the other patrons, but half a dozen stayed. The whole time, she stood there staring at Merl, who never once stopped glaring back.

The bartender walked over to a table on the far side and grabbed a man whose head rested on his arm. The bartender said something softly to the drunk, and then ended up dragging him out with help from another werewolf. Shawna waited while they cleared out the last of the humans.

A man sitting at a table about ten feet from her inhaled. "You're human."

She inclined her head. "I sure am."

"But you know about us." It wasn't a question. It was a statement. "You don't want to mess with Merl there, honey. Did he promise to mate you and then take off? Merl is just like that. He's always going after a piece of tail."

A man behind her but far enough away to not worry about laughed. "I don't smell pregnancy on her. Too bad. I'd love to see Merl taken down by a little redheaded mate."

"Forget that," another one laughed. "Don't mate her. Leave her for the rest of us. She smells damn good. I'll fight for a chance with her."

The bartender hesitantly took a few steps toward Shawna. "Listen, little girl. You need to leave. This isn't Disneyland, and we're not some tour for you to be walking through. Merl is trouble. I'll cover your back while you head out the way you came in."

She gave him a dark smile. "Thanks, but I don't need your help leaving here."

Shawna caught movement out of the corner of her reflective glasses. A man was inching up behind her, probably a friend of Merl's, or just some stupid werewolf with a desire to grab her.

She moved quickly and dropped her trench coat, going for her weapons. She reached for her .45 Winchester Magnum in the shoulder harness under her breast with her left hand as she slipped her right down to grab the other semi-automatic from a belt around her waist. She cleared the holsters and turned slightly, aiming one gun at Merl, and the other at the man behind her.

"I wouldn't do that," she warned loudly.

She heard a few sharp intakes of breaths around the room. The bartender backed up slowly. He softly cursed. "What in the hell?"

"Rambitch." Someone whistled. "Four guns. I'm impressed."

She smiled tightly. "Actually, six. I also have five throwing knives strapped...somewhere."

Another werewolf in the corner table took a deep breath. "What the fuck did you do now, Merl? The woman is loaded for bear."

"Never bear," Shawna said. "I'm loaded for wolf." She cocked her head at Merl. "You're going to look nice stuffed on my mantel, Merl. Want to be a good boy and change for me so you'll look even prettier in fur up there?"

A man at a corner table slowly stood up.

Shawna cut her gaze to him, really paying attention to his face—and felt a jolt when she recognized this particular werewolf. He'd been a teenage pup the last time she'd seen him, a nice one, but he was more than full grown now...and she hated that she couldn't trust him.

"Don't do it." Shawn adjusted the gun from Merl to a spot between them, knowing her old friend wouldn't recognize her any more than Merl did. "Sit your cute ass down, Wolfy, and mind your own business. I don't want you to get hurt."

He didn't sit, instead, he slowly raised his hands, palms out. "You know bullets are just going to piss a shifter off if you shoot him, don't you? It'll only be more dangerous for you."

"Silver-wrapped casings. They'll blow through his body and the silver will make it harder for him to heal. I guess I should also mention I'm an excellent shot. I don't miss. A few well-aimed bullets will solve all his problems—permanently."

"I'm Jason," he introduced himself, though she already knew who he was. It was the next part that surprised her. "I'm an enforcer for the Nightwind pack. If Merl has somehow offended you, why don't we go before our alpha? He'll hear you out. I'll personally assure you that no one will harm you if you just put your guns down."

She shook her head, her stomach lurching at the thought of the once-kind teen being an enforcer now. They were the quickest, hardest, meanest wolves of the pack, handpicked by an alpha to do their dirty work. Jason seemed the same, straightforward and honest, but that was the thing about shifters—they could change.

"No thanks. I'm familiar with your alpha, and I'd love to put a bullet in him too. Not to be cliché, but the only way you're getting my guns from me is if you take them from my cold, dead hands." She paused. "Good luck with that."

In her reflective glasses, Shawna saw the man behind her move, taking a step toward her as if to attack.

On instinct, she lowered her gun and shot him in the thigh without fully taking her gaze off Jason. The sound was loud and her would-be attacker howled, crashing to the floor.

Every man left in the place, seven of them with the exception of the one holding his bleeding thigh, was on their feet now.

"Woman," Jason growled, sounding shocked she dared pull the trigger. "I won't tell you again. Put down your weapons and I won't harm you. I'll take you before our alpha and you can explain your issues with Merl to him. That's how we do things here."

"I don't even know this crazy human," Merl assured him.

She flashed her gaze toward Merl. "Two words for you. Ralph Markum."

She watched as Merl paled and cast a concerned look toward Jason.

"Ralph Markum?" Jason frowned. "He isn't here anymore. He moved away a long time ago. No one's heard from him in years."

"He's dead," she said softly. "Merl killed him nine months ago over in Reddly."

Jason turned to Merl with a snarl. "That better not be true, and you *definitely* better not make shit up, because I'll know. You were never good at hiding that scared scent of lies."

"It wasn't here," Merl huffed in a grudging confession. "And it's nobody's business."

"You killed an ex-pack member? Why in the hell didn't you say something?" Jason's voice took on a low, animalistic growl. "I liked Ralph."

"Tell them why you killed him, Merl. Tell them how you attacked that girl in Reddly—the human you raped—and when Ralph tried to step in and help her, tell your enforcer how you killed him. Go ahead and explain that one, asshole." Shawna clenched her teeth and kept staring at Merl, but spoke to the enforcer as she whispered, "He killed Ralph for being a decent wolf who tried to protect a human. Did I mention she wasn't even twenty-one? She was walking home from college, not a care in the world...until Merl showed up. Now I get to watch him die for it."

"Can you prove this?" Jason still sounded more wolf than human.

"I sure can," she assured him. "Call anyone in Reddly. Talk to Ralph's folks. The girl escaped because Ralph didn't die easy. It took asshole over here a little time to fight him. She made it to safety and told the police what Ralph said to her attacker. Ralph called him by name. He told him to go back home and stay out of Reddly or he'd call the alpha. The police are looking for a man named Merl. Check that out.

"I heard the story through the grapevine and I *knew* who the hell did it. The girl even gave a description. I showed her a picture of his driver's license. She identified Merl instantly from a photo lineup of twelve men. No doubt in her traumatized head that I'm staring at the right asshole."

Merl just growled at her, like there were no human words vile enough for what he thought of her.

Jason just stared at him in shock. "What have you done, Merl?"

Merl huffed, and changed his tune, his voice becoming slightly whinny, "That's not all of what happened, she's got the facts wrong."

"Lying sack of shit," Shawna spat. "You killed Ralph. That's all I need to know. It's just a little extra pleasure for me that I get to take out a rapist in the name of revenge. Those are always my favorite."

"What are you?" Merl snarled. "Ralph's human piece of ass? You think you're avenging some lost love? Since you know so much about wolves, you do realize if he gave a shit about you, he would have mated you."

"I *know* how much he loved me." Shawna's voice cracked when she said it. "And now I'm going to show you how much I love *him*."

She opened fire.

The first bullet struck Merl in the face. The bloody destruction would've killed a human, but she walked forward as he went down and fired in all the major points, head, heart, stomach, and groin.

Determined to do the job right, she emptied the rest of the magazine into his chest. He wasn't going to heal up from that. Once the mag was empty, Shawna glared at Merl's bloody body with the ringing of gunfire still vibrating in her ears.

It never felt as satisfying as she thought it should, but this time, at least she did right by Ralph. He'd been a good brother. She owed him this.

Two of the shifters behind Shawna lunged toward her. She fired the gun in her left hand. At the same time, she dropped the empty one in her right, before she went for the sawed-off shotgun strapped to her back. She shot both her would-be attackers in the legs with buckshot, knowing wounds like that would be easily survivable for shifters. It was only when vital organs were taken out repeatedly that silver bullets worked. These injuries wouldn't cause any lasting damage, but they still went down screaming and cursing.

She turned so her back was to the wall and watched the men left standing. Jason hadn't moved. The pack enforcer had just stood there and watched her kill Merl and maim his defenders, which was a very un-enforcer-like thing for Jason to do.

That was something.

"Okay." She swiped her tongue over her bottom lip. "Now, I'm ready to leave. I'd like all of you boys to walk," she glanced at the three on the floor, "or crawl toward the pool tables. I apologize for leaving a mess at your door. I usually clean up my own kills, but he *was* your mess to begin with." Her gaze went to Jason. "Call Reddly before you decide to do your alpha's bidding like these fools and hunt me down for taking out a pack mate. Merl was guilty as hell. I want to believe you have a sense of right and wrong. He killed someone I loved, and now it's an even slate."

"Maybe." Jason kept his hands up. "But you know we can't let you walk out of here."

She lifted one of her guns pointedly. "You don't have much choice in the matter."

"If what you say is true, you'll be fine, but our alpha will have to clear this before we let you go."

"Oh, honey. Is that what you think? You'll *never* get me to your alpha. I'll shoot every single one of you to get out of here. No sweat." She didn't want to shoot Jason, he'd been a nice pup once, so she warned him, "I've been wolf hunting for over a decade, and I haven't survived this long by making mistakes. I did your boys a favor by only shooting them in the legs. I don't want to seriously hurt them or you, but I will."

Shawna saw Jason narrow his eyes in concern. "Wolf hunting?"

"Every pack has a Merl. Or worse. I tend to even out the odds between my kind and yours by taking out your rabid doggies."

He was silent for several heartbeats. "You leave it like this without speaking to our alpha, and we'll have to come after you. I don't want that, and you don't either."

Shawna tilted her head and questioned, "So, you're going to hunt me for killing a rapist? For getting justice on a rabid asshole who murdered a good wolf to protect a human? Do you ever once use that doggy brain of yours and think that might be fucked up? That grabbing a woman and raping her might be a little wrong? Do you still have free thought, or did your alpha finally beat it out of you?"

"What are you talking about?" He frowned. "We don't allow our wolves to rape humans."

She snorted. "Sure, you don't."

"*We don't.* Our alpha would have killed Merl himself if what you're saying is true. This is not normal Nightwind behavior."

Anger gripped Shawna. "Really, Jason?" She shoved her sawed off shotgun back into the holster on her back, freeing her hand, but kept ahold of her semi-automatic. She'd shoot anyone who moved toward her. She reached for the front of her jeans and unzipped them. Anger made her hands shake as she tore her jeans open and lifted up her tank top. She turned around, showing him her lower back. "Want to say that again?"

She stared at him over her shoulder, seeing Jason's gaze drop to her exposed back and the skin just above her black thong undies. She knew what made him pale. Claw marks that deep never healed over well, especially on humans. His horrified gaze flew up to her face with unspoken knowing.

"He'd have to kill *himself* first. These are from *your* alpha." She zipped her jeans and left her shirt un-tucked as she looked back to him. She pointed her semi-automatic at Jason. "Now I'm leaving. If anyone tries to stop me, I won't be shooting legs anymore. I have no fight with you, now that Merl is taken care of, so don't make me hurt you too. I just wanted Merl. Too bad he didn't shift as requested. I was serious about wanting to mount his furry head on my mantel. It would have looked nice with the five other ones I have up there—the worst offenders. Now clear a path, *enforcer*. I'm done here. Keep your pack in line and I won't ever breeze through your territory again."

Jason was still frowning, but he didn't move to stop her. "Everyone back away from her and do what she says."

"She killed Merl," one of them growled. "We just let were-hunters take us out now? We don't fight back anymore?"

"I said back away and let her walk," Jason snarled, glaring at the werewolf who'd spoken.

They walked or crawled toward the pool tables, all but Jason. He stood by his table, hands open, palms out, and silently watched her.

Shawna moved slowly; her gun trained so she could shoot anyone who came at her. She stepped back toward her coat and slowly reached for it. She tossed it over her arm. It would be a serious error in judgement to leave it. They'd use it to get her scent, instead of relying on memory alone, and losing them would be much more difficult. She didn't make rookie mistakes like that twice. She also grabbed her discarded gun and backed toward the door.

"We'll find you if you lied about Merl," Jason warned.

"Yeah, but I'm not a liar. That's not my way. Again, sorry about the mess on the floor. I tried to get him alone, but he practically lives at this bar. I have to be somewhere tomorrow, so I didn't really have a choice."

Jason shrugged. "We know how to clean up messes."

"Then why am I here?" She snorted in disbelief. "You should have cleaned him up a long time ago. He's been doing shit like this forever. He was always like that."

Jason frowned. "How do you know Merl?"

"I've just heard things."

"Who are you?"

"A ghost," she answered softly before she backed out the door.

2

*J*azz stared down at the bloody corpse that had once been Merl. *Go fucking figure this shit goes down on Desmon's day off.* Now Jazz was stuck with the mess.

Clearly it was not the day to be head alpha in charge.

Jazz removed his sunglasses and turned to look at Jason. "Explain fast."

Jason walked over to glower down at Merl's body. He curled his lip with distaste. "A human woman came storming in after Merl, claiming he killed Ralphour Ralph. Even if he left a long time ago, pack is pack. Merl had no right to do that."

Shock tore through Jazz when he realized what Jason was telling him. "Are you talking about Ralph Markum?"

Jason solemnly nodded.

"He's dead? Are you sure?"

"She was his girlfriend." Jason shrugged. "And her story wasn't hard to believe. She smelled honest. She seemed real torn up about it."

Jazz put his hands in his pockets to hide the shake in them. "Okay, let's hear the story, then."

"She claimed Merl raped a college girl in Reddly, only Ralph being Ralph, he stepped in and tried to save her. Like I said, it was easy to believe, sounds like something both of 'em would do. Merl's always been a waste of space," Jason spat. "She also claimed to hunt wolves. She wanted Merl here to change so she could mount him on her mantel along with a few other furry heads from earlier hunts. Those are her words, and I tend to believe that woman when she says she's got some of us stuffed on a wall. Damn, was she good with those guns. Ralph must've taught her. They were always his thing."

Jazz rubbed a hand over his face, trying to will the wolf under the surface to calm down. That name brought up so many painful memories, staying in skin was almost difficult.

He took another deep breath. "You believe her?"

Jason nodded. "Merl scented of lies as much as she smelled honest. His heart was beating so loud, I know I wasn't the only one to hear it."

"The Markums were always human friendly, and Ralph did like guns." Jazz groaned, feeling a wash of shame that it was one of his wolves to kill Ralph. It made everything so much worse.

"I thought of calling Des instead," Jason admitted softly. "But, you said—"

"No, let him enjoy his day off with his mate and son. He deals with enough shit. You and the guys need to clean up this mess before he sees it." Jazz stared at the one wolf with a bleeding hole in his thigh "And call the doc, someone needs to take Aaron to his place to dig the bullet out. This is a mess."

"She wasn't shitting about using silver casings," growled Aaron, the male by the pool table still holding his injured leg. "My leg won't stop bleeding."

"You probably shouldn't have let her do that," Jazz whispered under his breath to Jason. "You're telling me you didn't have one chance to stop her? You're on duty, asshole. You're paid to be an enforcer."

"He's okay." Jason dismissed Aaron before looking back at Jazz. "One silver-cased bullet won't kill him."

"Fuck you, Jason!" Aaron grunted.

Jason rolled his eyes, before he grew suddenly serious again. "When you call Desmon, you should ask him about that woman. She's saying things about him, which is the other reason why I decided to tell you instead of him."

Jazz frowned at Jason with confusion. "What things?"

"When I tried to explain to her that our alpha would need to talk to her, she freaked. Then, she unzipped her jeans and showed us the claw marks on her lower back, definitely from one of us." Jason swallowed hard. "She said our alpha was the one who gave them to her."

Shocked, Jazz grunted in denial. "She's lying."

"I know that, but one of our kind *did* mark her up." Jason sighed, obviously uncomfortable, since he had a human mate at home he worried about. "She was a small thing, and those scars were deep. Whoever did that didn't expect her to live."

"Great." Jazz grit his teeth. "And she accused Desmon?"

"Yeah, and the thing is…" Jason seemed to hesitate before he sighed heavily. "She smelled honest about that too. Real honest."

"It *never* happened. I've known him my entire life. You have too. He'd never hurt a woman. Ever. You're trying to tell me he marked her? She's lying about who did it."

"Maybe she has the wrong alpha," Jason suggested. "She's human. She might think this area belongs to the Goodwins. Maybe she thinks Leroy is our alpha. We *are* in neutral territory."

"Isn't anyone going after Rambitch?" Aaron growled impatiently.

Jazz arched an eyebrow. "Rambitch?"

"She's mean and loaded to the teeth with weapons," Aaron almost whined. "And my damn leg is still bleeding. It should have stopped by now."

Brandon bent over and lifted a piece of paper off the ground. "Rambitch forgot something. It fell out of her coat when she dropped it." He unfolded the paper, then cursed before he held it up for Jazz to see. "Look. It's Benny Boon. He's part of the Baker pack."

Jazz studied the paper copy of a blown-up driver's license photo and yanked his phone out of his back pocket. He searched his contacts, found the right one, and hit call. It rang a few times before someone answered.

"Hey, Nightwinds," came the low, raspy voice of Alpha Terry Baker. "Are you finally ready to get out of your territory for the full moon and accept the invite? You know we always have room for more out here."

"Thanks, but this is a business call." Jazz rubbed at the back of his neck as he tried to make his voice casual. "We had something strange go down over here and I was wondering if Benny Boon was okay?"

"Damn." The alpha growled. "What'd he do now?"

"We had a were-hunter blow into our bar tonight and take out one of ours who'd gotten in some trouble. The hunter dropped a picture of Benny on the way out, so I thought I'd give you the heads up and ask if he's still alive and kicking."

"Yeah, he's kicking all right." The growl was still heavy in Terry's voice. "Pain in my ass. Who'd you lose?"

Jazz sighed, and admitted, "It was Merl."

"I knew Merl. He used to wander over here sometimes. Made me glad he was your problem." Terry almost seemed relieved of the reminder that the Nightwinds had assholes too. "Do I offer my condolences?"

"You don't have to. It wasn't a great loss." Jazz flinched and turned to see if Merl's buddies were paying attention while one of them still sat on the floor bleeding. "Has Benny been in any significant trouble lately?"

"Yeah, I just had to bail him out of jail last week. Can you believe that? Dumbass got caught by humans. He attacked a woman while he was drunk, right out in the open. He roughed her up pretty good when she turned him down. He's facing charges on it, and his ma expects me to deal with human courts to save him. You don't want to know how much those lawyers costall to make sure he's not locked up and doesn't expose our kind to humans."

Jazz warned, "You better find Benny before that hunter does. It seems someone doesn't take too well to our kind messing around with human women. That's what Merl was guilty of. Human law enforcement was hunting for him up in Reddly. It probably sent up the same red flag."

"I ain't gonna look that hard. If it wasn't for Benny's ma, trust me, that wolf would've gone missing a long time ago. I promised her I wouldn't kill him since she's a sweetheart. I never promised I'd stop someone *else* from taking him out." Terry didn't sound too bothered one way or the other. "So, are you coming up for the running? Stay the week, bring a few of your wolves out of their territory for a while. It's good for them to try new things."

"If the invitation's open," Jazz tried not to wince as he said it, "we might take you up on it."

"Okay, then, I'll tell my pack." He sounded way too pleased. "You know the bitches will be excited. You need to get out more. It's not good for an alpha to stay lonely like you do."

"Yeah, I'll talk to you later, Baker." Jazz hung up, knowing Jason's wolf senses let him hear the entire conversation. "I guess I'm going to the Bakers for the running. I want to talk to this were-hunter. If she's carrying Benny's picture, he might be her next target."

"Might be." Jason gave him a look. "But you know I can't go with you to the Bakers for the running. Nothing against them, but they're just a little too free for my tastes. There's no fucking way I'm taking Brandi out there."

"Don't worry about it. I'm going to go hunt up Benny myself." Jazz did need to handle this on his own. He owed the Markums a hell of a lot, and if this hunter was Ralph's girlfriend, Jazz would try to protect her. "I'll take Miles with me. It'll give him something to do for the full moon."

Jason didn't look convinced. "If that's what you want to do."

"It is. Someone lock that door before a human wanders in. Put up the closed sign, Nester," Jazz ordered the bar owner, and then walked toward the back. "I'm using your office."

Nester nodded, waving him off as he locked up the bar and directed the men to the cleaning supplies. Jazz walked into Nester's small office and eased his large frame into the chair behind the cluttered desk. He stared at his phone, hesitating, and then dialed Desmon on his day off.

Desmon answered, laughing. "What's up?"

Jazz couldn't help but smile. "What's up with you? Why are you so happy?"

"Drew took his first steps today. I'll send you the video. Amber was filming it, got too excited, and tripped. It's funny as hell. I was about to rub the soreness out of her ass to make up for laughing at her. Can I call you back? Drew's down for his nap." Desmon let out a low, playful growl and warned, "Our window is narrow, Jazz."

"Merl's dead."

The laughter died in Desmon's voice. "How?"

"Oh my God." Amber's voice echoed over Desmon's grunt on the other end, since she was a werewolf now and had hearing as good as the rest of them. "This is going to drag up all of Katie's old issues. Not that I'll miss Merl, but yeah, how?"

Jazz understood. Merl used to date Katie, Amber's human sister, and it didn't end well for them.

Jazz took a deep breath. "A human were-hunter came into the bar. She shot a few of ours to keep them from defending Merl. They'll be fine. He sure won't be. The gun she used had silver-cased bullets."

The silence on the other end of the phone was lengthy, before Desmon grunted in shock. "A were-hunter? I haven't heard of one of those in...forever. And did you say it was a woman? A human woman? Are you sure she wasn't a vampire?"

"Jason saw it. The hunter is human," Jazz assured him. "I think he knows what they smell like. He *is* mated to one."

"Fine, smartass, then what the hell is going on?"

"I don't know, but it gets worse."

"How?" Desmon growled the words. "If she thinks she's coming after all of us, she'll be very disappointed."

"No, that's not it. She just wanted Merl. She claimed he raped a college girl in Reddly, which I tend to believe. The hunter said Merl killed Ralph Markum for stepping in to help the human." He paused, knowing Desmon would comprehend way too much when he admitted, "The hunter was Ralph's girlfriend, Des. This was revenge for his death."

"Fuck." Desmon grunted. "That is worse."

"That family has been through too much already," Jazz whispered miserably.

"How are *you*?" Desmon's voice was low with concern. There was a rustle of him crawling out of bed before he asked, "I know this is probably hitting you hard."

Jazz shut his eyes. "Well, it's not hitting soft, that's for sure. Now Ralph's dead, and according to this woman, one of our wolves did it. What are the fucking chances? It's like we're all cursed."

"We'll send someone out there to find Ralph's parents and offer them Merl's body." Desmon didn't hesitate to make that proposal. "Or invite them to the burning so they can see that he's really dead. We owe them that. They probably won't want to come back, but we should extend the offer anyway."

Jazz bit his lip, feeling the wolf stir in the back of his mind, stealing his grip on reality. "Do you think I should ask them about her? If they've heard from her? I know it's not the best time, but—"

Desmon softly growled. "Don't do this to yourself, Jazz. You *know* she died that day, even if you didn't get the closure of seeing her body. I'm so damn sorry."

"Yeah, I know. I don't want to hurt the Markums any more because of this pack. I get it." Jazz forced his eyes open. His tongue felt thick as he spoke. "But I'm going after Ralph's girlfriend. This woman is still wolf hunting. I have to stop her before some alpha kills her. Ralph's death must have made her crazy. Maybe they were mates but hadn't sealed the deal yet. I think I know her next target. I'll try to talk her down from the ledge before she gets killed."

Desmon sighed. "Are you doing this for Ralph or are you doing this because we couldn't save Marcy?"

Jazz flinched. "I thought we weren't going to say her name."

"I'm sorry." Desmon sounded it, but he was silent for a moment as though debating with himself. "You loved her. She was your intended mate, and there's no changing that. I understand wanting to do something for her family, but a were-hunter—" He growled in defeat. "Fuck. Go ahead. Just don't let the woman kill you while you're trying to talk some sense into her, all right?"

"Yeah. Thanks. I'll clean up the mess here before I take off."

3

---

*S*hawna bit her lip and shifted her weight in the tree. She hated heights but she was high enough that her scent wouldn't be easy to detect. She glanced at her watch. It was almost dusk. The bonfire had been lit and shifters were arriving slowly. A few were already dancing by the fire as the smell of cooked meat wafted over from the barbeques by the main house.

All packs handled their runnings differently. She knew the Nightwinds usually ran wild in the woods. They spread out, and it was easy to get a partner alone, but these shifters seemed to be more social about it. Unlike Nightwinds runnings, it wasn't rural, dark and quiet, with random wolf howls echoing from woods glowing in moonlight. This was one big-ass party, with no privacy in sight, and that complicated things.

Most shifters liked to have sex on the full moon, but werewolves were especially notorious for it. It was nature's version of Tinder for single wolves, and date night for the mated ones, where everyone fucked under the moonlight and walked around smiling and happy for the next week.

She had spied on a Nightwinds running as a teen. Her parents wouldn't have risked bringing her, even if she'd been adopted by the pack and her life had been with them. They claimed it was too dangerous for any human, but she'd wanted to know...especially after she agreed to mate with one particular wolf once she was old enough. Shawna considered it essential in the name of education, but like her parents, Jeremiah hadn't seen it that way.

He'd caught her before she could see much, tracking her to the spot behind the gas station where she sat crouched with binoculars, as if he'd known all along what she'd been planning. It wasn't one of her prouder moments, but she'd been a frustrated teenager. He, on the other hand, was always so desperate to protect her, and stubbornly determined to ignore the attraction between them until she was old enough to handle what he truly was.

Even if she hadn't wanted to wait.

Shawna shoved those memories away. After two marriages, she was pretty sure thoughts of her first love shouldn't still hurt but the ache only seemed to get worse.

Maybe if she'd slept with him.

Maybe if their love had had time to grow old and boring, then she wouldn't still feel the ache and burn of lost love most nights. She sighed softly.

There is no going back.

Shawna had been tempted a few times to check into his life. She hadn't done it. She didn't want to know who had become his mate and how many children they had. It would burn her up inside. That was the life *she* should have had. Any pups he helped conceive should have been *hers*. She should be the female he climbed into bed with every night and his face should be the one she woke up to.

Don't go down this road.

She still couldn't help doing it. When she was sitting sometimes, waiting for her target to show up, her mind tended to drift to why she'd ended up a hunter. Sad, lonely, and desperate to fill up that spot inside her that no amount of hunting could take away. And it all went back to Jeremiah Adam Zackary Zendell, otherwise known as the love of her life...whose father had destroyed everything.

She shifted her weight again, so her limbs didn't go numb sitting on the wide branch high in the tree. Miserable and uncomfortable, she remembered the day Jeremiah claimed her as his.

She'd been fourteen and had gone to a pack gathering with her folks. Her dad always warned her to be careful with the male wolves, to stay close to him and other adults. She'd been chasing after a baby bunny that had somehow become separated from its mother. It was a cute little thing, probably just a month or so old, and then suddenly she'd been surrounded on all sides by Dean Hills, Tommy Radcliff, and Joe Blackhawk.

She shivered at the memory. She'd gone to pack classes with all of them and knew their families. Suddenly she felt the danger as they surrounded her in the woods with dark looks in their eyes that didn't bode well for her. They weren't shifted, she'd have felt safe if they'd been in fur, but they'd been in their skin.

She had always been small for her age. Slight. The males in the pack were naturally taller and huskier. She'd looked up at the three boys she'd once played tag with and knew she was in deep shit. A day out from the full moon wasn't a time to end up alone with a bunch of horny teenage males.

They started to softly growl and close in on her, blocking off all escape. They'd sniffed at her, and she knew in that instant what they wanted. She'd had the birds-and-bees-and-wolves talk with her adopted mother. Wolf males had extremely high sex drives, but teenage pups had none of the control a full-grown male possessed— and they'd wanted *her*.

She didn't want to think they were capable of something terrible. But when Dean Hills reached for her, she stepped back and tripped. A scream burst out of her from the shock. She wasn't hurt, but she felt considerably more vulnerable sitting there in the dirt.

Before she could scramble to her feet, Jeremiah, the alpha's son, was suddenly there in the woods with his best friend Desmon at his side. Both of them growled at the other teenage males, their gleaming human teeth growing long and wolflike in warning.

"Who told you it was okay to corner her in the woods?" Jeremiah's voice was a low, animalistic growl of warning. "What made you think that was a good idea?"

"We were just trying to talk to her," Dean Hills growled back. "I mean, shit...smell her."

Dean's words were a mistake. Jeremiah jumped at the other males, already half shifted with blond hair sprouting from his strong arms and face. It made him look vicious, unforgiving, and extremely alpha. He had attacked all three boys, his fists brutal and fierce with surprising fury. She flinched, wanting to look away, but not daring.

"I think they got the point," Desmon warned Jeremiah after a few minutes. "If you can't control your wolf, you're as bad as them. It's a weakness."

Jeremiah growled, his light eyes narrowed as he met his best friend's gaze. He shared a knowing look with Desmon, then he let go of Joe Blackhawk's shirt and crawled to his feet. He took one step back, and then another, like he was waging a battle between fury and logic.

Desmon's words must've hit home. The hair on Jeremiah's face and neck receded. He finally turned his back and left his opponents bleeding and moaning on the grass. He walked over to her instead and dropped down on his knees. He studied her face, his blue gaze startling in the afternoon sunlight, and her breath caught with something other than fear.

Longing rushed through her body, warm and electric, as she looked up at him, and she hoped to God it didn't show on her face with all the boys around.

The truth was, she'd had a crush on Jeremiah for a long time.

"Are you all right?" His voice was still gruff.

She nodded and tucked a strand of hair behind her ear. "You had really good timing."

"I keep an eye on you. I saw you leave, and—" His face and neck turned red like it did sometimes when he was angry. He had to take a long, cooling breath before he went on. "That was dangerous, especially near the full moon. When you want to walk in the woods, come get me first. You're always safe with me."

He'd turned his head then, a deep growl coming from his throat and chest as if he was losing the battle once more. "She's mine," he snarled at the boys. "Next time you touch her, I'll kill you. Spread the word. *She's mine.*"

She'd been claimed that easy, a willing victim of young love. From that moment on, Jeremiah became her shadow. He'd been there to escort her to pack classes. He'd taken her to dinner in town, even if they weren't supposed to socialize much with humans. He defied his father to do so, because he wanted her to be near others of her kind. No shifter boys looked sideways at her without Jeremiah growling at them and threatening to kill any male who touched her. She was his, period.

It was old fashioned, completely misogynistic, and she'd loved it.

She loved him.

That's why she couldn't forget.

Shawna sighed softly again, remembering how they would lie out under the stars and talk about the future. When she turned eighteen, he planned to take her as his mate, and change her over. They'd have four pups together, one girl, and three boys to kill or maim anyone who even thought about hurting his precious daughter.

Jeremiah wanted to build a house in the woods by a stream, with a sunroom facing the water, and she'd been on board all the way. Most of their ideas were fantasies, and they both knew that. Pack life wasn't easy back then, especially for Jeremiah. It could never have been that simple. Alpha Albert's expectations weighed heavy on his shoulders. He pushed Jeremiah harder than the other pups. Being an alpha's son was a difficult existence, but Jeremiah never complained. He was fearless instead, and unapologetic of his love for the tiny human female the Markums adopted.

She'd have followed him to hell if that's where he wanted to go. Her parents worried about her being a future alpha's mate, but Jeremiah hadn't been concerned. He'd grinned and told her he'd change her and train her to fight, to defend herself, but most of all, he promised that he'd always protect her.

Jeremiah wanted to be her first. It meant everything to him. Her first love, her first lover, and he wanted to do right by her. He was determined to wait until she was older and mature by human standards. He'd even proposed marriage to her, something a lot of male wolves didn't do. The mating was enough, but he wanted her to be his in both worlds. They'd had so many plans...

And then a year later it had been ripped apart because she'd made one mistake. She'd trusted the wrong wolf.

Music playing suddenly snapped Shawna from her musings about the past. She was on duty. Hunting bad weres was her life now. Sometimes she even got paid for it. Not that she really needed the money. Her second husband had left her well off.

She felt another slice of pain slam into her heart. Ron had been a nice guy. Way too young to die, but he had. They'd wanted to try for a baby, and then he was just gone.

Maybe she was cursed.

"Damn," she sighed. "I hate this waiting shit. Too much thinking. Not enough action."

She scanned the woods around her that were bathed in the first pink streaks of dusk. Music sounded through the trees louder, as though other smaller parties were happening out of sight. There were a lot of younger members in the Baker pack. They were unmated, obviously, judging by the sheer number of members arriving. Why were there so many of them? She chewed on her lip.

Shit. This is really bad.

She lifted her binoculars and scanned the area around the bonfire. She observed everyone stopping to greet the alpha upon his arrival. It was customary and it was a courtesy. Her target would show. She knew he was single, and no single wolf would miss his chance at a full moon gathering to run as a pack. There would be females around with hormones going wild. A male's chances of getting laid was a hundred times better on the full moon, especially at a running like this.

Shawna finally spotted Benny almost half an hour later and felt a wave of relief wash over her. She didn't want to be up a tree for most of the night. Her latest target was good at hiding. She'd searched for him, but he never stayed in one place long since his arrest. He didn't go to the local hangouts. She'd asked around. He was probably lying low from the cops and that meant this was her one chance to get him.

She kept her gaze on him as Benny greeted the alpha and the alpha's mate. Then he turned north, heading into the woods. She bit her lip and studied the area around her. There were too many wolves, but she knew protocol if she was caught. She'd play the stupid human lost in the woods. The Bakers were always known for being a decent pack, and word was they hadn't changed much, even if they had a few Bennys in the lot. Chances were they'd point her in the right direction of a road, and she'd walk away. Hopefully she'd find her target before any of his pack found her.

She used the rope and slid to the ground. It was easier than climbing and a hell of a lot faster and quieter. She headed north, tucking her trench coat tightly around her. It was treated to hide her scent. She ran fast, her senses on alert for any movement. She had to duck once, seeing a large wolf coming in her direction. She knew that wasn't her target. She'd broken into his mother's house and gotten a photo of Benny while shifted. In skin or fur, she'd know him when she found him. They all had distinct markings in fur. Her boy had two white strips near his right hindquarters and a black streak under his jaw.

He was still in skin when she came across him. He was sitting on a rock, still clothed, and talking on his phone. He was so intent on the conversation that he didn't hear her sneaking up behind him.

"Look, asshole. You're getting paid to represent me so I don't have to be in court. The bitch is a slut. Prove it. She wanted it bad. I didn't do anything wrong. Earn your damn money or you won't get a penny. You don't get paid unless you get me the hell out of this nightmare. I—"

He finally noticed Shawna and jerked his head around. His green eyes narrowed when his gaze locked on her. He frowned and ended the call without a goodbye. He didn't stand up. Instead, he inhaled deeply and frowned.

"These woods are private property." He sounded irritated. "This isn't a safe place for hikers." His eyes seemed to darken in the shadows of sunset. "And I'm in too much shit with my alp...*my boss*...to bite."

There was a low growl to his voice, like it was taking everything in him not to attack. Shawna pushed her coat back, showing off the curve of her hip while wrapping a hand around the gun tucked into the holster she was wearing. *Male werewolves are so predictable.* All it took was a little flirting to get them to let down their guard. Being a woman hunter had its advantages.

"That's too bad." She gave him a long, sultry look, while tightening her fingers around the cool, comforting feel of her Glock. "Are you sure I should leave? You're really cute and we seem to be alone together."

She licked her lips, being sure he got the message as his gaze trained on her mouth.

After a long pause, Benny stood with a growl. "Works for me. My boss will never know, and I do like taking bites out of hot pieces of ass like yours."

Shawna's entire body tightened in anticipation. She was three seconds from whipping out her gun and pumping this worthless werewolf with enough silver to solve all his legal problems...permanently.

"You sure that's a good idea, Benny Boy?" a low male voice called out from the woods to the east of where she'd been hiding earlier. "How about we tell *your boss* what you're planning to take a bite of?"

Shawna acted without thought and spun around, her instincts telling her to shoot first and ask questions later. They were deep in the woods. She didn't expect company, and she wasn't ready to die—not for Benny. A few well-placed bullets would let her get away.

But the new arrival moved too fast. In the blink of an eye, she was facing the broad, muscular chest of a werewolf when he cleared the space between them too quickly for her human mind to comprehend.

Shawna knew immediately he wasn't an ordinary were.

This is an alpha wolf.

As if to confirm it, she heard Bennie hiss. "Shit. This isn't what it looks like."

The werewolf in front of her pulled her against him, and leaned down to whisper in warning, "I wouldn't. Benny doesn't know what you are, but I do." He ran a hand down to her forearm before wrapping his fingers around hers on the gun hiding behind her back. His breath was warm against her ear as he went on, "So, why don't we keep that a secret between us? The full moon is a bad time for *your kind* to get caught."

He easily pried her fingers off the gun.

Chills ran over her body in an icy wave when she struggled to break out of his hold, but he wasn't letting go. He was too strong. She swallowed hard as she fought to clear her mind and find her way out of this.

She knew better than to let one of them get their actual hands on her. Before now, she'd always used her guns to keep them at arm's length. Feeling helpless in a way that haunted her dreams, Shawna realized she'd rather die than end up prey to an alpha wolf...not again.

"I was a friend of Ralph's," the new werewolf assured her in another whisper, still not letting go of her arm. "I won't hurt you."

He sounded sincere, and even through the mad panic, a part of her almost believed him.

There's something about his voice.

She tried to get a better look at the alpha who had caught her. Shoulder-length blond hair, brilliant blue eyes that sparkled in the dying sunlight, strong jawline, full lips...

Shawna's world started to fall out from under her for an entirely different reason. The chills of terror morphed into a tidal wave of emotion. It pooled painfully in the center of her chest, choking her, but that didn't halt the hard, steady thump of fear now pounding in her ears.

She opened her mouth, still struggling to say something.

This can't be happening.

It's too much.

She'd been a fighter too long. She was completely overwhelmed, more than she ever expected to be. Everything in her told her to run.

Shawna kicked his shin on sheer instinct. She used the surge of adrenaline to finally jerk her arm out of his grip and take off when his hold loosened. The problem was, she was still completely thrown off, and her foot caught on a tree root before she could get more than two feet.

She heard him yell, "Oh shit!" as she threw her arms out in front of her to break her fall, at the same time he tried to catch her, wrenching one arm back in his attempt to save Shawna from herself.

She landed hard anyway. The solid crack of her head hitting something unforgiving on the forest floor was the last thing she felt or heard before everything went terrifyingly black.

JAZZ CURSED AGAIN AND LEANED OVER THE SMALL WOMAN. SHE WAS unmoving, clearly knocked out. He rolled her over and brushed away the strands of red hair escaping her ponytail to find a painful looking knot already forming on her forehead. He smelled fresh blood and spied a scrape on her arm. She was hurt. He gritted his teeth and slid his hands under her, adjusting her weight, and then hauled her up his body as he stood.

"That's not how I would've done it," Miles mused drily as he approached. "But it's your mission."

Jazz ignored his friend and studied her pale face as he held her in his arms. Then he looked to Miles, who was still standing there with an unimpressed expression. "I'm taking her to the SUV. I know this is a mess. Let's get the hell out of here."

"What about him?" Miles asked, looking to Benny, who stood there watching the three of them hesitantly. "We're technically kidnapping an unconscious human. He's probably seen too much."

"Hey, fellas, I have enough problems. I don't need a dominance fight with two alphas tonight. Have your fun. I didn't see a damn thing," Benny called out, obviously knowing they were discussing his future. "Unless you feel like sharing. I don't mind thirds."

"The world won't miss him," Miles whispered to Jazz. "I could solve this issue for you."

"You don't get to take your full-moon anger out on the Bakers' problems," Jazz snapped at him, holding the unconscious woman tighter. "We have more pressing concerns."

Jazz moved quickly through the woods, feeling more than a little guilty for her accident. Truth was, she'd shocked him too, and he wasn't totally sure why. She'd thrown him completely off his game. His wolf was half insane under the surface. The faster they got back into Nightwind territory, the better. He didn't smell a lot of blood, but he could barely breathe past the primal roar inside him.

He felt very...unsteady.

The SUV was parked at the edge of the woods. He opened the back and gently lay the unconscious woman down on the seat. He turned as Miles came out from the trees behind him.

"Hurry." Jazz tossed his keys onto the front seat. "You drive."

Jazz climbed into the back without thinking. It was instinctive to pull her onto his lap and hold her, though it did nothing to help her. He closed the door behind him, and then stared down at the small knot growing larger on her head by the second. His heartrate deafened him when he thought of how fragile humans could be. What if he'd killed her?

"You know, Jazz, I recognize this human's scent from somewhere," Miles mused as he pulled the driver's-side door closed. "Does she smell familiar to you?"

"What?" Jazz barked, because Miles's words were hazy behind the fear. His wolf was so panicked that hair was sprouting on his arms. He was like a teen again, having a hard time staying in skin. "Start the car! What if she's gravely injured?"

"She doesn't smell as if she's bleeding much, but she does smell—"

"Just drive," Jazz growled, ignoring his friend, when usually Miles's strong sense of smell made him an asset on a mission.

Jazz placed a hand over the hunter's heart, feeling the steady beat. She was breathing but passed out cold. That wasn't good, especially for humans. He wiggled out his phone from his sweatpants and placed a call to their doctor. Adam answered on the fourth ring.

"Meet us at the pack house. My room. I'm bringing in an injured human female."

"Great, it's one of those nights." Adam sounded mildly alarmed. "Do I want to know how she was injured?"

Jazz winced. "Someone startled her."

"And that someone was..."

"Me." Jazz huffed in frustration. "I grabbed her arm. It scared her. She freaked out, tripped, and hit her head on a rock."

Adam snorted. "We have to work on your running game, Jazz."

"That's really funny," Jazz mumbled distantly, and caressed the bump on her head. "She's unconscious. What if it's serious? She's completely human."

"Then we'll give her a little blood if needed, twenty-four hours to rest, and send her on her way." Adam didn't sound concerned. "Where was she hurt?"

"We were at the Bakers running. Miles and I had to scoop her up and go before one of them found her."

"Sounds like an interesting night you're having over there." Adam paused. "I might be a little late, but I'll make it eventually."

"Fuck that!" Jazz growled. "No, you'll be there in ten minutes."

"It's the full moon, and Mitch called four times saying Connie is birthing. It's a few weeks early for her, so I'm on my way there now. If it's her time, I'll send Jake over to you. He does a fair job, and it's good for him to practice on humans. If she just hit her head, I promise your human friend will be okay."

"Fine." Jazz hung up.

He studied the unconscious woman. He kept his hand on her shoulder. He could hear and feel her breaths. If she died, he'd have to explain to the Markums how he let Ralph's girlfriend die.

That wasn't going to happen.

4

---

*S*omeone was carrying Shawna. She frowned, waking up slowly, and realized the strong arms holding her were now gently laying her down on a soft surface. She opened her eyes, half-blind with the throb of a dazzling headache. It took her a second to focus, and the first thing she saw was a deep blue comforter. She turned her head to see who had carried her.

Shock came instantly.

Jeremiah.

He hovered over her with a frown, and she couldn't look away from him. It was pretty obvious he didn't know who she was. She let that sink in while she tried to get a hold of the crazy emotions that were swamping her. Jeremiah was inches away. She inhaled his scent. He smelled like the forest, and all things inherently masculine and wonderful. She soaked in the sight of his beloved face for one long moment.

Maybe this is a dream.

He'd grown taller, gotten much broader and far more muscular. His features weren't those of a boy anymore but had matured into hardened man. His eyes were the same shade of sky blue, but she saw some changes there too. He had faint laugh lines at the corners. His hair had grown longer. As a teen, he'd kept it in a short crew cut, but now his hair brushed his shoulders.

"How are you feeling?" he asked with concern. "Don't be alarmed. You're in my bedroom. I called our doctor to take a look at you. Where are you hurt?"

"I'm fine," she whispered. "What did you say your name was?"

"I'm Jazz." He touched her forehead gently. "You're still bleeding a little."

Jazz? Jeremiah Adam Zachary Zendell. His initials...J.A.Z.Z.

Shawna sighed when he stepped away from the bed and walked to the bathroom, knowing it made sense he didn't know who she was. She was wearing her green contacts tonight, and even still, it had been sixteen long years. She'd lost weight since her teen years. The attack she'd suffered had left her hospitalized for months, between her care and then her stay at a rehabilitation center. Years of hunting after her recovery made her body harder, more angular instead of soft and curvy. She had let her hair grow and dyed it red, very different from her natural color, which was a soft brown.

Still, the pain hit her. She was supposed to have been his mate...and he didn't recognize her. She opened her eyes and pushed up on the bed. A sharp ache instantly jolted down her arm from her shoulder. She softly cursed.

Jazz was coming back from the bathroom with a washcloth. He hesitated and then sank slowly to sit on the edge of the bed. He held out his hand.

"Give me your wrist. It's scraped. We'll clean you up a little while we wait for the doctor."

She did so, glancing around the bedroom. He said it was his. She frowned. "*This* is your room?"

He nodded. "In the pack house. You know what they are, right?"

"Yes." She winced as he placed the wet washcloth on her still-bleeding wrist, but he was gentle. "You live here?"

"Not really." He winced too as he patted her arm to clean the small scrape. It wasn't life threatening, but he treated the wound like it was. "I keep a room here though."

She hesitated. "I thought an alpha's living space in a pack house would be bigger."

"I'm not really alpha." He smiled. "I mean, I'm alpha, but I'm not the head of our pack. It does makes me second-in-command, even when I don't want to be."

Shawna felt pure, raw, unfiltered terror, realizing his father must still lead them and jerked her arm out of his gentle hold. "I have to go now."

"I scent fear on you. Strongly." His frowned deepened. "What's wrong? No one will hurt you here. I told you, we're going to have a doctor see you. He's delayed, but he's coming."

She rolled off the other side of the bed. "I don't need a doctor."

He stood quickly. "I give you my word that I'm not going to harm you. I didn't hurt you in the woods. You fell. You remember that, right?"

"You aren't the one I'm afraid of." She memorized his features, wanting to remember every detail later. "I have to go."

He moved in front of the door. "I can't let that happen. My alpha wanted to meet you as well. He'll be here soon."

She backed up. A window out of the corner of her eye caught her attention. She turned and lunged to open the curtains, and saw they were on the second floor of a very large building. This pack house was new since she'd left. She saw a roof slanting under the window. The garage was under it. The drop from the garage to a side wall was just a few feet. She took in the wall next. It backed into an alley between the warehouse next to it, which was probably used for pack storage space.

"Let's talk about this," Jazz coaxed. "No one is going to harm you. Our pack knows all the Markums. That means you're safe here."

She turned to face him. "Please just trust me."

"You shouldn't be walking around. You were unconscious."

She bit her lip hard enough to draw blood. Terror was pounding through her. *Jeremiah—no*, she mentally corrected herself, *Jazz doesn't recognize me. It doesn't mean the alpha won't.* She had to get the hell out of there *now*.

She heard the rattle of a doorknob, and Shawna felt her heart jolt. A brown-haired woman opened the bedroom door, saw Jazz, and grinned. She put her hand on her hip and winked at him. "Found you. You can't hide forever, Jazz."

Jazz glared. "Not now, Krystal."

Krystal sniffed and turned her head fast to stare at Shawna.

Shawna studied the wolf. She knew the woman wasn't human.

The she-wolf frowned and was obviously not pleased to see her. "Who's this?"

"It's pack business. Leave. I'll call you later."

Krystal looked pissed. "Fine." She turned and slammed the door.

Shawna couldn't hide the pain in her voice when she asked, "Is she your mate?"

Jazz shook his head. "No. She's an unmated female. She wanted to talk to me about something. That's all."

Shawna was shocked. The female werewolf had sent enough signals to Jazz in those seconds for Shawna to know she wanted him sexually. "You cheat on your mate? Does she know that?"

He appeared stunned. "What?" A door slammed loudly in the house. Jazz stopped speaking and cocked his head. "My alpha just arrived. He'll be here in a few minutes."

"Fuck," Shawna groaned softly.

She'd run out of time. She desperately needed to get out of there. There was a table next to the window, a decorative wood box sitting on it that seemed sturdy, like a male version of a jewelry box.

"Stop being afraid," Jazz coaxed. "You're terrified and there's no reason to be."

"No reason to be?" she snapped at him. "Are you on drugs or did you go brain dead since I left?"

He gaped at her. "What in the hell does that mean?"

"I want to leave *now*. You said you won't hurt me, so let me go. Because I'm about to get seriously hurt."

He didn't budge. "I don't know what in the hell you're talking about but *no one* is going to hurt you."

Terror and panic were a bad combination with Shawna. Her past had left her with a fuckload of PTSD. Without warning, she grabbed hold of the wooden box next to her and pitched it at him.

It struck him in the head.

She yanked at the window, forcing it open. She had to get out of there before her worst nightmare walked back into her life. She scrambled to crawl out, but a large hand suddenly grabbed her ankle.

Shawna felt a hard tug and was knocked down. Pain shot up her already injured shoulder despite the carpet breaking her fall. She gasped, tears of frustration blinded her, and she blinked hard. She turned. Jazz had a hold on her. He'd thrown himself on his stomach, stretching his arm out to catch her.

"Let me go!"

His forehead was bleeding, and he looked grim and pissed off as he glared at her without releasing her ankle.

He touched his forehead with his free hand and stared at the blood on his fingers. "What the hell is wrong with you? You're like a feral human. I didn't think they existed."

She heard someone coming down the hallway. The wood floor creaked. Terror made her whimper. "Damn it, Jeremiah, let me go!"

He stilled, stunned, before he let out a growl of shock. "How do you know my birth name?"

"Let me go. I don't want to fight you," she begged. "Please, don't let him get me again!"

"Who?"

"Your damn *father*!" she almost sobbed, and then kicked hard, but he wasn't letting go. She didn't want to hurt him, but she wasn't going to let Albert touch her again.

"My father? You knew him?"

"I can't believe you don't know who the hell I am! I'm sorry, babe. But I'll *die* before your father ever touches me again!" She kicked him harder the second time.

He grunted and let go. She got the impression it was his shock rather than her superior fighting abilities that let her get away, but she wasn't going to stay around to find out.

Shawna got to her feet quickly. She reached the window again, putting one leg outside and turning back to look at him. Jazz sat up as someone knocked on the door. Loudly. He ignored it and met her gaze, looking pale. She raised her hand, blew him a kiss just like she used to, then fled, going out onto the roof.

She moved fast. Years of practice made her balance pretty amazing. She ran across the slanted roof. One misstep and she knew she'd be sliding off the roof to fall a story below. Once she reached where she wanted to be, she turned and slid down to the pitched roof of the garage.

She glanced back, unable to resist the urge. Jazz stood inside the open window, staring at her. His face was in shadows since the light was behind him.

"Marcy?" His voice sounded raspy with disbelief.

She knew it was time to go. She took a single second to gaze back at him before running across the garage roof and then dropping down to the wall. Two more movements and she was landing hard on the alley floor. She felt pain shoot up her legs, but she knew it was just the result of a hard impact. She turned, ran, and kept going until she hit a main street.

She found a place to hide and waited for a vehicle to drive along the nearby road. The driver wasn't anyone she recognized. Shawna reached down into her boot and withdrew some cash she kept there. She never carried anything that identified her on a hunt, including her phone, just in case she was ever caught, but money for emergencies was a must have. She flashed some bills at the driver. He slowed to a stop, allowing her to walk up to his lowered window.

"I'll pay you fifty bucks to give me a ride. My car broke down and I don't have time to wait for a tow truck." She was counting on his greed. Fast, easy cash was always a motivator.

"Yeah, I can take you where you need to be. Get in."

She walked around his truck and climbed into the passenger seat. "Thanks." She counted out the money and slid it his way.

The driver pulled away from the curb. "Where do you want to go?"

"Take me to the River Motel."

"Sure thing."

She leaned back and shut her eyes when he stepped on the gas.

Jeremiah knew who she was. Her heart still pounded. It sent a shiver down her spine, the good kind. Even after all the years that had passed, seeing him had made her feel weak in the knees. That wasn't a good thing though. They could never be together.

She grit her teeth. She was a damn idiot for even feeling anything for him anymore. That's what she was.

Jazz heard the bedroom door break open behind him. Desmon and Brandon entered the room. Desmon had a deep scowl on his face.

"Why in the hell didn't you answer? And why are you standing at the window ignoring us? I thought that woman had hurt you." Desmon glanced around the room. "Where is she?"

"She escaped."

"Shit." Desmon gripped Jazz's chin. "You're bleeding. She hit you? You let a human hunter get away from you?" He laughed. "Are you getting old?"

Jazz stared at Desmon. "It was *her*."

"Who?" Desmon quirked an eyebrow. "The hunter? I know."

Jazz turned to Brandon. "Leave us. Shut the door on your way out."

Brandon nodded and fled the room, doing as he was told. He had to slam the broken door twice for it to stay shut. Jazz listened to him walk farther down the hallway before he took a step closer to his friend. His legs felt unsteady. Hell, his hands were shaking. He suddenly gripped Desmon's shoulders.

"It was Marcy," he whispered. "She's the hunter."

Desmon gave him a skeptical look. "Marcy *who*?"

Jazz dug his fingers deeper into Desmon's shoulders. "*My* Marcy. She's not dead! Oh God, she was in my room. She was here! She..." He choked up with emotion.

Desmon shook his head. "Jazz—"

"I swear, Des!" Jazz looked at his friend, feeling sick to his stomach when he realized his shock was too much. He let Marcy get away. "It was *her*."

Desmon studied him with concern. "Sit down. You're bleeding in two places."

Jazz sat hard.

Desmon crouched in front of him, locking gazes with his best friend. "Are you sure?"

"She's thinner and her face looks a little different. Her hair is longer now too, and she changed the color to red. Her eyes were altered, but humans have contact lenses to do that." He stood, unable to stay still, before he rounded on Desmon. "She called me *Jeremiah*. Then she freaked out when I said—" He paused, then cursed. "I told her my alpha wanted to see her. She was terrified. That's when she attacked me and I was so shocked it took me a second to react. She doesn't know my father's dead. She said something about him hurting her before and she'd never let him hurt her again. *Damn it!*" He suddenly roared, raced toward the window and tore the curtains down. "She was here but I let her go!"

"You're *absolutely* sure?"

Jazz nodded, still shaking. "It was Marcy."

"It explains her being a hunter, doesn't it?" Desmon mused. "After what was probably done to her, I can see her killing our kind."

"She wasn't Ralph's girlfriend. She's his sister." Jazz crumpled on the bed again and dropped his head into his hands. "I carried her. I *touched* her. I was holding her wrist in my hand and I didn't fucking know! *She* knew. Damn it, she knew. She had to have realized it was me in the woods. That's why she reacted that way."

"We'll track her down. We'll let Marcy know your father is dead and that I'm the alpha now. She'll realize she's safe."

Jazz growled. "I wish I'd been the one to kill him."

"I'm sorry. But at least you took out the enforcers. All of them. I couldn't have fought him fairly without you doing that first. We took over this pack *together*."

"I remember." Jazz stared sightlessly at the wall, thinking about the past. "It happened the way it should have. I'm glad you have the job. I'd hate it. You saved my life because that asshole would have killed me, Des. I was already half dead from the fight with Deacon, Barney, and Paul. I just think about what he did to her...and I want to kill him over and over again. He's dead but I couldn't take my rage out on him. It's still there, eating me up."

Desmon softly cursed and sat down next to Jazz on the bed. "We'll find her."

"She never called me or came back. She let me think she was dead, Des." Jazz choked on the words, fighting tears. "All this time she's been alive, but she let me grieve her."

Desmon reached over and put his hand on Jazz's shoulder. "I'm sure she didn't mean to hurt you, man."

"She obviously hates me for what my father did. She hates me so fucking much that she let me suffer all these years, thinking she was dead."

"When we find her, you can ask her why she never called you, all right? Calm down."

Jazz shook his head and growled again. "She was *here*, damn it. Even if my father was alive, did she actually think I was going to stand there while he hurt her again?"

"I'm sure she didn't think that. If you'd been around the first time he attacked her, you would have died protecting her. She knew that."

Jazz got to his feet. "I need a drink."

"I'll drive." Desmon followed him rather than fight it. "I have a feeling you might need to be carried home."

Jazz couldn't deny wanting to get falling down drunk as he turned back to his friend in a daze. "Marcy's alive…"

"We'll go out tonight, let your wolf drown his sorrows, and tomorrow we'll find her."

Jazz wasn't so certain of that. "Maybe I should go looking for her instead of that drink."

She'd been missing for sixteen years.

Tomorrow was too long to wait.

5

---

*S*hawna stripped out of her clothes. She turned on the bathroom light and lifted her chin. She stared at her body reflected in the lousy motel bathroom mirror. Other than the collection of cuts and bruises which wasn't unusual in her line of work, she looked good for her age. She worked out. The only permanent marks scarring her body were from the alpha of her family's pack.

Yeah, that's it, just a few bone-deep scars.

She replayed the long-ago day in her mind, on purpose, to remind herself what had made the woman looking back at her in the mirror.

JEREMIAH'S FATHER HATED THAT HIS ONLY SON WANTED TO MATE WITH A human girl, and he hadn't been secretive about it. Marcy knew to avoid him, but that late afternoon when she saw him pull up outside her parents' home, blowing the car horn, she knew something was desperately wrong. The alpha's face was bright red, and his breathing was labored when she ran outside to see what the commotion was.

"Get in, Marcy. It's Jeremiah. He's been in an accident in the woods."

Shock tore through her. "What?"

"A rotten tree fell on him. It was huge, and he's trapped. They're working frantically to get him out. He might be dying. Get in, damn it! He's been calling out for you. We need to hurry."

Marcy didn't think. She didn't even stop to write a note to her parents, who had gone into town for supplies. She yanked open the car door and threw herself into the passenger seat. The image of Jeremiah trapped under a tree brought tears to her eyes. She was terrified for him. Everything was fuzzy under the fear as his father maneuvered the car through the winding mountain road like it was urgent that they get to his son.

She fought more tears as Albert turned off onto a dirt road. He climbed out of the car and ordered her to follow him. She didn't hesitate, she was desperate to get to Jeremiah.

She was running after Albert, and her attention was on the ground. She was being extra careful not to trip over anything in the woods and slow them both down. She never saw it coming.

Albert's arm suddenly flew and his elbow struck her hard in the face. She fell backwards into the grass and was left gasping for breath when the fall knocked the air from her lungs.

She blinked after a few long seconds, still sprawled on her back, bleeding from her nose and mouth, to find Albert standing over her. He looked really pissed off. She was so stunned, she just stared up at him in shock.

"You think you're good enough to mate my son? Do you think I'm going to let some human bitch rule my pack one day? Turned or not, you'll never be strong. You're nothing but a mutt the Markums took in. You're worthless for anything but being a pack whore." He unfastened his pants. "Once my son returns, he'll never want to touch you again. No one would ever let him live it down, knowing you were mounted by his own father first."

The raw shock rolled over her, mixing with the pain. Her face hurt badly. She rolled and started to cry, trying to crawl away. Her head throbbed and she felt dizzy.

Albert roughly knocked her flat onto her stomach. She looked over her shoulder and saw him change as she stared in horror. He became part man and part beast. He lifted his hand and she watched, sobbing, as his fingernails grew and thickened into claws.

That's when he slashed the full width of her lower back, tearing her open.

She screamed. The pain...The agony ended up being a blessing. It was the kindest thing he'd ever done. She'd passed out and couldn't remember most of what had happened. He'd raped her still, she found out later. Then he must've walked away, leaving her to die.

She had flashes of his enforcers dragging her down to the river, laughing as they tossed her in. The shock of pain and cold water was enough to steal the rest, and she passed out again.

Her next memory was of someone lifting her. She opened her eyes and saw the face of an old man. He was a stranger, and human. He dragged her out of the water and was yelling for help, demanding for someone to call an ambulance. He'd held her as a second man had come rushing toward them with a blanket. Between the two of them, they'd wrapped her up and laid her on the grass. They hovered over her, talking to her, telling her to hang on. Help was coming.

She'd woken up in a hospital with her adopted mother and father on each side of her. Her mother cried. Her father was enraged. He leaned over her, gripping her face.

"Who did this to you?" he growled. She knew the fury wasn't directed at her. She saw his eyes and knew he was going to kill someone.

"The alpha," she got out. "Deacon. Barney. Paul."

She'd seen shock on her father's face. "Albert?"

She tried to nod but pain stopped her. She reached up. Her broken nose was bandaged. "Yes. He said..." She started to cry again. "No human bitch was going to be his son's mate. He said I was a pack whore." Sobs took her then. "He hit me and—" She couldn't even talk anymore.

Her father stood suddenly and pulled off the sensor leads attached to her. Then he reached under Marcy and lifted her gently. The motion tore the IV from her arm.

"Henry!"

"She's not staying here, Rosa! She's not safe. We're leaving *right now*. We need to get her far from here. We'll give her blood along the way. It'll keep her stable."

The doctor had tried to stop her father, but he had help getting her out of the hospital. Her brothers were there too. Ralph and Morgan shoved the staff out of his way until they got to the fresh air of the parking lot. Her father had climbed into the backseat when Morgan pulled the car up, still holding her in his large arms.

"It's going to be okay, baby." He started rocking her gently. "I'm getting you to safety. They'll never find you or hurt you again. Never."

She pulled herself from the past and wiped at her tears. Grateful for the distraction, she stepped into the shower and let the hot water run down her body. Her father and mother had taken her away, all right. They'd checked her into a hospital two hundred miles north under the name of Shawna Hensky.

There was an underground agency that helped werewolves acquire human identities, and her father was owed a favor. In his haste to protect her, he'd quickly chosen her middle name and her birth mother's maiden name. She'd lived under that identity until she'd married.

Life had been hard. She'd recovered physically. Her injures had been bad, and she missed her family. Though they had left the pack, she was safer away from all werewolves—especially marked as she was.

Instead, she'd lived with a human friend of her biological mother's for three years until she'd hit eighteen. Then she worked for a security outfit. She'd answered phones and gotten to know a lot of the guys. That's where she'd met Allen, her first husband. He was a cop during the day and a part-time security officer at night.

Her nightmares had driven Allen to suggest she get counseling over her "bear attack". That's how she'd explained the scars on her back. He never questioned her, but the vicious marks always made him uncomfortable. Maybe as a cop, a part of him suspected there was more to the story.

She dealt with her anger by taking self-defense classes. She built emotional walls to protect herself...and ended up keeping her husband out too. The marriage had broken up in a matter of months. He wanted a different kind of wife, one who didn't spend all her spare time at the gun range. He wasn't her ideal, either. Allen wasn't Jeremiah.

But he was still her friend—even now. He helped her out sometimes, like getting Merl's driver's license copy for her.

After their divorce, she'd started hunting the dangerous werewolves, true predators like Merl, and Allen was usually good for the occasional tip from law enforcement. He had covered her ass a few times too, when werewolf hunting almost put her in legal hot water. It helped ease her rage and the painful loss of Jeremiah, but it wasn't the most lawful of professions.

Then she'd met Ron while sitting in a hospital waiting to interview a woman who'd been attacked by a "big, strange dog" in a park. Ron was recovering from a round of chemotherapy. He'd been a friendly guy who'd asked her out to dinner, and she'd accepted.

Months later, she'd married him when he gotten the news that his cancer was in remission. She'd happily said yes and retired from hunting. The fourteen months after her second wedding were the best of her life since Jeremiah.

She'd been happy with Ron. They'd had a friendship kind of love that was comforting. He made her smile and laugh. It was flat-out unfair that his cancer came back and stole her future once again.

Shawna finished her shower and dried herself, her mind continuing to relive the past. She'd gone right back to hunting after Ron's death. Sometimes she got paid. Word got around, people who knew what they were dealing with offered her money to solve the problem. Like the case she'd had five months ago.

She sighed. A woman had dated a were, knowing what he was, and shit turned bad fast. It happened sometimes. The guy had grown tired of her being a girlfriend and had shown up with a few of his buddies. The woman had been forced into their small pack of wild wolves and changed against her will. Unmated females with no one to protect them led a hellish existence in packs like that. The woman wanted out, to escape, and she'd heard about Shawna.

Shawna had killed the ex-boyfriend and two of his friends, because they'd threatened to track the woman wherever she fled. Shawna helped her get to safety in another state, in an area known as were-free territory. It was hard to find somewhere that weres didn't live. They were a tough breed. They could survive any element, but for some reason they didn't like desert communities.

Shawna smirked. It was probably the heat with all their thick fur. Palm Desert, California, was werewolf free. The extreme heat waves during the summer probably made the place feel like hell on earth. One werewolf lived there now, and she was happy to be free.

Shawna lay down on the bed and stared up at the popcorn ceiling of her hotel room.

Jeremiah is now known as Jazz.

The shock on his face when he'd realized who she was would haunt her. She could never go back to being the girl she'd once been. Now she was Shawna, and she liked herself just as she was. Marcy had died that day in the woods, and there was no way to bring her back.

Hell, she was on the edge of running right now, but she'd leave first thing in the morning. She needed to rest, then retrieve her Jeep from the woods in the next county.

She was worn out since she'd been hunting for months without a break. Her defenses were low, but looking back never did anything other than leave her feeling bitter. Albert had ruined her future and taken Jeremiah away from her. It was too late to change things now, no matter how badly she wanted to.

She needed a drink...badly.

The urge was strong enough to make her climb out of bed and open her suitcase that she left there when she checked into motel before she went after Benny. She pulled out a pair of faded jeans and a black long-sleeved blouse. It would hide her bandaged wrist that she had wrapped with supplies from the first-aid kit she traveled with.

Shawna put on a pair of boots. They had sharp heels with steel tips. She grinned as she stood. They were her shit-kicker boots. Whatever she targeted with them screamed "shit", that was for sure.

She grabbed her leather jacket last and pulled her hair into a pony-tail, not bothering with makeup. She wanted a drink, not a man hanging around her.

6

The bar was just a short walk down the street. It was upscale and trendy, with fluorescent-blue lightning, nu-disco playing in surround sound, and two-for-one happy hour martinis advertised on the sign by the door.

It definitely wasn't a werewolf bar.

Shawna studied the patrons. It was preppy hell, with men in suits and women in corporate dresses. Shawna knew she stuck out but that was more than fine with her. She headed for the bar and took a seat. The bartender came over, looking tired of his job.

"What can I get you?"

"An extra-dirty martini, very dry, please."

"Okay." He walked away without a backwards glance.

Shawna glanced around the bar, careful not to make eye contact. That might encourage some suit to approach. She felt gazes on her, and knew they were probably curious about the chick in the leather jacket and vicious boots. The bartender returned with her drink and she paid him in cash.

She took a sip and had to stop herself from grimacing. The bartender did not know how to make a dirty martini. He had the right ingredients, but it was mixed for shit. She looked down the bar, saw what everyone else was drinking, and rolled her eyes. *Preppy hell.* They had what she called "foo foo" drinks in their hands. She sighed and worked on finishing her cocktail. It wasn't bad but it wasn't good either.

A man sat down next to her and bumped her elbow. She turned, knowing at first glance that he was drunk. It was obvious from the stupid grin on his face and his wide, dazed gaze. Then there was that other hint—he stunk of strong booze.

"Hi, beautiful," he slurred. "Wanna come rock my world tonight?"

She let her gaze rake up and down him. He was about five-eight, a hundred and fifty pounds, and wore a brown suit. He looked like either an insurance adjuster or a car salesman.

"No thanks, I'm not in a band."

He laughed far too much and almost tumbled off the barstool. "That was so damn funny."

She took another sip of her drink. "If you say so."

"I love your red hair. Let me take you home with me. You'll like my place. It's got an awesome view of the stars at night."

She gave him an unimpressed look. "No offense but I'm not interested. Time for you to leave."

He didn't leave. Just her luck. Instead, he moved closer and touched her jean-covered thigh. Shawna looked down at his hand, and then quickly grabbed his wrist and twisted hard enough that he cried out in pain.

She made a point to look him dead in the eye. "I said, time to leave."

He almost fell out of his seat, but he managed to stagger to a table in the corner. The woman seated there looked understandably miserable about her new table mate, and Shawna felt a pulse of guilt.

"Hello," another male said softly from behind her.

She turned, now more than annoyed—and felt the color drain from her face.

Jason smiled and took the stool next to hers. He reached over and rested his arm on the back of her chair when she turned instantly and tried to jump up.

Another man, one she'd never seen before, dropped his ass to the chair on her other side and gripped hers as well. She was trapped.

She turned back to glare at Jason.

He studied her seriously, really staring at her face.

"You could've just told me who you were, you know." A scowl marred his forehead. "I'm still a good guy."

"You're not a guy, you're a werewolf, and werewolves change," she stated softly, giving him another side glare, even if her words lacked real anger. "I couldn't trust you, Jason. Sorry."

"Fine, hate the rest of us. I can't blame you, but Marcy, you know Jazz—"

"Marcy's dead," she snapped at him. "I go by Shawna now."

"Okay, Shawna. You're the last person I want to fight with tonight. Believe it or not, we're all really happy you're alive." Jason sighed. "And I came with a message."

She swallowed hard past the emotion and nodded. "Then let's hear it."

"There are teams of us looking for you." Jason leaned in closer to speak, keeping his voice low. "You've got Nightwind wolves tracking you all over the area, and we were told to let you know a few things if we found you. First off, we're supposed to tell you Albert isn't alpha anymore. Desmon is. He killed Albert a long time ago. We're a peaceful pack now."

Shock tore through Shawna. "You're lying."

The man on the other side of her growled softly. "We aren't lying."

She scowled at the stranger but then turned back to Jason. "How do I know you're telling me the truth?"

He shrugged. "You'll have to accept my word for it, unless you want to take a night drive to the cemetery and go dance on Albert's grave. He's buried over in Eternal Hills."

She let that sink in. "Desmon Nightwind? How long ago did he take over?"

Jason was silent for a moment before he answered, "Right after you disappeared."

"He was so young!"

"Yeah, but he was pretty fucking angry too." Jason gave her a pointed look. "I guess he was big enough to take out the asshole who killed his father and marked his mother as a pack whore."

She flinched but tried not to let it show. "And Jer—" She paused. "Jazz?"

"He's happy to be second wolf in charge. Too much paperwork and politics for his liking. He's well liked and generally fun to be around —as long as no one brings up his lost mate."

She sighed. "Ouch."

Jason reached into his inside jacket pocket and pulled out a piece of paper. "Jazz's number. He'd like you to call him."

She read the paper and then took it. Her hand shook, and she knew he saw it. "Anything else?"

"That was it." He moved slowly as he released her chair and stood up. "Have a good night."

She was shocked as she watched Jason and the other werewolf leave. They hadn't tried to grab her. She feared they would. She glanced at the paper in her hand. That was Jeremiah's number.

Jazz.

She had to learn his new name...and she did think Jazz fit him better. She stuffed the paper into her pocket, shut her eyes, then sipped her drink.

Albert was dead and Desmon was the official pack alpha...not Jazz.

Shawna finished her drink and stood. She turned and studied the bar on her way out but didn't see anyone out of place. Jason and his friend weren't lurking in the corners, waiting to grab her.

Outside, she paused, careful to look around again. She half-expected to be ambushed, but there was no sign of anyone waiting on her. She forced herself to relax her shoulders and walked down the street, still on alert the entire time.

Nothing happened.

Shawna made it back to the motel safe, and locked the door behind her, making sure to use the deadbolt. She was half-tempted to grab her stuff, order a ride to her abandoned Jeep and move on tonight.

Instead, she yawned.

It had been a long day. She figured if the Nightwind pack meant her harm, they would have jumped her coming out of the bar. She hadn't been followed. She was sure of that.

Maybe it's all true.

Or maybe it isn't.

Either way, Shawna planned to leave before she was curious enough to find out for sure—first thing in the morning.

She took the number out of her jacket as she stripped it off. A part of her was tempted to call him, but she stopped herself, cursing aloud. She wanted it more than anything, but that boat had sailed a long time ago.

She was still trying to wrap her mind around the claim that Albert was dead and Jazz hadn't taken control of the pack. He'd been groomed to be leader since the Nightwind pack fell into his father's hands. They all assumed he would be in charge one day.

Did he feel any bitterness that Desmon had taken over the pack? Were they still best friends now that Desmon was Jazz's boss? A hundred questions went through her mind. None of them would be answered unless she called Jazz.

She wasn't going to do it.

In the suitcase, she found her boxers and a tank top. She removed the rest of her clothes and donned her sleepwear. Then, she dug out the spare gun at the bottom of her suitcase, flipped off the safety and took it with her to the bathroom to finish the rest of her nighttime routine.

Shawna yawned again as she headed to bed. She left the bathroom light on and climbed under the covers with her teeth brushed and hair combed. She turned to face the door and tucked the gun under the pillow next to her, so it was easy to reach. Letting her eyes close heavily, she sank into an exhausted sleep withing minutes.

7

-----

*J*azz abandoned the idea of a drink. He started looking for his mate instead. The phone on the passenger seat didn't finish the first ring before Jazz answered it with a growl. "What's going on?"

"We found her," Jason replied. "She was nursing a drink at that new upscale joint on Fifth Street. I gave her the message and your number."

Jazz pulled over. He had all the available pack enforcers looking for Shawna, but he hadn't expected them to find her that fast. His heart pounded with anticipation. "What did she say?"

"Not much. She didn't believe me when I told her that Desmon is pack alpha. I invited her to go see Albert's grave. She looked shocked."

"Did she say she'd call me?"

Jason hesitated before he admitted, "No, she just looked at the number and put it in her pocket, but—"

"I'm on my way there."

"She left the bar. We followed her. She's at River Motel. Room thirty-six. We're sitting in the parking lot."

"I'll be there in ten minutes. Keep watch. If she tries to leave, delay her, but *no one* hurts her. Do you understand? I don't give a damn if she shoots one of you. No one is to harm a single hair on her head."

Jason was silent for a long moment. "You know we wouldn't hurt her, Jazz."

"Not without orders," Pete added, making it obvious he was listening to their conversation while sitting next to Jason in the car. "But damn, she kills our kind and Jazz is actually planning on climbing into bed with her every night? He's nuts."

Jason laughed. "You know he likes living dangerously."

"No shit." Pete sighed. "But I never pegged Jazz for being suicidal."

"I'm hanging up now."

Jazz pushed the button on his phone and tossed it back on the seat before he pulled out of the parking lot and headed toward River Motel. It didn't take long to get there, especially with the way Jazz was driving.

Jason climbed out of his black SUV and walked over to Jazz as he opened the car door. "Need some backup?"

Jazz arched his eyebrow, and then he growled menacingly. "I don't share my woman."

"I have a mate," Jason reminded him, clearly annoyed. "What I meant was, do you want us to stick around in case she shoots you? 'Cause I'm not sure she's in the mood for a growling alpha wolf bursting into her room and informing her that she's still his mate. It's been almost sixteen years, Jazz."

"She's mine. She was always mine."

"What if she's already married to a human?"

Jazz growled. "Too bad for him."

"What do you want us to do? Go or stay?" Jason took a step back, and warned, "I think Des would tell us to stay."

Jazz sighed. "Stick around. If you don't hear gunfire or I don't call you in an hour, then you can take off. If you hear gunshots, you should probably come in, but don't harm her. Just restrain her and take both of us back to the pack house if I'm shot."

"Shit. Don't forget, she killed Merl. You didn't see it go down like I did. She isn't the Marcy you used to know. She did *not* hesitate with that shit. I know he wasn't her first execution."

"She won't kill me. She might injure me, but she won't go for a kill."

"How in the hell can you be so sure? Didn't she knock you in the head earlier to get away?" Jason looked pointedly at Jazz's forehead. "You healed up, but that's beyond having a feisty bitch, Jazz. She's dangerous."

Jazz smiled widely. "Nothing easy in life is worth a damn, but she's worth everything."

Without another word, he turned and headed for room thirty-six. He stopped at the door and didn't hesitate before he kicked it open.

SHAWNA SAT UP IN BED AND HAD A GUN LEVELED AT THE INTRUDER IN A blink. Eyes wide, heart pounding, she saw the dark shadow of a tall, broad man standing in the frame of her broken motel room doorway.

"Are you going to shoot me, babe?" he asked casually.

Shawna was stunned. Jazz was in her room. He wasn't entering. He just stood there watching her silently.

Was she going to shoot him?

Never.

She swallowed hard and lowered the gun. She saw Jazz's shoulders sag a little, as though he was relieved.

He shut the door slowly, tried to lock it, but it was broken. He just left it shut and flipped the switch on the wall. Fluorescent light poured into the room and Shawna had to blink to adjust. Jazz stayed by the door, rather than come at her. Seeing that as an act of nonaggression, she set the gun on her lap and stared, still hungry for the sight of him —whether she should be or not.

"What are you doing here, Jeri— Jazz?"

He scowled. "You didn't call me."

"I just got your number," she eyed the clock, "about forty-five minutes ago."

"And you didn't call."

"I wasn't ready to talk to you."

He let out a snarl that made her jump. "Why didn't you tell me you were alive?"

"I couldn't—" she started, feeling the shame wash over her.

"I'm furious, damn it!" he growled before she could finish. "I searched *years* for you. I hired private detectives. You were just gone. You didn't even call your family. They were worried sick! They thought you were dead too."

She looked away from him and admitted, "No, they knew I was alive. My family helped me get away when they realized I wasn't safe at the hospital."

"Bullshit! They knew Desmon took the pack before they moved. They knew Albert was dead. They were pack. Of course, they knew!"

That truly stunned Shawna.

Her family knew that?

It took her parents time to pack up their house and move once they decided to leave the pack. In hindsight, it wasn't that hard to believe they'd kept that information from her while she'd been recovering in the hospital, but the shock must've shown on her face.

"Unless they never told you my father was dead," Jazz whispered after one long, silent moment where Shawna just stared at him in shock. "They didn't tell you because they didn't want you mated to me."

"Maybe." Shawna remembered the aftermath too well. They'd have done anything to protect her. Even lie, which didn't come easily to werewolves. "My attack scared them. I was still a teenager. They wanted me away from *all* shifters back then. I'm not surprised that they would keep Albert's death a secret."

"Really? 'Cause I am. They're wolves. They know what losing a mate does. Not just to me, but to you too. Are you happy hunting rogue wolves and living out of shitty motel rooms?"

"It's not all my parents' fault." Shawna wanted to defend her parents somehow, even though they'd lied to her too. "They haven't known where I've been for a long time. Over the past few years, I've been moving around a lot. I don't tell them where I am because of the hunting. I couldn't risk the Shifter Alliance coming down on them for their association to me if I got caught. That's why I didn't hear about Ralph until just last week. If I'd been talking to my parents, do you think it would've taken me nine months to avenge my brother?"

"They could've told me you were alive! They knew I was worried sick and frantically looking for you."

She studied him. "Why?"

"Why?" He sounded shocked. He took a step forward and then stopped. He fisted his hands at his sides and repeated, "*Why?*"

"Yeah. Why?"

"You were supposed to be my mate!"

She felt tears rise and fought to blink them back. "Not after that day. They knew it was over between us. It was kinder to let you believe I was dead. It was kinder to me too. Having you reject me would've been too much. I can't blame them for lying to both of us."

He leaned back against the wall and ran a hand through his hair. "What happened that day didn't matter to me, damn it!"

She blinked at him. "My place in your pack was forever changed. Don't deny it. You couldn't mate with me after that."

He growled and dropped his arms. "Bullshit."

She felt anger course through her. "You couldn't mate with me after what your *father* did, Jazz!"

He looked furious. "Says who? Did I say that? Did you? Who the hell said that, Marcy?"

"My name is Shawna now. No one calls me Marcy. She's dead and gone. I'm Shawna."

His mouth tensed. "I'm sorry. Who the hell said so, Shawna? Who the hell said you still weren't going to be my mate? If you'd stuck around long enough, gotten in touch with me one damn time, I would have told you I wanted you—no matter what."

She shut her eyes and fought tears. When she finally felt in control, she opened her eyes to find Jazz was closer. He stood at the end of her bed. The look he gave her was heartbreaking. He seemed so...sad.

She lifted the gun and sat it on her pillow next to her. She slowly shoved off the blankets, then stood on shaking legs. "Who said?" She cocked her head. "Look at me, Jazz. Really look at me."

Shawna's hands trembled as she turned her body. She stared at him over her shoulder as she lifted her shirt. She saw his gaze lower to her bare back, and he flinched. It made her feel dread in the pit of her stomach.

He looked back at her face, and she saw tears reflected in his light gaze. She understood his pain. She felt it too. "He not only raped me, he marked me. Everyone will know—always." Her voice cracked "That's why he did it. He said it to my face. After that day, I could never be your mate. That dream died."

"No, it didn't." He met her gaze and blinked hard. "It doesn't matter."

"Bullshit." She let the tears fall. "The claw marks don't lie. This is done to women who are considered worthless in a pack except as a whore, for anyone to fuck if they need to get off. We both know it. If I'd returned right after the attack, every time you stripped me, you'd have to look at *his* mark. You would have wanted to change me over. Everyone in the pack would have seen those scars when they saw my wolf. What would that do to you over time, if you'd have mated with me, Jazz? It would have driven you insane, and you'd have always had to protect me from horny wolves who thought I didn't have the right to say no. It would have destroyed us both."

"You should've given me a chance." His voice cracked with emotion. "I loved you more than I hated him...always."

She lowered her shirt and turned. "Jazz, this mark will be there forever—reminding both of us, and the rest of your pack, what happened to me. Do you know what I had to tell my husband to explain the nightmares? That I was attacked by a bear. That it was nightmares of a bear that had me waking up at night, covered in sweat, screaming my head off."

Jazz backed up, his face pale. "You're married?"

"We divorced, but that doesn't matter. I made the decision a long time ago to never come back. I knew every time you saw these scars they would be a constant reminder that your own father had raped and marked me. To the pack. To any visiting werewolves who saw them."

He took a step toward her. "The mark, I don't give shit about. I care about *you*, Shawna. Just you."

She wiped at her tears. "Why are you here, Jazz? Let's stop torturing each other with the past. It's done and gone."

"Get dressed. There's somewhere I'd like to take you."

"Where?" She didn't trust so easily anymore.

"Please, Shawna? You know I'd never hurt you, don't you?"

She looked into his eyes and nodded. "I know that."

"Then trust me. Put on some clothes and let's take a drive."

"Should I bring my gun?"

"There's no danger where I'm taking you. I swear."

Shawna went to her suitcase and grabbed a pair of cotton pants, silently calling herself an idiot for going along with this. She pulled them on, and then tugged an oversized sweater over her head. She snagged her slip-on flats from the floor and lastly grabbed the plastic motel room key. She turned back to Jazz.

"Are you bringing me back...because getting a ride around here isn't easy? I still have to retrieve my Jeep."

"I'll bring you back."

She shrugged. "Let's go."

Jazz opened the door and studied the damage. He shot her a look. "I'll have that taken care of right now. The owner is in our pack."

"Shit. He is? He doesn't look or act like it."

"He's older, at least three hundred. He moved to California from up north for the warmer weather, but he ran a motel up there too. Both places mostly cater to humans." Jazz shrugged. "He's had years to learn to fit in."

He led her to a blue sports car and opened the passenger door for her. She flopped into the seat. He shut the door behind her, and she turned around to watch him walk around the car. He stopped at the back, and Shawna was surprised to see Jason come out of the darkness. He nodded at something Jazz said, and then started walking in the direction of her motel room.

When Jazz climbed into the driver's seat, Shawna asked, "What did you say to him?"

Jazz met her gaze. "I told him to get someone over to repair the damage to the door, and to stay in front of your room to protect your things until it's fixed."

She chewed on her bottom lip. "Thanks. That was nice of you."

"I broke the damn door," he growled. "It's my responsibility to fix it and have your things guarded." He started the car. "Don't thank me for doing what's right."

She shut her mouth. Jazz was angry. She wasn't afraid, but she did give him a cynical, uncertain look as he drove, knowing he was heading for Hollow Mountain. When he turned off the main road onto a paved driveway a few miles later, she frowned and shot another glance at Jazz.

"My home," he informed her softly. "I thought we could talk there without being interrupted."

She tensed. "Where's your mate?"

He growled. "I don't have one. When I get lonely, and I can't leave the pack, usually Krystal can help me out. We aren't in a relationship. It's her *paid* job to see to the needs of unmated males. She has the right to say no to anyone. She's not forced."

Shocked, Shawna gasped. "She sleeps with your pack for money?"

He shrugged. "She's a nice woman to boot. Don't judge her. She likes her life."

"And you fuck her? You fuck a woman your entire pack has done?"

He sighed and looked away. "It's not as bad as you make it sound. It's not the entire pack, not even close. Most of the unmated males in our pack don't have issues finding companionship. It's just a few of us, those who are busy and aren't as inclined to look for company."

"You mean, males who've lost their mates," she realized. "That's who she takes care of."

Jazz nodded. "There's others, for different reasons, but that's it for the most part."

She studied the man sitting so close to her. He was a different from the one she'd left behind. The Jazz she knew had wanted to wait until they were married to have sex. He wasn't a virgin at that time, but he'd not slept with anyone after staking his claim on her because he said the wait would be worth it. He'd been kind of prudish, actually. Now he was sharing an unmated female with his pack mates.

Jealousy burned through her, and worse was the sadness, the awful pain in the center of her chest thinking about Jazz being so lonely.

"She looked pissed that I was there," Shawna whispered.

"I keep avoiding her. She's been after me to help with Desmon and Amber's anniversary party. Krystal loves planning parties. She's always looking for a reason, and I hate that kind of crap. If she was mad, it was because of that."

"So, you're friends with benefits?"

"We're friends." He nodded. "I turned her."

She looked out the window rather than say anything.

Jazz sighed. "You're upset."

"It's none of my business. When I got married the second time, my husband encouraged me to not let shit get to me that I couldn't change."

Jazz growled. "You're married to someone else?"

"Not anymore."

"How many ex-husbands do you have?" he snarled.

"One ex. My second husband died."

Jazz grew silent.

So did Shawna.

When she spotted lights ahead of her, shock hit hard as they pulled up to a large two-story structure set in the woods. It was a nice house. Nicer than nice. It was beautiful.

Jazz parked his car in front and turned off the engine. "Welcome to my home," he said quietly. "Let me get your door. Don't move."

He climbed out of the sports car, and Shawna sat there waiting, feeling fidgety and nervous as he walked around and opened her door. She climbed out, then stomped toward the house before she got ahold of her common sense and changed her mind.

Jazz followed, unlocked the front door, and held it open for her. "After you."

She paused. "Do you live with anyone?"

"No."

She walked into the house. The lights were already on, showing off Jazz's large living room. Most of the furniture was light-colored wood, but the couches were black leather. The fireplace was made from smooth, large gray rocks.

She turned with a jolt when the door shut firmly behind her.

Jazz stepped into her personal space, close enough that she had to tilt her head to look at his face. His blue eyes were hooded, and his emotions were hidden.

"It's a nice house," she whispered.

"I had it built ten years ago."

She chewed on her lip again and released it. Jazz was silently watching her. She wished she knew what he was thinking. She felt like a basket case. Half of her wanted to run right now and never look back.

It was the other half—the lost, in love, broken half—that kept her rooted to the spot.

Why did he bring me to his house?

"What did you want to talk to me about? You said you had something to show me. Is this it? Your house?"

He shook his head. "No. There's something I'd like you to see."

She hesitated as he went to the stairs that curved to the second story. He paused on the second step and his haunting blue gaze studied her once more.

"Follow me, please."

She sighed in defeat and started to walk, following him up the stairs. They passed silent bedrooms. She counted three of them and a bathroom. The room at the end of the hall had double doors. They stood wide open. Jazz approached the dark room and turned, blocking the entrance.

"You might have walked away from me, but I never walked away from you."

He flipped on the light and moved out of her way.

She stepped into the room and looked around. It was the master bedroom. He had heavy wood furniture. The bed was a four-poster with a canopy. A large, twelve-drawer dresser took up most of one wall. He pointed toward it, and she noticed that framed pictures littered the top.

She stared at him warily, but curiosity got the better of her. She stepped close enough to really see the pictures—and gasped.

Before she could stop herself, she reached out with shaking hands and lifted one of them. It was her and Jazz at a pack dance they had in the spring for all the young weres. They were both smiling for the camera, appearing very much young and in love. They looked so happy and innocent, she barely recognized herself. This wasn't her; this was Marcy.

Shawna put it back, but there were so many of them to look at.

There were several other pictures of them together. And many more just of Marcy, back in the days when Shawna wasn't even something she could conceive of. Dozens of them. She turned, shaken, and met his gaze.

"Welcome to the hell I've lived since you left me."

"Why? Why would you have all of these?"

"Why?" he growled. "You were fated to be mine. Did you think I took that lightly? Did you think I'd just shrug you off? I thought you were dead. I looked for you for years. *Years!* I didn't want to give up, but everyone kept telling me you were dead. That if you were alive, you'd have returned to me. That you wouldn't have walked away from a love like ours. That you would know this is where you belonged, with me. I kept these pictures in my bedroom for sixteen years. Sixteen damn years of suffering and hurting and missing you."

She blinked back tears. "Jeremiah—"

"Jazz," he reminded her. "Jeremiah's dead, just like Marcy."

"You're breaking my heart, Jazz."

Jazz suddenly moved. He gripped her hips and lifted her effortlessly. She gasped, putting her hands on his shoulders rather than fight him.

Their faces were inches apart. "You broke mine. I think it's only fair."

She felt hot tears roll down her cheeks. "I'm sorry I went with him. I'm so sorry. Albert told me you were hurt. I never should have trusted your father."

Jazz looked away. When he turned back, his eyes were also glassy with tears. "He betrayed us both. He took you away from me. I tried to kill him when I found out he'd done something to you. All four of them had your blood on them. I smelled it. His enforcers attacked me to protect him. The bastards wouldn't allow me to challenge him. I took out all three of them, but I was severely injured. I still tried to go after him but I'd lost too much blood to win.

"Desmon jumped in and had to kill him. I couldn't do it. I'm sorry. I did take out Paul, Barney, and Deacon. I killed them all, Shawna. I made them suffer greatly before they died. I did get *some* justice for you."

She was overwhelmed. "Jason forgot to tell me that part. I didn't know that's how it happened."

"They touched you. I knew that they had hurt you. I swore to kill any man who ever did that. Did you think I wouldn't? Then I waited for you to come back to me. To be my mate. To be my other half. Yet... you never came. You let me think you were dead."

"It was for the best. I couldn't be your mate. All I could be was an unmated female. What were you going to do, Jazz? Kill every male wolf who thought they could touch me because of the marks Albert left?"

"*Yes.* Our pack isn't like that anymore. Those are old rules that no one follows."

"No one? You forget, I hunt weres. I see it all the time."

"Not in our pack. Not even in most. The Alliance forbids marking females like that. Things are changing—and I know you've heard about it. You can't tell me your parents aren't keeping you up to date."

"Maybe, but there are a lot of packs out there. Were you going to kill them all?"

"If that's what it took to keep you safe. I would have mated you. Changed you. Killed any man who dared even look at you wrong. Do you think I gave a damn how you were marked? It didn't change a thing, babe. Not one goddamn thing."

"Put me down," she ordered softly. "Your arms are going to get tired."

He growled. "I'm never letting you go again."

She pushed at his shoulder. "You can't do this, Jazz. You can't. If you care about me at all, you won't even say that."

"You'll be my mate, damn it! You *are* my mate."

She shook her head. "You know I can't be your mate. No one would respect it. If you turn me, Jazz, you'll be putting a big target on my back. Don't do that to me. The only protection I have is being human, and it being against the rules to rape a human."

He growled and turned, dropping Shawna on the bed. He reached for his shirt and pulled it over his head. "I won't turn you—but damn it, you're *mine*."

8

She stared up at Jazz as he kicked off his shoes. She was still frozen in disbelief as he tore his belt open and threw it down on the floor. He went for his pants next, pushing them down his hips, along with his underwear.

She couldn't help but take in all of him, since he was standing there... so bold and naked.

He had scars on his cut, beautiful body. Fight scars. On male weres, they were a mark of pride. He had many of them, and she noted each one. There was a wolf tattoo on his arm with *Nightwind* inked underneath. He was perfect. Sexy.

Her gaze went lower, and she stared at his arousal. She felt a second of apprehension. Jazz was a big man all over and it had been a while for her.

He slowly moved to the bed. "Don't fear me. I won't ever hurt you."

"Tell that to the weapon on your front." She looked at him pointedly. "Jesus, Jazz."

He followed her gaze, staring down at himself before he glanced back at her with a sad smile tugging at his lips. "All for you, babe."

He moved onto the bed, and she lay back, unable to hide her anticipation. Jazz climbed over her, caging her body with his arms and legs, and stared down at her. His eyes were dilated, his breathing loud.

Shawna put her hands on his broad shoulders. "This is a mistake."

"Does it feel like a mistake?" he asked in a low, raspy voice.

She shook her head. "No."

He licked his lips. "Kiss me."

Shawna shut her eyes, wanting him so badly it hurt. She ran her hands around to the center of his back, pulling him closer rather than pushing him away. Her mouth touched his...

And the sensation was unlike anything she'd ever felt. Molten lava. It stole every ounce of common sense. She moaned into his mouth and wrapped her arms around his neck.

He lowered his body, pinning her to his bed.

She loved the feel of him on top of her, the delicious weight of Jazz crushing her into the mattress. His skin was hot under her fingers, all hard male and tense muscle. He was fantasy come to life, and suddenly her clothes were a huge issue. She fisted a hand in his blond hair, at the same time trying to kick off her sweatpants. Jazz helped, and together, they pulled off her clothes between fevered, hungry kisses.

When she was completely naked, already breathless with anticipation, he shifted his thigh and she felt his hairy leg brush along her shaved one. The sensation was incredible. She arched her chest into his, rubbing against his body. Sensations were dancing over her skin as Jazz moved against her, adjusting his weight so he didn't crush her. Their mouths were moving, locked together, and Shawna felt like Jazz had literally set her on fire.

When he finally pulled back, Jazz was breathing hard. Her eyes opened and their gazes locked. "You are mine, babe," he rasped.

"Don't turn me, Jazz. Swear to me you won't bite me during..."

He nodded. "Even if it kills me, I swear I won't."

She let her hands glide down his shoulders to his chest. He was so broad that she had a lot to touch. Her nails raked him, but she was careful to not cut his skin. He'd heal fast but she didn't want to do that.

He blinked at her. "Have you ever been to bed with a shifter?"

She stared at him. "You mean besides when I was attacked?"

He flinched. "That doesn't count."

"Then no. I don't remember much, Jazz. I was in too much pain to stay conscious. I lost too much blood."

She saw tears in his eyes. "Do you remember any of it? Of..." His voice broke.

"Bits and pieces. Pain mostly, but I try not to think about it." She squeezed his bare shoulders as she reminded him, "I was married twice, remember? I've been with men, Jazz."

"But I'm not just a man." He shut his eyes and took a few ragged breaths, before he looked back to her. "Don't be afraid. Please, baby. Don't ever be afraid of me. I won't hurt you. I'm having a real hard time controlling myself right now. You bring out too much in me. I might slightly shift. I swear to God, I won't bite or hurt you. Will it scare you if I lose some control over my wolf?"

She shook her head. "No. I always thought you were hot when you went slightly furry."

He suddenly smiled. "You used to say that to me, but I was always afraid I'd terrify you if we had sex for the first time together and I lost control of my skin."

She reached up and caressed his cheek. "It's okay."

He nodded. "I might not lose control, but I didn't want to terrify you if I do. You have no idea what you do to me, babe. What you've *always* done to me. I've never wanted anyone the way I want you. I've never *felt* anything that even compares to what I feel when I touch you."

"I know." She took another shuddering breath and admitted, "I feel the same way."

He groaned softly and then he eased down her body. Shawna watched as he lowered his head to her breast. She curved into his strong hold, seeking his mouth. His tongue was rough. His lips warm and wet. He sucked on her nipple and she moaned. She dug her hands into his hair, letting her fingernails lightly scrape his scalp. Jazz growled deep in his chest and she felt it vibrate against her lower stomach.

"Jazz," she moaned. "You're making me ache."

She opened her thighs under him, spreading them slightly. She arched into his stomach, wanting him to take her now. She knew she was soaked and ready for him. Her body was screaming for him to be inside her. Aching. His mouth left her breast and moved to the other one. She whimpered and arched again, restlessly wiggling under his body.

"Easy, babe," he growled before he sucked her nipple.

"Now, Jazz! Please?"

He released her breast and lifted his gaze. "Not yet. Let me savor you a little first."

He moved farther down her body, using one large hand to spread her thighs wide.

"Jazz? What are you doing?"

His glanced up and smiled. "Tasting you."

"But..." The human men she'd slept with never went there the first time. But Jazz moved fast, and Shawna gasped when he buried his face between her thighs.

All ability to speak flew right out the window. He was gentle, and she still jerked a little when he swiped his tongue along the seam that was spread open to him. She was so sensitive, everything was heightened.

Shawna moaned when he circled his tongue over her clit, and then gently sucked. She arched at the intense feeling and gasped his name. His tongue shoved at the hood covering that sensitive bundle, and Shawna went nuts. She clawed the comforter and threw her head back.

"Jazz!" she panted.

He growled and vibrated against her. He released one of her thighs, and Shawna almost sobbed when she felt one of his fingers rubbing against her slit. She bucked her hips into his face when he pressed into her deep and growled again. His finger eased out, and she felt him slip in another as his mouth and tongue tormented her with pleasure.

"Oh, please," she panted. "God, Jazz."

His fingers moved, thrusting into her slow and deep. Then he turned them inside slightly and found a spot that made her scream. He sucked on her, and his tongue moved quicker. His fingers pumped into her faster and he kept hitting that spot that was driving her insane. Over and over, until her body tensed and she jerked under him.

Shawna screamed again as she climaxed. Her body bowed. Jazz tore his mouth away from her and slowly pulled his fingers out. Spasms made her shudder. She felt Jazz moving, his larger frame sliding up her body.

She forced her eyes to open, staring up at him in awe.

Jazz's eyes were changed. He had fur. His mouth was elongated. She saw sharp teeth.

She reached for him and cupped his face. There were so many emotions. *Too many.* So she just wrapped her legs around Jazz, needing him. He was large and so hard as he pressed into her. Her body took him as he pushed his hips forward. She shut her eyes and arched, moaning, as he entered.

"Jazz," she cried out.

"Babe..." He kept going, slow and steady, making the need burn bright.

She jerked, her muscles still twitching. Her body fought the thick length of him as he slowly pushed inside her.

He growled.

Shawna forced her eyes open as Jazz threw his head back. He wore a pained expression as he arched his back, his chest pushed into hers. The small amount of fur that had sprouted rubbed her hard nipples. Sensations were slamming into her body as Jazz continued to push, until she wondered if there was enough of her to take all of him.

He froze when he was finally buried deep inside her. She felt her muscles gripping him, trembling around that thick, incredibly hard length.

He withdrew and thrust. She shut her eyes and moaned loudly. Her legs wrapped around his wider hips, locking around his back. He buried his face in her shoulder and neck.

He growled and withdrew, thrusting into her again.

Withdrawing.

Thrusting.

He made a soft, almost whimpering sound. Then he was moving faster.

Shawna stroked her hands down his back. She felt fur, skin, and muscle moving under her fingers as Jazz thrust faster, deeper, and she moaned his name when the climax crashed into her.

Nothing in her life had ever felt so incredible. She'd been married twice but nothing had come close to this.

She was completely overwhelmed.

Jazz tensed, his entire body turning to stone. He shook almost violently—and then Shawna's eyes flew open as she felt wet heat shooting into her, gush after gush.

Jazz shivered again and again, before he finally collapsed. He managed not to crush her by holding up his chest. He was panting. She felt the fur under her fingers and along her body slowly disappear.

Jazz turned his head and kissed her neck. "Son of a *bitch*, babe."

She smiled and hugged him. She was locked around his body with her arms and her legs. "That was incredible."

He chuckled. "More than."

She hugged him harder, holding on. "I don't want to let go."

"Don't. I'm not letting go of *you*."

She suddenly laughed. "We'd die of starvation if we never got out of bed, and we'd get pretty ripe if we didn't shower regularly."

"That's true." He laughed and rolled them over slowly, so she was sprawled on top of him. She straightened her legs along the outside of his since they were still joined at the hips. "Okay, I think we can safely stay together in my house. We'll live off take-out."

She lifted her head and smiled at him. "I wish we could."

"I'm not kidding." He sounded serious. "We could do it."

She reached up and cupped his face. "Don't tempt me."

She felt him throb inside her. He was still hard, and he growled softly, "I want you so much."

"I'm with you."

"I know I can't mate you, but I still want a mating night."

"A mating night?"

He nodded. "Didn't your parents tell you about it when I claimed you?"

"My mom said things would work out between us. They gave me the basics of what a mating meant and how it was done."

He grinned. "Sit up on me."

She sat up, straddling him. She moaned softly and lifted, savoring the friction when she dropped down back down. Jazz groaned and gripped her hips.

"I want your desire to match mine." He sat up so they were chest to chest. "Will you trust me?"

"You know I do, Jazz. I wouldn't be here without weapons...hell, I wouldn't have gotten in your *car* to go somewhere unknown at the time if I didn't trust you."

He wrapped one powerful arm around her. "I want you to take some of my blood."

She stilled. "We can't end up mated."

"We won't. Just a little won't cause a full change, but my blood when I'm turned on like this will drive you into a kind of mating heat."

She blinked at him. "Could I get pregnant?"

"You're not ovulating. I wish you were. I want to plant my baby in you. A dozen of them if you'll let me."

She shivered in a good way at his words and his husky voice. "Heat, huh?"

"Yeah," he grunted in a low, possessive voice. "You'll want me as much as I want you."

"I already do."

"Babe, I'm a wolf. I can fuck you for hours. You're human. I'll wear you out fast, and I don't want that. My blood would temporarily protect you too. It'll make you a little tougher. It'll give you more endurance."

She licked her lips and nodded. "Okay."

"Kiss me." He grinned. "And ride me, babe. I'll bite into my arm and you drink while we make love. Just a little though."

She shivered again. Jazz slid his hands down her back and cupped her ass. He moved her, setting the pace. She whimpered at the sensations Jazz created deep inside her. Her body quivered. She was already so turned on, she wondered what would happen with his blood. Could she want him even more?

She kissed Jazz as she rocked on him and moaned into his mouth.

His hands pulled her tighter against him, urging her to move faster. She gripped his shoulders for leverage and rode him with everything she had. Jazz growled and made small noises, but he remained in his skin. He tore his mouth from hers and gripped her hips, locking her in place.

Their gazes met and held, then Jazz lifted his arm to his mouth and she watched his face slightly change. He bit into his wrist. She saw his eyes narrow, almost flinching from the pain, but then he was holding his arm up to her as his face shifted back.

"Drink. Not too much...but drink."

She closed her mouth over the bite. Jazz's blood was warm and tasted slightly metallic, but she wasn't repelled. She sucked gently. Inside her, Jazz pulsed and a sexy groan tore from his lips. Shawna took a few swallows before Jazz yanked his arm away.

"This is so damn illegal," he confessed with a broken laugh. "I don't want you taking too much. I want you to remember all of it."

"Illegal?"

He nodded. "Very. I just broke a major shifter law—and I don't give a damn. This is only something mates do. My hormones will hit you in a few minutes, Shawna. Then you'll know how much I want you. You'll feel it."

She stared into his eyes and licked her lips, cleaning his blood off her mouth. Jazz watched her with a hooded gaze. She moved on him, but he held her hips, locking them down so he was buried deep inside her but she couldn't move.

"Not yet, babe. Wait for it."

She felt her heartbeat start to accelerate. She'd ached for Jazz before, but now that ache became a pain. A *real* pain.

Her eyes flew wide open and she inhaled his scent. He smelled so damn good that it made her mouth water. The passion became something larger, a ravaging hunger that rose up from someplace deep inside She tried to move on him, but he still held her firmly, refusing to let go. She whimpered.

"You're feeling it, aren't you?" Jazz smiled. "Does it hurt, babe? That's how I hurt for you. That's how much I need to feel you, touch you, and be inside you."

She threw her head back and fought his hands.

Shawna ached.

She burned.

She needed.

She whimpered again, frantically touching him. She lowered her head and met his eyes. She saw passion burning in those blue depths. Her nails raked his skin, scoring red marks.

"Fuck." He released her hips and threw himself back on the bed. "*This* is how much I want you. I feel what you feel. My need is your need. My heart is your heart."

She rode Jazz, bucking hard on him, throwing her head back at the wild rush of pleasure. She felt her climax building and she found the release quickly, screaming. Jazz arched up, thrusting into her, and his body tensed. He shouted out as he came.

Shawna collapsed on his chest, completely breathless.

"It can't get any better," she panted. "I couldn't survive it if it did."

Jazz chuckled. "But wait, babe. Just wait. It *does* get better."

She felt the ache return immediately. She wanted him again.

She lifted up and started to move on him, when he grabbed her and rolled them over.

"I know what you need," he growled. "Hang onto me and I'll give it to you."

He moved fast, riding her, driving into her quicker, harder. She held onto him, her nails digging into his skin. The sensation of him inside her was making her scream and moan. It was too much pleasure. It felt too good. She felt another climax seize her and shrieked out his name.

She took Jazz with her again, and he hoarsely shouted her name in response as his body jerked. When the wave passed, they were both left breathless and fighting to get air.

"Tell me if I hurt you. I'm not hurting you, am I? God, babe. Please tell me none of those screams are pain."

She shook her head frantically. "You're going to kill me, but I wouldn't mind dying this way. You feel so good I feel like I'm drowning it."

"Me too." He hugged her tighter against him. "You're killing me too, babe."

The ache started again, and her eyes flew open with shock. Still, she wiggled her hips. "Again."

"That's what I want to hear. I want to fuck you until neither of us can walk tomorrow."

He moved slowly this time, pumping into her languidly, over and over. It was torture. She writhed under him, moaning, pleading. "Faster. Harder!"

"I don't want to make you sore," he rasped.

"Take me, damn it," she shouted.

She heard a snarl and opened her eyes, watching him change. He sprouted fur in a few places but remained in human form, and their eyes locked. He braced his arms on the bed, lifting his chest off of her. He moved his hips, thrusting into her faster, harder, just like she asked.

Shawna moaned and screamed his name. The pleasure was so intense it felt like pain, but she wanted more. He moved even faster—but not harder. She realized he eased up, not going so deeply into her body. She locked her legs around his waist and tensed. Again, she came, shuddering and screaming.

Jazz withdrew, and she gasped when he flipped her onto her stomach. She smiled when she felt Jazz pulling her up, holding her hips. He entered her carefully and slowly from behind, then his hands sought hers. He weaved their fingers together and kissed the scars on her back...softly, gently...before his tongue traced up her spine. He kissed her neck reverently, licking at the tender spot behind her ear.

"I won't do it...but you have no damn idea how much I want to sink my teeth into you while I'm inside you, Shawna. You have me drooling over the idea." He kissed her earlobe. His hot tongue traced her neck and then the line of her shoulders. "No damn idea. You're mine, Shawna. *Say it.* Promise me, so I know I don't have to mate you to make you mine. Swear to me, babe. Swear."

"I swear, Jazz. I swear I'm yours—and you're mine."

He growled deep in his throat and thrust into her. He rode her hard, and she clung to every decadent sensation of him fucking her from behind. She'd never liked doggie style sex...until now. The bliss grabbed her tighter this time, wringing her dry as wave after wave of sheer ecstasy slammed through her. Behind her, a howl tore from Jazz's throat.

In the next moment, they both lay panting on the bed. Jazz lifted her hair out from between their bodies. He spread it on the bed next to them, working his fingers gently through the tangles

"Swear to me that you'll never leave me again. Start over with me, babe. I can't survive losing you again..."

She turned her head. Her body was starting to ache with need again. She met his look head on. "The marks."

He leaned back and his gaze left hers. He traced his finger over the claw marks that scarred her. "Sexy. Totally fucking sexy—because they prove you're a survivor. You're powerful. I have scars too. So what? They won't drive me crazy. I promise you. I love everything about you. I always have. Nothing could ever change that. *Nothing*."

She stared into his eyes...and understanding filled her.

He meant it. He wasn't repulsed by the scars. He didn't care what those markings meant. A wolf who held no regard for his upbringing was caressing her scarred skin, and all she saw in his eyes was love and desire.

"I swear to you, Jazz," she whispered. "Let's see what happens."

He smiled and kissed her. He traced his hands up her body to her breasts. He moved slowly inside her, teasing her with every shallow stroke. She moaned and wiggled her hips against him at the rush of bliss.

"Don't cheat on me," she moaned. "I'll kill you."

He chuckled, still moving inside her, his strokes getting a little faster, a little more demanding. "I swear, babe. No one but you. You're all I have ever needed."

She expected him to make her promise the same, but he didn't. He started fucking her with intent, driving them both mindless, until they came together yet again. She knew she was going to hurt tomorrow but she didn't care.

She turned onto her side, panting, with Jazz curled around her back, still inside her. His breathing tickled her neck.

She bit her lip. "Jazz?"

"Yeah, babe? Are you getting sore?"

"A little, but that's not what's on my mind."

He brushed a kiss on her shoulder and then her neck. "What *is* on your mind? Talk to me about anything."

"Don't you want me to promise to be loyal to you?"

He tensed behind her. "I don't have to do that."

"Why not?"

"Because it goes without saying that you won't want another man. I'll keep you so satisfied and tired, you won't have the strength to lust after anyone else."

She laughed, relaxing. "That sounds like a perfect plan to me."

Jazz nuzzled her, and slowly started to move. She moaned. The frenzy seemed to be leaving her system, but it wasn't gone yet. She reached back and caressed his hips. "That feels so damn good."

"I know," he grunted. "It sure as hell does."

She groaned softly. Jazz put his arm around her. He brushed her clit with his finger, making her moan louder.

"You're heaven," Jazz groaned. "Having you here, it's heaven. We need new pictures."

She pushed back, meeting his hips. "Yes."

"Yes, to the pictures, or yes, you're close? You're milking me, babe." He groaned. "God. Yes!"

He moved faster. She felt the orgasm building inside her. Jazz shifted his hips, driving into her higher, hitting her just right. She cried out his name as she climaxed. He kept moving, drawing it out for her, and then stilled. She felt him throbbing inside her as his seed shot in fast bursts, warming her entire body.

Jazz wrapped his arm around her waist and withdrew from her minutes later. He lifted her, shifting them to a more comfortable position. They ended up sprawled together across the bed with Jazz on his back and Shawna on top of him.

She smiled. "Amazing."

He lifted his head and smiled back. "We're amazing together."

"Yes." She yawned. "But I'm tired."

"Me too."

"Jazz..." She inched closer so their bodies were pressed wrapped around each other. "I love you," she whispered.

"I love you too, babe. Sleep. Rest." He hugged her tighter. "*Really* rest. I'm not done with you by a long shot tonight. I'm just giving you a few hours to gain your strength."

"Good."

"Pictures, Shawna? Was that a yes?"

She laughed. "Yes."

He ran his hand through her long hair and twisted the red strands through his fingers. She lifted her head, looked at his hand, and arched an eyebrow.

"I'm worn out, babe. I promise. I just don't want you getting away."

"Leashing me to you by my hair, huh?"

"I'd handcuff you, but I think you wouldn't sleep comfortably in shackles."

"I'm not going anywhere, Jazz. Besides," she gave him another long look, "I'm not so sure I can walk so well right now. Someone turned me to jelly."

"Mmmmm. I love jelly."

She laughed. "One of us should get up and turn off the lights."

"I guess I could," he groaned.

She scooted over and lifted her leg that was pinned between his thighs. "You *are* the big, bad, strong wolf."

He unwound her hair from his fingers and climbed off the bed without complaint. He walked naked to the doorway and flipped off the light. She watched him as he returned to bed. He was so incredibly sexy. Masculine. Handsome.

And hers. Finally.

Jazz lay on his back and pulled her into his arms. She snuggled against his skin. He was so warm, she knew she wouldn't get cold. Weres ran a little hotter than humans. His hand wound through her long hair again and she just laughed. He chuckled with her.

"I'm not taking any chances. I love you, Shawna. I have always loved you...from the minute I laid eyes on you at the first pack meeting you were brought to."

She lifted her head to look at him. "Really?"

"You were so tiny...even for nine. But you had those big blue eyes, and you smiled at me. So brave. I was ten, and you melted my damn heart on the spot. I thought to myself, one day she's going to be my mate. I just knew."

"I fell in love with you the day you claimed me. If anyone else had made a statement like that, I would have argued, but I looked into your eyes and just thought...lucky me."

"Sleep." He caressed her shoulder. "I'm giving you two hours before I drag you out of this bed and into a shower with me. Then I'm going to use my mouth on you until you scream my name and beg me to be inside you again."

She shut her eyes and sighed. "I can't wait."

Shawna drifted to sleep within a minute.

9

*S*hawna shrieked with amusement, swiftly dodging Jazz's grasp when he tried to grab her. She took off toward the kitchen with him hot on her heels. His laughter followed her closely. She rounded the island, keeping it between them, and grinned smugly as he studied her.

"Come here." Playfulness gleamed in Jazz's light gaze

She shook her head. "No way."

He ran his tongue over his bottom lip. "I just want to give you a hug."

"Bullshit," she snorted. "You're going to tickle me. It was just shaving cream."

"In my pants." He looked down pointedly. "And it doesn't belong there."

"You thought I was going to do something really sexy when I unzipped you while you shaved, didn't you?"

"Yeah." He wagged his eyebrows at her. "When you went down on your knees, I had a *very* different idea of what was going to take place."

"What?" She stayed on the other side of the island for protection. "Didn't you imagine I was going to grab the shaving cream and foam you up?"

"Now I have to shower again. The least you could do is come wash me."

She giggled when he made a move to grab her, barely dodging him. "You make my undies wet all the time, so this was just a little payback."

"I'm trying to do it again if you'll just stop moving."

She saw an opening and ran out of the kitchen. She heard Jazz let out a bark of amusement, coming fast behind her. He caught her around the waist and swung her off her feet. Shawna gasped when he twisted her in his arms, and suddenly she was over his shoulder. Rather than fight it, she reached down and grabbed one beefy butt check, admiring how firm it was in her hand.

"I love your ass."

"I love yours too." He lightly slapped her butt over his shoulder, and then hooked his arm behind her legs. "Now let's go shower again."

He moved for the stairs, but the chime of a doorbell stopped him short. Rather than set Shawna back on her feet, Jazz spun and went for the door with her still over his shoulder.

Her laughter died. "Put me down! We don't know who it is."

"It's fine. You're safe." He didn't put her down. Instead, he unlocked the door and yanked it open.

Shawna felt a rush fear. She couldn't see who was at the door but Jazz's body didn't tense. Still hanging over his shoulder, she heard a male snort of amusement.

"I guess you found her."

"Yep," Jazz answered. "Do you want to come in?"

"Sure." The male had a deep laugh. "Obviously, I'm interrupting something. I apologize. You weren't answering your phone, and I wanted to make sure that you weren't passed out drunk. You weren't in the best of moods last night. Last you told me, you wanted to be alone to search for her. Hello, Marcy."

She tensed. "It's Shawna now."

Jazz gently put her down. Once she was standing on her feet, she turned and he wrapped his arms around her, holding her against his body. Shawna looked up at the new arrival standing inside the door.

She recognized the tall, powerfully built werewolf instantly, but the last time she'd seen him, he was a teen in jeans and a t-shirt. Now he was a full-grown alpha, his long black hair pulled back, and he was sporting a tailored three-piece suit that made him appear more than a little intimidating.

"Hi, Des." She smiled at him hesitantly. "I see you've grown up."

"I see you have too." Desmon smiled as he tilted his head and quirked an eyebrow at her hair. "I wouldn't have recognized you either, except for your eyes. My mate is going to want to meet you badly."

She stiffened. "Why?"

Jazz's hold on her tightened. "That wasn't a threat. Amber was human. She's very nice. I keep telling you that no one here is going to want to hurt you, babe."

"I also give you my word that's true." Desmon's tone grew solemn.

Shawna leaned back into Jazz. She felt safe with him near. "You can't really say that and mean it. You can't control everyone—especially weres."

Desmon inclined his head. "That's true, but I'm making it known if anyone even considers trying to hurt you, Jazz and I will kill them."

She stared up at him, a little shocked. "Why would you do that?"

"Jazz is like a brother to me." Desmon sighed. "I realize some of our pack and others won't be very happy that Jazz is mating with a were-hunter, but we'll make sure it's known you only hunted the ones who *needed* to be put down."

"But Jazz can't mate me. I'll just be his human girlfriend."

Jazz softly growled behind her. "If you won't let me mate you, then you'll at least let me marry you."

She turned her head and stared back at him, before slowly nodding in agreement. "It's rash, but...I can do marriage."

Jazz relaxed with a broad smile. "Deal."

"Why won't you let Jazz mate you?" Desmon scowled at her. "The man has torn up the entire country looking for you. He's *always* remained fixed on you. You're the only woman he's ever loved, Mar —Shawna."

She met his gaze, rather than lowering her head in shame. "I'm marked, Des."

Desmon looked past Shawna to Jazz. "I don't understand."

Jazz held her tighter. "I keep telling her it doesn't matter."

Desmon frowned. "Marked how?"

Shawna took a deep breath. "I wasn't just attacked when I was sixteen. I was *marked*. Albert marked me as a pack whore."

She saw the look of shock cross Desmon's face, and he lowered his gaze for one long moment, his jaw clenching. "No one ever told me. I'm sorry you have a physical reminder."

"So Jazz can't mate me."

"I can understand why you feel that way." Desmon sighed. "You know Albert marked my mother, too. Do you remember that Jazz and I share a sister?"

"I do," she whispered. "How is Hope?"

"I sent her and my mother away after we took the pack. I understand your fears."

"Des," Jazz growled at him. "You better be on my side with this!"

"Let me finish." Desmon gave Jazz a look before he focused on Shawna. "We did send them away to a sanctuary pack in Arizona, but that was a long time ago. They would be completely safe to move back to Nightwind territory now, but my mother has a close friendship with the alpha there, and she's happy. Hope has her friends. They're her pack, and we wouldn't dream of taking her from where she's happiest. She still visits from time to time. So does my mother—even marked, she comes here, and she's safe. Always. Nightwind is not like you remember. We protect our females, Shawna. Jazz and I make sure of it."

"See." Jazz leaned down to whisper in her ear, "I wasn't lying. You're safe here."

"There would be precautions to take," Desmon went on. "She'd be safe from our pack. There's no doubt about that, but we'd have a problem with other packs if they saw her scars—and you know they would, when the packs merge to run together. If you changed her, you couldn't take her outside of Nightwind territory for runnings, that's for damn sure. It's not fair, but like Shawna said, we can't control everyone."

"What if it were Amber?" Jazz asked, sounding more resigned than defiant.

Desmon held his best friend's gaze. "If it were Amber, I would mate her, but I'd be very careful about who saw her shifted. You're safe running around here, but I'd keep her far away from the Goodwin border. You can't ever relax your guard around them."

"It's still a lot to risk for me," she pointed out.

"It is, but most things are," Desmon reminded her. "I can't speak for all packs, only mine, and I'll assure you again that you're safe here. That's no guarantee in the rest of the world...but if I were betting man, I'd say your odds of survival are better here, mated to Jazz, rather than hunting rogue weres out in the wild as a human. Just my two cents."

"Maybe." Shawna couldn't argue with that logic. "I'll think about it."

"Then I guess I've said my piece." Desmon tilted his head to the door. "I'll let myself out."

Jazz let her go to follow Desmon to the front door. "Thanks for checking on us."

"Yeah, you know I had to make sure." Desmon stepped onto the front porch and turned back to smile at Shawna. "I'm really glad you're back. It's a miracle we never counted on."

She bit her lip to distract from the sting in her eyes. "Thanks."

Jazz locked the door after he left.

Shawna studied him for a moment, and asked, "Does it bother you that you're not leading the pack? You were groomed for it."

"No." Jazz didn't even flinch over the word as he walked back to her. "I lost all interest. It cost me the most important thing in my life."

She swallowed hard and bit her lip once more.

"You. If you were wondering."

"Yeah...I thought that's what you meant."

"My father took you from me because he wanted me to take over the pack." Jazz reached out, took her hand in his larger one, and pulled her into his arms. "I want to mate you, Shawna. We deserve it. Both of us."

She shook her head against his chest, hugging him back. "You aren't going to die trying to protect me. That's even worse than being alone like I am now."

"Then we won't leave our territory if you're shifted. There's no rule that says I have to go on runs. I'm not the damn alpha. Don't forget that, Shawna. I don't have the responsibilities that go with the title. Desmon and I run the pack together but it's all voluntary on my side. We could do this. I have fifty acres of land. We'll run here when we want to stretch our legs."

"You make it sound so easy."

"It can be." He tilted her chin, until she was looking up into his light gaze that burned with raw determination. "It really can be. We can do this together, Shawna. We can have it all. Sixteen years apart was too long...but still nothing. We'll have so many more years if you let me mate you. Fully mate you. We'll be wolves together, we'll run in the woods, just like we planned. Give me those years to love you. Let me finally have the chance to make you happy."

"I need to think about it." She couldn't say no and truly mean it. It wasn't in her, not after last night...but she was still scared. "I'm not going to drop dead from old age tomorrow, you know?"

"True.

"It's a lot, Jazz. Even without the markings, there are a lot of weres out there who aren't going to like the fact that I'm a hunter."

"You *were* a hunter." He frowned at her. "You need to give it up. I need you safe. Please, babe...for me...*please* give it up. You said you wanted children, and I do too. You can't do that and risk your damn life all the time. Leave putting down bad weres to someone else."

She stared up at him and found herself nodding, even if a part of her still worried. "I promise you that I'll give up the hunt—unless I feel it's absolutely necessary. I can't stop being who I am completely, not even for you. If there's a bad guy out there, hurting humans, and no one else stops him, then I have to. I can't turn my back, not when *I* know how it feels to be hurt. It's the reason I started hunting. It's what kept me alive a lot of times when I didn't have a reason to get out of bed."

Jazz opened his mouth.

Shawna put her fingers to his lips. "But if I get pregnant, then I swear to give it up no matter what. I don't want to leave my children without a mother. I lost my birth mother, then my adopted mother, and I don't want to do that to our children—or you."

"That's fair. Any bad weres show up on the radar, I'll have them taken care of before you can even blink." He gave her a wide smile. "Now, are you going to walk up those stairs willingly or do I carry you up there?"

"Beast." She snorted, though her smile probably gave her away. "Making me go up there to get naked with you."

He started guiding her toward the stairs. "Don't forget hot sex. I'm going to make you have hot, steamy sex with me in the shower."

"If that's the case..." She broke out of his arms and ran up the stairs.

Things had gotten too serious, and she missed their little escape from reality. She reached the top and called out, "Hurry up, damn it!"

Jazz followed her lead, right on her tail as she ran into his bathroom. Shawna tore at her clothing and bent over in front of him to turn on the shower. She took her time adjusting the water, feeling his hot gaze on her. She didn't turn until the temperature was right, but the look on his face stole her breath.

"I love you, Shawna." His voice cracked with the confession as he reached forward and grabbed her, holding her tight once more. "I love you so damn much."

She wrapped her arms around his waist. "I love you more than the moon and the stars. I never forgot."

Jazz whimpered, as if the memory sliced through him. They used to say that to each other when they were teens. "I'll die if I lose you again. I'll fucking die, babe."

She held him tight. "I'm never going to leave you again."

Jazz didn't let go, as if afraid she might disappear.

Finally, Shawna wiggled in his arms and reminded him, "It's hard to have hot, steamy sex if you just hold me."

"Okay." He released her and pulled his shirt over his head. "I'm coming."

"I hope we're both coming really soon." Shawna stepped into the shower stall. "Get in here."

Jazz stripped fast and followed her under the spray.

When he went to his knees, Shawna looked down at him and arched her eyebrow. "What are you doing?"

He pushed her back against the wall and lifted one of her legs, resting it on the top of his shoulder. He dipped his head down, and Shawna moaned as he spread her open with his fingers without a word. She threw her head back when he boldly swirled his tongue over her clit.

"That feels so damn good."

He licked the full length of her. "You *taste* so damn good."

Shawna shuddered and gripped the top of the shower door to help hold herself still. Her hips bucked toward Jazz's mouth. She wouldn't last long with him licking her. Teasing her. The tension was almost unbearable. Her eyes were squeezed shut. She could feel the moist steam flooding the bathroom, making her warm all over.

She panted and moaned, completely frantic, and still Jazz didn't stop.

Shawna screamed out as she came, shaking from the waves of pleasure. She was still trembling when Jazz climbed to his feet and grabbed her hips. He lifted her up his body, and Shawna instinctively wrapped her arms and legs around him.

He pushed her back against the cool tile and entered her slowly. The thick length of him stretching her, claiming her, filling her up completely, drove Shawna wild. She lowered her face to his shoulder and bit him.

She just couldn't help herself.

Jazz growled and started to pump frantically. "Harder!"

She bit harder.

He drove into her, fast, powerful, his growls growing more and more primal. Shawna tasted blood in her mouth and licked at the wound she'd made with her teeth. She knew what was coming, with his potent blood in her system.

She grinned, clinging to him, grateful Jazz was all hers for the next few hours.

JAZZ CLIMBED OUT FROM UNDER THE COVERS AND STOOD THERE NAKED, studying Shawna. She was sleeping on her stomach, her bright red hair spread out over her naked back. He loved seeing her in his bed. Everything about her cuddled up in his sheets looked perfect.

His gaze strayed to the scars. Pain and anger battled inside him. His *father* had done that—because he didn't approve of his son mating to a human. He'd hurt her, nearly killed her, and cost them so many years apart.

He closed his eyes, smelling her in his room, and calmed. Shawna was alive and back in his life. That's what he needed to focus on. His father was dead and couldn't hurt them ever again.

He looked to the clock. They'd missed lunch and dinner, and very little of that time was spent sleeping. His body ached, which meant Shawna was probably going to be sore as hell.

His smile died.

If Shawna had let him change her, she'd heal while she napped, but human Shawna was going to be tender when she woke.

Thinking about it made the wolf in him irrational, so he turned away to take a shower. Jazz took his time under the water, letting the warm spray ease some of the tension he felt rolling under the surface.

He assumed Shawna would be up by the time he was done, but still she slept. She was exhausted. Half of him was proud of that fact, while half of him worried. He'd probably taken her too many times. He should have been gentler, but Shawna responded so passionately, even without his blood in her system. It was impossible to not lose control. Shawna was his woman.

His mate.

He turned away once more, wanting her to get the rest she needed. He dressed quietly in a pair of sweats and walked out of the bedroom, keeping his steps light.

The house was silent and dark.

Jazz turned on lights in case Shawna woke, knowing she couldn't see like he could. He went to the kitchen, still thinking about his mate. Shawna needed to eat. He needed to eat. It was just after ten at night, and he decided on an early breakfast instead of a late dinner.

He started pulling out the ingredients for his special omelet. All the guys at the pack house asked for seconds and thirds when he made it. It was a favorite, one of those things he saved for really special occasions.

His mate was home.

He couldn't think of a better reason to celebrate.

He was just finishing cutting onions when movement caught his attention. He grinned and turned, expecting Shawna.

It wasn't her.

His smile died. He'd been so lost in his thoughts that he'd missed hearing the other woman approach. The strong scent of onion probably didn't help either.

"Hey, Krystal." Jazz shook off his shock and went back to cooking. "What are you doing here?"

"You can't avoid me forever, you know." Krystal grinned at him, her gaze raking over his body. "We need to make some decisions about the anniversary party for Desmon and Amber. You're Desmon's best friend and co-alpha. Tag, you're it."

"Please just plan it and I'll pay for it. Tell me how much to make out the check to you."

She leaned against the doorway and put her hands on her hips. "Ah. You're being a man."

"Yeah, well, I am guilty." He looked down at himself with an arched eyebrow, and then reached for the bell pepper on the counter. "You plan it and I'll pay for it. Fair deal. There're plenty of other wolves you can recruit for help."

"Fine. I can do that." Krystal laughed and eyed the food. "Hungry?"

"You have no idea." He thought about Shawna again and smiled. "I missed lunch and dinner."

"Want something besides food? I miss you, Jazz." Krystal walked in the kitchen. She hopped gracefully onto the counter, opened her thighs wide and scooted to the edge as her mini skirt hiked higher. "Why don't you drop the sweats and come say hello."

He frowned. "Krystal..."

SHAWNA WAS PISSED. SHE'D STOOD ON THE STAIRS, LISTENING TO JAZZ and the woman from the pack house.

Krystal.

Jealousy, curiosity, and a healthy amount of distrust had Shawna standing there fuming—until that bitch made it clear she was after more than party money. Something much darker than distrust swept over Shawna then, and she moved fast, storming into the kitchen.

Jazz spotted her and paled. "This isn't what it looks like, babe."

The woman on the counter slammed her thighs shut, just as Shawna grabbed the knife where Jazz had laid it down after cutting his vegetables. She tested the weight in her hand for a split second before letting it fly.

It sank hard into the cupboard about three inches from the other woman's face.

Shawna was furious. "Get out—or the next one won't miss."

Krystal paled. Her gaze flew to the knife stuck in the cupboard near her face, before she glanced back to Shawna with wide eyes.

"I'm serious. Get the fuck out. And by the way, leave the key," Shawna snarled in warning. "You ever walk into this house again without being invited, I'll take you out. Got me? And keep your damn legs shut around Jazz. *He's mine.*"

"Shawna, I was just about to tell her. Krystal didn't mean anything."

"Bullshit! She's a wolf, isn't she? Don't tell me she couldn't smell me all over this house!" Shawna rounded on him. "How many other bitches have keys?"

Jazz flushed a little.

"Jesus. *How many?*"

"A few."

"Asshole." Shawna wanted to lash out at him...but she knew it wasn't actually his fault that he'd been lonely. She turned to Krystal instead. "Out—and don't come back!"

Krystal hopped off the counter with werewolf grace and dashed quickly out of the kitchen.

Shawna followed after her. "Don't forget to leave the damn key!"

Krystal reached into her purse. She dropped a key on the table by the door and fled, slamming the door behind her.

Shawna stood there in the ringing silence until she felt Jazz behind her.

She turned and gave him a long look.

"I'll get the keys back and let them know we're together," Jazz said quickly. "I didn't invite her to come over, and I promise I would've told her to get off my counter if you'd waited two more seconds. I was about to tell her about you."

"I may have been married twice, but I never had a string of men climbing into my bed." She glared up at him. "I didn't hand out my house keys like a doctor does lollipops."

His frown deepened. "Shawna...why are you *really* so upset? Do you think I would have taken her invitation? Did you see me moving toward her? No to both."

"You were talking to her." Shawna's voice cracked. "Like it was no big deal that she let herself into your house!"

"We're all pack. We walk in and out of each other's houses all the time. You know that. I didn't even think she wanted anything else until she hopped up on the counter. Babe, you know how wolves are."

"I know." She fought the urge to cry. "I'm just pissed. Get the damn keys back—and the next woman I find in the kitchen flashing you is *dead.*"

She stormed toward the stairs.

Jazz softly cursed and followed after her.

She stopped at the top and folded her arms over her chest. "I want you to take me to my motel."

"No. I didn't cheat on you. Damn it, I was making us dinner! Krystal let herself in. I didn't know she was coming. We were talking about this party for Des and Amber. Having a mated alpha couple is a big deal to the pack. They like celebrating their anniversary. It's a surprise thing they're planning. When the conversation turned, I was going to tell her to leave."

"I want you to take me to my Jeep."

"You aren't leaving me," Jazz growled. "Not over this. I would *never* cheat on you. I'm sorry for what happened. I had no idea she would come over. I have no interest in her at all. I'm a wolf. You're *my mate.* You know how all that works."

"And that is the *only* reason I didn't use that knife on *you.* I want to be taken to my Jeep, then the motel."

"Babe," he growled.

"Don't you babe me!" she snapped at him. "I want my guns."

He blinked. "You aren't leaving me?"

"I want my guns." She folded her arms stubbornly. "She's a were. In a fight, she'd tear me up. I'm defenseless without my shit, Jazz. Since your house seems to have an open-door policy to all your ex-fucks, I need my weapons."

He stared at her. "I'll have the locks changed. I'll call every damn female I've slept with in the past ten years and let them know they aren't welcome anywhere near me. Please calm down."

"Tell me how calm you would have been if this was *my* house, and you walked into the kitchen and found a man you knew I've had sex with standing there with his pants around his ankles."

His blue eyes narrowed, and a low growl rumbled from the center of his chest. "I understand."

She cursed and stormed into his bedroom, looking for her clothes. They were on the floor. She yanked off the borrowed shirt of Jazz's and started to get dressed.

Jazz suddenly grabbed her, throwing her on the bed. She fought, but he was stronger. He pinned her under him, holding both her hands above her head.

"Babe," he whispered, rubbing a thumb against the inside of her wrist. "Please calm down. I belong to you. I'm sorry."

She narrowed her eyes at him.

"And you are anything but defenseless." He arched an eyebrow. "You ran Krystal right out the door. She was afraid of you. You don't have my sense of smell, but trust me, she was terrified."

"I'm pissed, Jazz." Shawna sighed and shut her eyes. "I know it's not reasonable. I *know* that...but I'm still angry."

"I don't think it's unreasonable," he argued. "She let herself into my house and offered herself to me. It happened so fast that I didn't see it coming, or I would have cut her off when she started talking about Desmon and Amber. I would have told her about you immediately. I assumed she could smell you too."

Shawna snorted. "You think she couldn't? I hate to break it to you, but that's *why* she did it."

"You're probably right." Jazz looked apologetic. "I'm so sorry."

Shawna didn't say anything after that. She kept her eyes closed and fought her temper. She knew he'd slept with other women. Hell, she'd been married twice in the years they were apart. But that woman had walked into Jazz's place like she owned it and offered herself to him with Shawna still in the damn house.

"Babe?" Jazz leaned down and nuzzled her neck with his lips. "I love you. You're the only one I want."

She shook her head. "Let me be alone for a little while. I'll calm down."

"I'm not leaving you alone. And I'm not taking you anywhere tonight. I'll change the locks tomorrow, and I meant it about making sure everyone knows we belong together. They'll all know you're the woman I want, the *only woman* I want. I'm yours. Look at me, Shawna. Please?"

She opened her eyes, seeing the torment in Jazz's brilliant blue gaze. If only it didn't hurt her so much to see him sad.

"I understand your anger. Trust me. I'm putting myself in your shoes, and I get it," Jazz went on, not releasing his hold on her wrists. "I hate thinking about the two husbands you had. Just thinking about them touching you pisses me off. I'd go more than a little crazy if I walked into a room to see a man you used to sleep with trying to seduce you. I promise I get it, babe. I should have called everyone right away and told them. That was my mistake. I'm really fucking sorry. I was too caught up with you. I never once thought that anyone would come over here."

Some of her anger eased. "It hurt," she acknowledged.

He hugged her. "And I don't ever want to hurt you."

She nodded into his chest, and he kissed the top of her head. "How can I make this better for you? Do you want me to make those calls right now? You can listen to every word."

She shook her head. "I don't want to know how many damn calls you have to make, Jazz."

He tensed. "Okay. Good point."

She slapped his arm hard. "Slut."

"I was single. If I knew you were coming back into my life, I would have lived like a monk." She heard amusement in his voice. "Honest."

"Asshole."

He chuckled. "Is that an offer? Because I would love to try that with you."

She punched him and laughed. "No way, no how, Jazz. You're huge."

"Fair enough." He sighed. "Now, I'm starving. Let me go finish our dinner and we'll have a picnic on the bed."

She nodded. "Okay. I think I should avoid the kitchen for a little while."

"Good idea." He caressed her cheek. "I love you."

"I love you too...slut."

He grinned. "Not anymore."

"Only because you want to live."

He laughed. "Damn straight. My woman is *fierce*."

"And good at throwing knives," she reminded him.

"Let me go get the food." He caressed her cheek once more. "If you're really good, I'll turn on the television and let you have the remote. See how much I love you? I'm a man offering up the remote control."

"Okay." She gave him another side-eyed glare, while trying and failing to resist the smile tugging at her lips. "I so get the remote after that kitchen scene."

He grinned. "Yeah, you do."

10

*T*he early morning sun was hidden by the trees, but sparks of it found their way through. The glimmers danced on the muddy forest floor, casting ominous shadows as Miles Nightwind walked quietly through the woods, keeping his steps light.

He lifted his bow and arrow, wishing he had his lever-action Winchester rifle instead. He just hadn't expected to smell trouble when he set out before the sun rose to hunt. Now he was tracking the scent of blood and death instead of a cougar that had been lingering around the area.

Most Nightwind wolves avoided this side of the north border, and not just because it bordered Goodwin land. This section of the woods was particularly dense, which left things wet and mossy. The scent of mildew permeated the air, making it hard to smell anything else for most wolves. Losing a sense was scary, which was exactly why Miles had built his house here.

He liked places where it was easy to hide his scent. In the swampy darkness of his tiny corner on the north border, only the best trackers could use their noses to survive.

It gave him the edge.

And for a werewolf who couldn't shift, tracking, staying in the shadows, knowing his enemy before he could see them—these things were all vital to survival according to Miles.

That meant he was likely the only one who could smell the faint odor of fresh decay on the wind. He decided to deal with it now because situations like that only got worse with time.

It didn't take him long to find the problem.

He stepped over a rock, now lingering right on the edge of Goodwin land, where he spotted blood on the roots of a towering redwood. This wasn't a wild animal like he'd hoped. It scented of werewolf blood—one that seemed vaguely familiar. He turned on his heel, trying to find a body, but the smell of it was everywhere.

That's when he stepped on a hand—just lying there on the forest floor, all by itself.

"Oh hell." He whipped his head around and spotted a lone ear hiding under some leaves. "Fucking werewolves."

He stopped looking and reached for his phone instead, knowing the discoveries were only going to get more gruesome. Since this was clearly a message and not a full-blown attack, he set his bow down and put the arrow in the quiver on his back. Then he called his cousin.

Desmon answered on the second ring. "You're calling me. That's not good. What time is it? Am—"

His mate Amber answered, "It's seven-fourteen."

"Oh Jesus. That's too early," Desmon grunted into the phone. "I'm going to have to leave the house without coffee—I already know it."

"Are you done?" Miles sighed with annoyance.

"Is it a serious issue?"

"Well, yeah. I'm calling you at seven in the fucking morning, Des," Miles barked at him. "I found a body near the north border, right past the big redwood on the east end."

Desmon groaned out loud. "What kind of body?"

"The werewolf kind."

"One of ours?"

"Smells like it." Miles sniffed the air again. "It's familiar, but I can't place it."

"And you can't just look at it?"

"That's part of the issue." Miles winced as he glanced around. "The body's kind of—scattered."

Desmon was quiet for a long moment. "It's a message."

"Very likely." Miles hated to admit it. "I found it right on the edge of the border. Obviously the Goodwins are getting serious about this territory war—enough to break laws."

"I thought they were trying to be good for the Alliance. They've been kissing political ass since everything that went down with Amber. Now they're just tossing dead wolves over the border and ruining their supposed good reputations?"

"Yup," Miles agreed.

"I have to go meet Miles up by his place," Desmon huffed to his mate over the rustle of sheets being pulled back. "This is a big problem."

"I figured." Amber sounded concerned. "You sure you don't want me to make you some coffee before you go out?"

"No, I'm running up there in fur. Miles, try to find out who it was."

Miles grunted, but started searching again, using his nose as a guide. He stomped around the woods for a few minutes while Desmon bitched and moaned about putting on a harness, which would allow him to run in fur and carry weapons in case he needed them.

Miles spotted light blond hair in the mud and walked over, finding a head. He moved it gently with his booted foot, grimacing as he looked down, finally placing a face with the scent. "It's Scotty, that new wolf from Santa Barbara we accepted in."

"Oh, God. He was on guard duty last night." Desmon sounded gutted. "He was a seasoned enforcer. He had years of experience, but maybe with the territory still being new he was caught off guard or something."

Miles glanced away, feeling guilty too, wishing he would've heard something last night, but his place was too far. "Des, it's not your fault. They crossed our border and probably ganged up on him. We didn't expect them to pull any shit right now with them kissing Alliance ass."

"Yeah, good luck proving it. They'll just tell the Alliance he wandered into their territory. They'll make up some bullshit and claim it was their right to kill him."

"They left an old-school war message," Miles reminded him. "That's serious."

Desmon was quiet for a moment before he sighed. "I'm going to call Jazz on my way out, and then I'm heading your way. I won't take too long."

Miles nodded. "Okay."

Desmon hung up, and Miles looked around, surveying the damage as he slipped his phone back into his pocket. He decided to start cleaning up before Desmon got there.

His cousin had enough to deal with.

Miles didn't want to tell Desmon, but if the Goodwins were starting a territory war now, he was worried Nightwind might not win.

Jazz stretched out in bed, feeling incredibly warm and cozy. Shawna's skin was so smooth, and she smelled amazing first thing in the morning. All snuggled under the covers, he wrapped both his arms around his mate and sniffed her hair.

"What are you doing?" Shawna asked with a giggle.

"Smelling you," Jazz admitted without shame. "More specifically, smelling me on you, and both of us mixed together. It's my new favorite scent in the world."

Shawna tilted her head, smiling at Jazz over her bare shoulder. "That's sweet."

"Well, I'm a sweet wolf." He kissed her neck. "Want me to prove it?"

Shawna looked at him again, her gaze becoming soft and inviting in a way that drove Jazz wild. "I wouldn't say no."

He growled and buried his face in the curve of her neck, licking and kissing her skin until Shawna moaned. She rolled onto her back, spreading out beneath him, her red hair vibrant on his pillow...

And his phone rang.

The growl that came out of Jazz was less than friendly, especially when he rolled over to grab his phone off the nightstand and saw it was Desmon calling early in the morning.

That wasn't good.

Against his better judgement, Jazz answered. "You know I just found my mate after sixteen years of living without her. Is someone dying?"

"Dying? No." Desmon paused. "He's already dead."

Jazz fell back against his pillow with a groan. "Who was it?"

"Miles found Scotty's body out on the north border this morning —scattered."

"Damn." Jazz ran a hand through his hair. "Scotty didn't seem like an aggressive wolf. The Goodwins must have attacked him."

"You know it's a warning."

"I know." Jazz looked over to Shawna. "Shitty timing."

"It's never a good time for a territory war," Desmon grunted. "Look, I know it's hard to leave your mate after finding her so recently. I'm going to help Miles clean up and figure out what happened. Have some coffee. Take a shower. Wake up. We'll meet at the pack house in a little while to figure out new patrol schedules. We're going to need four times the manpower on the Goodwin border—at least."

"What you mean to say is you and I are going to be out there," Jazz clarified. "Sniffing around on the muddy, nasty side of the north end all night—every night."

"Go drink your coffee. I'll meet you at nine."

"Yeah, okay." Jazz grunted, "See you then."

Jazz dropped his phone after he hung up, and just lay there staring up at the ceiling. He wasn't mad at Desmon, but he was frustrated with the real world showing up and ruining his safe, cozy morning with his mate.

He'd spent years dreaming about mornings like this.

"Bad news?" Shawna whispered into the silence.

"They found one of our wolves dead on the north end. I have to go meet with Desmon to deal with it."

"I'm sorry about the wolf you lost. Tough to be a boss. You carry a lot of worry on your shoulders." Shawna was surprisingly understanding. "What time do you have to be there?"

"Nine."

Shawna leaned over and picked up his phone, looking at the time pointedly. "A lot can happen before nine."

Jazz raised his eyebrows, loving her more than ever, and had to agree, "Yes, it can."

SHAWNA PARKED HER JEEP IN FRONT OF THE MOTEL. SHE HAD TO GO TO the office to get the new key to her room since the door and lock had been replaced while she was gone. She considered the owner with apprehension, while he studied her back with a cold, grim gaze.

She gave him a weak smile to break the ice. "Sorry about the door."

"Jazz took care of it." He just stared at her for another long moment, before he announced, "I want you packed and out immediately. Leave the key on the dresser."

Shawna was stunned but managed to hide it. "Fine."

What did she care? She was checking out anyway. Shawna took the key and left the office. She felt a chill down her back, and almost wished Jazz were with her, but he left to his meeting in a rush when they ended up stepping out the shower well past nine o'clock.

After he left, Shawna managed to get a car to pick her up way out in the middle of Nightwind territory, and had the driver drop her by her Jeep. Might as well run some errands while Jazz was busy instead of waiting around his place. She didn't need a bodyguard anymore. She'd fought her own battles for a longtime without Jazz around.

Shawna packed her things quickly. She made sure to strap on her weapons and slipped her arms through her trench coat to hide them. Just in case. She stepped out the door with her bag over her shoulder, but stopped short when she found the owner, Dan, and six other men waiting by her Jeep. She knew a few of them, but Nightwind must have really grown in the past sixteen years. Most of these werewolves were strangers to her.

Not good.

She tensed hard and was grateful she had her long coat on. She slipped a hand to her side and gripped the handle of her semi-automatic hidden in her tactical belt.

She stayed at least twenty feet from them and asked, "What's up?"

Dan growled at her, showing long canine teeth. "We want you to leave Nightwind territory and never return."

"So I see." She frowned at the group of them. "Too bad Desmon Nightwind, your alpha, said I could stay."

Dan growled again. "You're a damn were-hunter. Unless you want to be the one hunted, you'll get your ass out of our territory. Are we clear?"

"Do you know who I've killed?" Shawna was pissed. "Merl raped a human girl. Do you have any daughters? Any nieces? How can you stomach that? Luckily, another werewolf came along before he could kill her. He pulled Merl off her, and Merl killed *him* for the effort. That wolf Merl killed was my brother." She glared at Dan. "It was my right to take Merl out for what he did to my family."

Shawna saw a few of the men frown at Dan with confusion.

"That's not what we heard," Dan snapped. "You just don't like weres. All weres. You kill them for the fun of it."

"You heard shit. Weres *raised* me. I'm human, but werewolves took me in when my biological family was killed in an accident. I love them. They're great people. I said Merl killed my brother. He wasn't changed over. He was born a werewolf. So was the rest of my family."

The men all looked surprised, and she realized none of them knew she used to be Marcy, and that was fine by her. She didn't want them to know who she was. Then they'd think she definitely hated all shifters because of what had happened to her thanks to their old alpha. She studied the werewolves standing in front of her.

Shawna's gaze settled on Dan.

"I don't have a problem with your kind unless they go rabid. That means going after helpless humans for no damn reason but to inflict pain—like raping a defenseless girl. If you believe I shouldn't have killed him, then the next time I come across one like that I'll give him your address, and you can live with the next Merl. How about that?"

Dan took a deep breath. "Desmon would have taken care of it if someone had told him. Most Alphas would. We don't need humans to take care of our business. There's no need for you."

"Desmon is a good alpha," she agreed. "Not all of them are."

Dan eyed her. "True."

"And if I knew Desmon Nightwind was your alpha, I would have just called him instead of taking out Merl myself. I thought your old alpha was still in charge—and he wasn't a good man."

"What do you know about it?" one of the others asked defensively.

"Like I said. I was raised by weres. I heard plenty of shit about Albert Zendell."

Dan glared. "Fine. You can stay—but we're watching you."

"I didn't know I needed your permission." Shawna arched an unimpressed eyebrow at him. "Now can you please move away from my Jeep? I'm not exactly feeling the love from your welcoming party, so excuse me if I'm a little on edge. I'd like some space between us."

A vehicle entered the motel parking lot. The driver was speeding. He locked the brakes, making the SUV rock violently. Shawna tensed and tightened the grip on her gun. *What now?*

Her eyes went to the open door of the SUV and Jason stepped out. His gaze darted over to Shawna and then locked on Dan.

"What in the hell is going on?" Jason snarled.

Dan paled a little. Shawna watched the exchange. Jason was a pack enforcer. That meant he was one mean fighter and could likely take any man in the pack who wasn't alpha.

Jason looked furious. He was dressed like a biker with a leather jacket, torn jeans, and black leather boots. She noticed he stayed a good distance from her, but he put his body between hers and the men by her Jeep, his back to her. He was a huge werewolf, but his position still surprised her.

He'd turned his back on a known were-hunter. He either didn't consider her a threat, or he trusted her to not attack him.

"I asked a question." Jason's voice was like gravel, rough and harsh.

"They were just saying goodbye and they were nice enough to ask if I needed help with my bag on my way out," Shawna lied.

"Bullshit." Jason turned his head and shot her a glare. "I know trouble when I see it. I want you to tell me the truth."

She dropped her suitcase to free up her hand and saluted him. "Yes, sir."

He sighed with obvious exasperation. "I don't envy Jazz. You're a handful, aren't you?"

"I try. I hate it when life gets boring."

Jason's frown melted and he smirked. "Jazz is very brave. Could you please let go of the gun at your side? You're making me a little nervous."

She eased her hand off her semi-automatic and pulled it out from under her coat. She showed him her open palms. "Not a problem."

Jason winked at her, and that surprised her too.

He turned his back on her again to growl at Dan. "You were told she was off limits to everyone. She's with Jazz. He's claimed her. The woman you're harassing is Jazz's future mate. If I don't scare you enough to keep your noses out of trouble, then worry about Jazz. He finally found a woman he wants to settle down with, which none of us thought would ever happen. Can you imagine how nuts he'd go if you hurt a single hair on her head? What in the fuck were you thinking? You're trying to chase away *his mate*."

Dan spoke, looking hesitant, "We heard she was declaring war on all of us."

"You heard wrong," Jason went on. "Someone is making up fiction. Yes, she killed Merl. That was no big loss and her story checked out. I personally called Reddly and talked to a contact in the police station. Merl attacked a human and raped her. He killed an innocent werewolf who came to that girl's defense. Merl was always a problem, and now this woman has solved it. Thank the short little shit—but don't ever attack her. It will be the last damn thing you do. Are we clear?"

Dan nodded. "Very, Jason."

Jason studied Dan and the other werewolves slowly. "See that coat she's got on?"

The men glanced warily to Shawna, before their gazes returned to Jason.

"If she'd dropped that coat, every last one of you would have been dead. I've seen her in action. Just because she's little doesn't mean a damn thing. Shawna? How many weapons are concealed right now under that coat?"

Shawna smiled. "I'm actually carrying light today. Just a sawed-off shotgun, two semi-automatics, a few knives and a can of bear mace."

Shawna saw shock on the men's faces around her. She opened her coat and let them see some of her weapons. They all collectively stepped back.

Jason turned and studied her, before a wide smile spread across his face. "Where's the bear mace?"

She grinned back. "A woman has to have some secrets."

Jason snorted before he sobered again, turning to glare at the other werewolves. "She's off limits—and if anyone is stupid enough to try to go for her, remember today. She's not just a woman. She's a warrior. Are we clear?"

The men around Dan all nodded grimly. Jason ordered them to leave. As the parking lot cleared, Shawna stood there and waited until Jason turned around to face her again. She gave him another smile.

"Thanks, but I had it handled. I think they were starting to like me."

"Sure." Jason snorted. "I could tell by the way they all looked so damn happy."

"They were hiding it well, but they dug me."

Jason threw back his head and laughed. "Maybe Jazz isn't crazy. You grow on someone, don't you?"

"Yeah, but I've been told I'm cuter than fungus."

Jason shook his head. "Sorry I was late. Domestic trouble with a pack couple." He flexed his fists. "Someone forgot my 'don't hit women ever' policy so I had to remind him."

"What are you late for?" Shawna put her suitcase in the back of her Jeep. "I wasn't expecting you."

"Jazz wanted me to ride shotgun with you while you're running free around town. For some crazy reason he thinks you need to be protected. I told him I was pretty sure you could handle yourself, but I just take orders. Jazz told me to get my ass here, so here I am."

Shawna frowned.

"Don't get pissed at me." Jason opened her passenger-side door and sat in her Jeep. Then he clicked a button on his keychain, locking his SUV. "I think you can handle yourself but I'm still going to do my job. You don't have to worry about me stepping out of line. I'm happily mated these days. Totally safe. Probably why he picked me."

"It's not that. Sorry. Jazz ordered you?" She stood there scowling at him. "I'm confused. I know my pack info is out of date since I haven't lived with shifters in almost two decades, but I thought no one could give an enforcer orders except the pack alpha."

"Usually true, but we're a progressive pack. We like change. Desmon leads, but Jazz is like his second-in-command. We all take orders from both of them. It's been that way since the beginning and it works great."

Shawna gave up and crawled into the driver's side of her Jeep, knowing it wasn't in a werewolf to disobey an order from their alpha. "So, what is Jazz's title or place in the pack?"

Jason buckled his seat belt while Shawna started the car. "He's just Jazz. If Desmon isn't around, then Jazz is."

"That's weird."

"Maybe, but it works for us. Are you heading back to Jazz's place, or do I need to worry about another stop to terrorize more weres?"

She gave him an unimpressed look. "I was planning on taking a nap."

"Works for me. Easiest job I've had all week." Jason leaned back against his seat, looking very comfortable. "You can nap and Jazz will be home soon. The meeting won't take that long. They're mainly going over schedules. We're having massive patrol issues."

Shawna glanced at him as she started driving toward Jazz's house. "What's the issue or is it a secret?"

"No secret. The Goodwins want to expand into our territory, and they aren't exactly subtle about letting us know."

"The dead body this morning," Shawna remembered.

"It's a huge problem, and we have so much space to defend. We're strong, but we're still a smaller pack. Desmon likes it that way. He lets a few in, but with too many new faces, that's asking for a lot of trouble. You know there's a lot of old-school weres out there. They come in here and don't want to follow Desmon's new laws. Goodwins, on the other hand, they've been growing a lot, and they want our land. We've been on the verge of a full-out turf war since Desmon mated Amber. That's one thing that hasn't gotten better. It's a lot worse than you remember."

Shawna was shocked. "Jesus."

"Yeah. Exactly." Jason gave her a knowing look. "That's why Jazz couldn't miss that meeting."

"Would we win?"

Jason hesitated. "Maybe. They have numbers we don't. I wasn't lying about that."

She bit her lip. "Is that the only reason he doesn't expand the pack? He's afraid there will be problems?"

"Yup. We have the money and the area to expand. It's crazy how land rich Nightwind is. It's just that we don't want the trouble. It only takes one bad wolf to ruin the party... Merl, for example."

She took a deep breath. "Tell me where Desmon is."

"Why?"

"Is this meeting with the other pack?"

"No. It's a meeting with Desmon, Jazz, Miles and a few of the other enforcers, making guard schedules and going over contingency plans."

"Let's go."

He gave her a look. "Why?"

She put on her sweetest smile. "Because I asked so nicely?"

"Fine." Jason surprised her by giving in. "But if they're upset, you tell them you threatened to shoot me."

"Deal."

11

The last place Shawna wanted to visit was the pack house, but she parked in front of it. Jazz and Desmon were in there and she needed to speak to both.

Shawna sighed and put on her coat as she climbed out of the Jeep. She saw Jason's eyebrows rise but he shrugged.

"I'm not stupid. Not everyone is happy about me being here."

He scowled. "I'll handle any trouble that comes up, all right?"

"I'm used to looking out for myself but if you want to put yourself between me and someone else, be my guest. If it goes bad, though, keep away from me. I maneuver better with some space."

Jason threw back his head and laughed as he walked up the steps. "Damn, does Jazz have his hands full with you."

He opened the door, stepped in first, and then held it open behind him. Shawna walked in. She gripped a knife handle under her coat. She didn't want to shoot anyone who lived in the pack house unless she had to. Pack houses usually housed single males, and with a war looming, everyone was valuable.

She didn't want to piss off Desmon either.

Shawna saw a large living room area, complete with two pool tables. She couldn't help but grin. Male central. The house was obviously built and furnished for men. An open pizza box rested on the coffee table. Beer and soda cans were scattered around on most flat surfaces she could spot besides the pool tables. Both of them were currently in use. She saw seven male heads turn in her direction. Noses flared and eyes narrowed.

"Hello, gentlemen," Shawna said sweetly. "Sorry to interrupt."

Jason uttered a curse, and then scowled at the other werewolves. "She's claimed by Jazz so put your tongues back in and drop your eyes."

He grabbed Shawna's arm and led her down a hallway. Out of curiosity, she turned and looked over her shoulder. No one followed. That was good.

Jason led her down the hall. "The kitchen is this way."

Three other tall werewolves slipped past them, like they couldn't wait to get away, and then Jazz appeared from around the corner.

"What in the hell are you doing here?" he snapped, making it obvious he had smelled her in his vicinity.

Jason backed away, but Shawna just smiled up at Jazz when he stormed over to them. "Hi, babe."

Jazz caught her hand in his and pulled her into the kitchen. He swept his gaze up and down her body. "Was there trouble? Are you all right?"

"I'm great."

Jazz grabbed Shawna's coat and pulled her into farther into the kitchen. "You shouldn't be here, Shawna. I haven't had a chance to make a formal announcement. Did anyone give you trouble coming in?"

She shook her head, and then turned to look around, ignoring Jazz's hold on her jacket. The kitchen was a large and open, with dark wood cabinets and highline, stainless-steel appliances. Miles Nightwind was leaning against the counter, looking similar to his cousin with his long black hair tied back, but instead of business attire he wore jeans and a purple t-shirt. She saw scars on him that she didn't remember from her youth—lots of them.

He arched an eyebrow at her as he took a sip from his cup of coffee, as though daring her to say something.

Miles was an intimidating male, a lone alpha wolf, easily one of the most feared types of werewolves. Last she heard, he was working for the Alliance, which was common for alphas who didn't have a pack to lead.

Shawna realized three full-grown alpha males were living in this pack peacefully. That was no small feat for Nightwind, and it certainly made them stronger—and unconventional.

Her plan could work.

Desmon stayed seated at the kitchen table where papers were spread out in front of him. This time his business suit was navy blue and accented with a silver tie. He smiled at her, and she grinned back before Jazz's hands inside her coat distracted her.

"Watch the Magnum," she said softly. "I don't want you to accidentally shoot me."

Jazz growled. "Why are you wearing this?"

"I'm used to it...and oh yeah, not everyone is happy with me being here."

Jazz slid her coat down her shoulders, and she didn't protest. He carefully took it off her and laid it over an empty kitchen chair like it might explode. She chuckled. Jazz shot her a dirty look and then moved back to her. He pulled her up against him and sniffed her neck.

She pushed him lightly. "I'm fine. Put your nose away."

"I was just checking."

"For what?"

"To see if anyone scared or touched you."

"He worries," Desmon chuckled. "What brings you here, Shawna?"

She turned back to Desmon. "I have an idea."

"About what?"

Jason spoke first. "She asked what the meeting was about. I told her about the Goodwin issue. It wasn't a secret, was it?"

"No, it's common knowledge at this point. Everyone knows we're having territory issues." Desmon sighed. "Have a seat, Jason. You can stay."

Jason just leaned against the entrance to the kitchen, while Desmon studied Shawna. She pushed away from Jazz. He reluctantly released her but stayed so close she knew if she moved at all, she'd brush against his body. She gave her full attention to Desmon.

"I'm dying of curiosity." Desmon held up a hand expectantly. "What's your idea about our problems with the Goodwins?"

She licked her lips. "May I sit?"

"Of course." Desmon gestured to a chair on the other side of the kitchen table. "Be my guest. Make yourself at home."

She pulled it out and plopped down. "Nice place. This is the fanciest pack house I've ever seen. You really stepped things up."

"Thanks."

"If you're looking for more members, I'm your girl."

Desmon blinked. "I don't understand."

"I've been hunting for fifteen years, on and off. I've gotten to know a lot of weres who would fit right in here. They'd love to move somewhere with an alpha like you."

Desmon shook his head. "I'm not sure I follow."

She leaned forward. "The Coleman family. Ted and Amy. They have six sons, all good men. They range from their mid-teens to early thirties. They have three daughters in the same age range. They were banned from their pack. I see your frown, but just wait to hear the explanation.

"They were in a pack where the females were auctioned off to the highest bidders because their alpha was in deep debt. The family refused to allow it. They lost everything when the pack forced the issue. Their home was burned down. They sent in men to kidnap the girls. One of the men who bought the youngest girl—seventeen, by the way—was a nasty bit of work. I took him out after they contacted me to help them get their daughters back. I didn't even charge them. They're good wolves, Desmon.

"Trust me when I say those boys can fight too. They fought with me to get their sisters back, and we succeeded. They've been exiled from every pack ever since. They only want a place to belong. They're a tight family, and they treat women right. You'd never have a problem with them. They just don't want their girls sold off or hurt, now that they're safe again. They want their daughters to find mates they love."

Desmon studied her silently before he mused out loud, "So we'd get six good fighters."

She leaned back and studied him. "Yes. There are more families I could tell you about. Good people who ended up in bad packs. The Riley brothers. Four of them. Meanest sons of bitches you never wanted to face in a fight—for a reason. Their pack was short on females, so their alpha turned to the mated women to breed. Two of the brothers were mated. All four were in service to the Alliance at the time and not home.

"One of the mates committed suicide after they were attacked, and the other one fought anyone who tried to touch her until they killed her. The Rileys came home to find their mates dead." She paused. "The brothers killed every damn male in the area who'd touched those two women. They were banished, and they don't have people anymore. No one's willing to take them, knowing they killed their own pack mates, but they were fucking animals who raped and caused the deaths of their mates, Des. I think you'd actually like them...and they have elite training with the Alliance. Men with honor who would stand at your back and die protecting it. When shit hits the fan for me, and I find myself in over my head, I call them. I'm human, but they've always come to save my ass—every single time."

Jazz growled. "Have you slept with any of them?"

She turned and gave him a look. "No. We've been over this. You already asked me if I'd slept with any shifters, remember? I didn't lie. They're my friends. That's it."

Desmon gave Shawna a skeptical look when she turned back to him. Then he glanced toward Miles in a silent communication that made it obvious the cousins were close.

"I don't know," Miles grunted, and shook his head. "But we could use more help guarding the borders. We're outnumbered. We're better fighters, but it won't matter if the Goodwins keep recruiting like they have been."

"There are more. So many more," Shawna added. "If having low numbers is endangering the pack, I can give you a list of names."

Desmon seemed hesitant. "I'd have to meet them."

"Of course." She nodded. "There's only one problem—if you *see* it as a problem—with the Riley brothers."

Desmon arched an eyebrow. "What?"

She hesitated. "They have some unmated females with them. About a dozen. It's not like a harem thing going on, either. They protect them. They help people like I do, and over the years, they've found several unprotected, unmated women who were abused. The Riley brothers took them from their packs and now they protect them like they're sisters. If any of your men went after those women, the brothers would take it...badly. They have a real problem with anyone screwing with a woman against her wishes.

"I wanted to warn you because if you take them on, they'd bring the women with them. The women are nice. I've hung out with some of them. Their stories are common. Their mates died and they got tossed to the pack, or they had small families and their males couldn't protect them." She paused. "There are a few kids too. Some of the women have pups from their dead mates or from being abused."

Desmon blinked. His face was unreadable. "That's a lot of unmated women to keep track of and protect."

"The Riley brothers will protect them. They're tough bastards who have a real soft spot for helpless women and kids. I'm giving you names of people who would follow that law to the letter, and hell, help you enforce it big time."

Desmon glanced to Jazz. "What do you think?"

Jazz sat next to Shawna and looked her in the eye. "You're sure about these people? The last thing we need is fighting in our pack."

"They'd follow you both to hell and back if you gave them a home where their women will be safe." Shawna glanced from Jazz to Desmon. "They want to be a part of a pack again. You know the longing they feel to be part of a group. They want to live in a place where their women and kids are safe from being raped, sold, or enslaved. It lines up with the kind of pack you've built, right?"

Desmon nodded. "Yes, it does."

"The Coleman men and the Riley brothers are incredible fighters, Des. They've been out on their own, protecting their families, and it's made them tough as hell. I'll personally pay for their relocations here, so it won't cost you if they need financial assistance."

Jazz cleared his throat. "That could get expensive, Shawna."

"I have the money. Trust me. It isn't an issue."

Jazz gave her a look.

"My second husband was an investment broker," she explained, a bit impatient. "He came from old family money. When he died, he made sure I was taken care of. All the money I've been paid from hunting, I donate to families that need it. I can afford to relocate dozens of shifters here and set them up without breaking my bank account."

Jazz's frown deepened. "How much money?"

"It doesn't matter." She turned to Desmon. "I'm just offering, okay? If you meet them, and you decide to offer them an invite to the pack, I can and *will* happily shell out the money to see them get set up here."

"That's real generous, Shawna." Desmon looked a little stunned at the generosity. "Thank you."

She breathed a sigh of relief. "Give me your number and I'll text you their information. Strengthening your pack with good men who can fight would force the Goodwins to leave you alone."

"Us," Jazz said softly, and reached over to squeeze her hand. "It's your pack too, Shawna. We're lucky to have you."

Her chest tightened with emotion. It took her a second to catch her breath and smile at Jazz. "Yeah. Our pack."

Desmon handed Shawna a notebook with his number written in a neat, concise way. "Send me their contacts. If you could include some info about them, that would help. I'll talk to each one, gauge if they're interested, and we'll see how it goes."

Shawna started entering his number into her phone.

Miles cleared his throat from where he had been quietly listening. "You know, Des, if this works out, we could possibly get approval from the Alliance to register as a sanctuary pack like the Hunters in Arizona." He took another drink of his coffee, and went on, "The classification isn't easy to get, but it's worth trying. They're untouchable. Challenging their borders is like starting a war directly with the Alliance. No one lives to tell the tale after that."

"I know. That's why we sent my mother and Hope there." Desmon appeared thoughtful. Then he smiled at Shawna. "It's a good idea. Thank you."

She grinned back. "You'd be helping me. I worry about all of them. It would be nice if they had a safe place to live in a community that will accept them and not hurt them anymore."

Shawna looked to her phone after that, paging through her contacts and sending Desmon the ones she felt would suit Nightwind pack best. She included quite a bit of information on each of the potential new pack members, which took time. The room was silent while she worked. Clearly, no one wanted to do anything to mess this up.

"That's the last one." She finally glanced up from her phone as the final chime sounded on Desmon's.

He studied her for a long time, but she didn't shy away from his assessment of her. Finally, he sighed. "You were hunting shifters to save *other* shifters for the most part, weren't you? Not just for humans?"

"Yes." She gave him a tight nod. "It sucks to be the little guy, regardless of your bloodlines."

Jazz wrapped his arm around her shoulders and pulled her close. "I want to take you home now."

Shawna turned to study him for a long moment, before she gave him a small nod. "All right."

Jazz smiled. "You make me so hot."

She laughed, standing when Jazz pulled her to her feet. He released her and carefully lifted her coat off the chair. He hesitated before handing it back. "You don't need this anymore, you know."

"I'm keeping the coat." Her smile died. "Sorry, Jazz. Just in case."

He frowned. "It's my job to protect you now, babe."

"And it's my job to watch your back while you do it. I'm not the helpless type anymore. It's not like when you used to snarl at boys who looked at me wrong. When I was young, I was constantly terrified, and I *needed* you to protect me. That hurt both of us. Now I can handle myself for the most part. It makes life easier for me. So don't think I'm going to give up my weapons forever."

"Fine." He sighed. "Let's go home."

She studied him. "You're angry."

The look on his handsome face was raw and determined. "I can protect you."

"I know you can. I'm just saying that in case you ever need some help, or if you aren't around, I don't want to be defenseless. I'm not a shifter, Jazz. I don't have claws. I don't have sharp teeth or kick-ass ninja reflexes. What I *do* have are my weapons. Please don't try to take them away from me."

His blue gaze locked with hers. "All right. I get it."

"Thanks." Shawna slipped on the coat.

"She has bear mace in there somewhere," Jason said. "She wouldn't show me where it was."

Jazz turned and growled. "Why do you want to know?"

"I was just curious." Jason backed up a step and dropped his gaze. "Come on, man, I'm mated. I couldn't even if I wanted to, which I don't, 'cause she scares me. No offense, Shawna, but I like my mate just how she is, without the scary coat. You two are perfect for each other."

Shawna smiled. "We are, aren't we?"

"Let Jazz be possessive." Desmon chuckled. "It's a good thing to see. It's nice to have a mate to protect."

"I know." Jason flashed Desmon a dirty look. "But it's easy for you to say, he's not growling at you."

Jazz grabbed her hand and the two of them walked toward the door. Shawna suddenly stopped and turned to Desmon. "Oh. One more thing. Are you prejudiced?"

"No." Desmon shook his head. "Why?"

She smiled. "Just checking. Talk to the Riley brothers. You really want them. Just remember you aren't prejudiced when you talk to them."

Desmon looked to Jazz. "What the hell?"

"Beats me." Jazz shrugged. "Talk to you later."

Shawna waved goodbye to Jason. Since Jazz was going home with her, Jason was released from his babysitting duties. Jazz put his arm around her and let out an actual growl at the other males mulling around the living room of the pack house. Now that Jazz was fine with her keeping the coat, Shawna thought his big bad wolf act was kind of cute.

Once they were out the door, Shawna noticed Jazz's sports car was nowhere in sight, which was kind of funny for a knight in shining armor. She turned and arched an eyebrow at him on the porch. He was still wrapped around her, in full alpha-wolf-protection mode. "I take it you need a ride."

Jazz just grinned. "Not necessarily. I could strip down and go back the way I came."

"You ran here shifted?" she asked in disbelief. "That's a serious run. I guess I'll see you in an hour."

He leaned down and whispered in her ear, "Yeah, but I run *a lot* faster than you remember. It'll be ten minutes tops."

"Mmm-hmm." She didn't doubt it, but she also didn't feel like encouraging a territorial, full-grown alpha wolf to show off. "How about I take your word for it and give you a lift instead."

Rather than complain, Jazz opened the driver's-side door for her when she pushed the button. She grinned at him and slipped behind the wheel. Then he happily went around to the passenger side and let Shawna drive him home.

The ride was quiet as they drove back, but mostly pleasant...until Jazz cleared his throat as they pulled up in front of his place.

"I have some calls to make before dinner." Jazz gave her a hesitant look. "Important, 'so you won't kick my ass' calls."

She rolled her eyes. "I thought you would have already called your harem of women."

"Someone made me late for my meeting with Des, so I didn't have time."

She grabbed her bag and hopped out of the Jeep. "Fine. I'll go unpack."

He eyed her bag. "Let me carry it up for you."

"I can manage. Stop stalling and make those calls."

"I'm not stalling." He got out of her Jeep and closed the door. "I'm trying to be a gentleman."

"Yeah. Right." She closed the door and headed for the house. "You just don't want to make those calls. I'm not kidding, Jazz. You need to start dialing."

"All right." He laughed. "I'll get it over with."

SHAWNA HEARD JAZZ ON THE PHONE HALF AN HOUR LATER. HE WAS still making calls. She grit her teeth. How many damn women had he been sleeping with? She raised her hand to knock on his door as Jazz's voice carried into the hallway.

"Yeah, well, that's how it is, Marla. You know how these things go. I found my mate." He sounded so proud. "She's amazing. I love her more than life."

Shawna knocked before she heard something else. If only Jazz wasn't so damn charming about the whole thing. It made it hard to be mad at him.

She heard Jazz saying goodbye before the door opened and he peaked around it. "Hi." A small smile tugged at his lips. "I'm almost done."

"Almost? How many women are you calling?" She held up her hands. "Or maybe I shouldn't know."

Jazz reached out and grabbed her around the waist, pulling her to his chest. "Babe..."

"Don't babe me. I'm mad." She tried to wiggle out of his hold, but Jazz wasn't letting go. He just held her tighter when she turned in his arms, showing Jazz her back. "I can't help it. If I slept with men in numbers that equaled a football team, you'd be pissed off too. I probably need an STD test instead of dinner."

"I don't have STDs. I can't catch them. I'm a shifter. You know we're immune to human disease. And I'm sorry. I was a single guy. *Single.*

You know werewolves have a high sex drive. It's all done and over with now." He squeezed her affectionately from behind. "I've called all but one. They know I belong to you. I told them there's never going to be another woman in my life, and that's exactly how I want it. You know you believe me."

"Maybe." She looked up at him over her shoulder. "Are there any women in this town that you *haven't* slept with?"

"Plenty. I usually saw women from other territories. It kept things less complicated—or so I'd thought."

She sighed.

"Shawna, I believed you were dead, and I had sworn to never take a mate." Jazz sounded a little desperate. "I never realized my sex life was going to come back and bite me in the ass. I'm going to be apologizing for the next decade, aren't I?"

She relaxed in his arms. "I don't know—maybe."

He buried his face in the curve of her neck, hugging her tighter. "Look on the bright side."

"I can't wait to hear this one. Go ahead."

"Practice makes perfect—so I'm a really fantastic lover for you."

She snorted. "Great."

He spun her in his arms and lifted her so she was facing him. He was grinning. "Maybe I should distract you from being mad."

"I'm going to the store. Put me down."

"Okay." Unfazed, he kept carrying her down the hallway instead.

She turned her head, watching where he was walking them. "Where are we going?"

"Family room."

"I see that. Why?"

He grinned. "Because I've missed you and I love you."

"I said, put me down." She gripped his shoulders. "I'm buying new locks today and you're going to put them on. I don't want any more women in this house."

"In a minute, Shawna. I really need you right now."

She frowned at him. "I'm still angry."

"Don't worry. I'm going to distract you."

He stopped and bent, until she ended up on her back on the coffee table. Jazz went to his knees, then he yanked off her boots. Shawna didn't stop him. He reached for her jeans next and unzipped them. She half-heartedly swatted at his hands, but he had her jeans torn down her legs in seconds.

Jazz chuckled and gripped her hips, pulling her to the edge of the table. His gazed roamed her body, hot and possessive, as he slid his hands up her thighs, over her bare stomach, before he grasped the edges of her button-down shirt. He tore it wide open, sending buttons flying everywhere as she gasped.

"I liked that shirt."

"I'll buy you another." Jazz gripped her underwear and slid them down her legs, a low growl coming from the back of his throat. He tossed them somewhere across the room. "I'll buy you more of those too. Did I tell you how much you turn me on, Shawna?" He met her gaze, and she saw his light eyes were dilated with need. "Have I told you how much I love you?"

She stared up at him and opened her mouth to say something, but gasped instead when Jazz caught her ankles and draped them over his shoulders. He bent over her, then buried his face between her open thighs.

Shawna shut her eyes and gripped the sides of the table. "Jazz!"

He growled against her, and she arched into his mouth. He slid his hands under her ass and lifted her a little off the table, holding her against his mouth. He sucked on her, making her moan, before his tongue moved strong and fast against her clit.

Relentless.

That was the word that flashed in her mind as she bucked and cried out. The pleasure built fast, and she fisted his hair, feeling her legs shake.

She screamed his name as she climaxed. Her body was still twitching with satisfaction as Jazz pulled her to a sitting position. He released her and tore down his sweats, letting her glimpse how aroused he was. In the next second, his hands were on her again. He lifted her and gently eased her on his lap as he sat. Shawna met him halfway, shifting her hips, letting him slide in slowly, stretching her in the most exquisite way possible. He was so thick. It felt incredible.

She moaned and wrapped her arms around his neck as he buried himself fully inside her. "Jazz..."

"Right here, babe. I love you, Shawna. I love you so fucking much."

He moved, the friction sending shivers of white-hot pleasure through her as he held Shawna pinned in his arms. The only choice she had was to just feel him, over and over, as he used his strength to move inside her. He was torturing her with slow, deep strokes. She dropped her forehead to the top of his shoulder and moaned into his skin.

She was close to coming again when he eased out of her body and lifted her off him.

Shocked, she stared into his eyes. He smiled at her and eased her down to the carpet on her hands and knees in front of him.

"Am I forgiven?" He came down over her, easing back into her body.

"God," Shawna moaned. "That's not fair."

He reached around her and brushed her clit with his finger, teasing. He thrust once inside her, deep, and asked, "Am I forgiven?" He punctuated his words by moving his finger again, rubbing her, and Shawna whimpered from the rush of ecstasy. "I love you, Shawna. Tell me you hear me."

"Yes," she cried out.

Jazz growled and withdrew, thrusting into her again, then again. Shawna moaned loudly, clutching the thick carpet under her fingers. Jazz's body was wrapped around hers. He moved faster, rubbing her clit with his finger in time with his rapidly thrusting hips.

Shawna shut her eyes, just feeling. Nothing had ever felt as good as Jazz did when he was inside her, touching her. He growled, and she moaned louder. His pace increased until he was pounding against her, burying himself deep.

"Come for me," he snarled. "I can't hold off much longer."

Her body tensed and she screamed out as she climaxed. She heard Jazz softly curse, and then he was following her. She felt him pulsing hard inside her as he slowed his movement.

She almost collapsed on the floor when the pleasure started to fade. Jazz held her up. He moved his hand from between her thighs and opened his palm wide on her stomach, holding her in place.

He kissed her shoulder. "I want to bite you so damn bad."

She smiled. "No biting."

"Would you forgive me if I ever lost control and bit you?"

She jerked her head and looked at him over her shoulder. "You can't bite me."

"Damn." He withdrew from her body and slowly released her. He straightened, jerking up his sweats. He reached for her and pulled her to her feet. "I want you to be my mate."

She stared up at him. "You can't. I'm sorry, Jazz. If I wasn't marked, I'd say yes in a heartbeat."

"I want you to smell like me. I want you stronger, damn it. I want you to…" He cursed. "I just want all of you."

She bit her lip and eyed him. "You can't take me in full wolf form. My mom said she and my father conceived Ralph that way in the woods. She said it was different and wild to mate in shift. Even if you did change me, I'll always be too human for that."

"If you were furry and had a tail, you'd totally want me to mount you if I was furry and had a tail too."

"Sorry. I can't do you when you look like a dog. It's one thing when you do the half thing. You're hot that way, and physically still more of a man than a dog."

"I'm not a dog." He looked offended. "I'm a wolf."

"Dog. Wolf." She laughed. "Not much difference."

He grabbed her, pulling her against his body. He looked down at her with narrowed eyes. "Wolves are stronger, faster, and smarter than dogs. Ask anyone."

"Sorry. Are we a little touchy on the subject?"

He started to shift in her arms. It was a weird feeling to have his skin sprout fur against her bare body. He only partially shifted, so he was upright. He lifted her in his arms and backed her to the wall. His hands gripped her thighs and spread them. He entered her fast.

Shawna moaned and gripped his shoulders. She locked eyes with him. They were Jazz's blue eyes, but they were shaped differently. She couldn't kiss him. His nose and mouth were extended and his teeth were noticeably sharp. He tilted his head, and his tongue was rough as he licked her neck. She moaned when he withdrew and thrust into her again.

"I'm not a dog," he growled. His voice was deep and guttural now. "Feel the difference?"

Shawna gasped as he moved inside her. Jazz was so unbelievably strong. He pinned her to the wall so she'd have no chance to fight him. She didn't want to when he started fucking her harder. She just dug her nails into his shoulders to hold on. She felt his fur receding again and she turned her head.

Jazz was back to himself. He caught her mouth with his and kissed her as he moved inside her. She moaned against his lips and came minutes later.

Jazz brushed his mouth over hers gently before he lifted his head and met her gaze. "If you were changed, we could go at this for hour after hour. I could do you until you could barely walk and when you rested up a little, you wouldn't be sore. You're going to be sore tomorrow now. Let me bite you, Shawna."

"Don't use sex as a weapon. It's not fair to me, Jazz. You know how much I love you and want you. It makes me feel like I'm denying you the air you breathe or something. The guilt is awful for me...because I know if you were with someone else, someone not damaged, you might be happier. Do you want me to leave?"

He softly cursed and eased out of her body. He put her on her feet gently and released her. "Damn it! *No*. I love you! I'm sorry." He stormed away.

Shawna watched him walk away and shut her eyes. He was taking the whole 'can't mate' thing really hard. She took a few deep breaths and went to find him, knowing she could soothe his hurt—but for how long?

12

Shawna fought tears as she climbed out of her Jeep and walked into the bar she'd been to a week before. The preppy bar didn't have werewolves or any other kind of were. No respectable shifter would come to a place like that to drink. She walked up to the bar and ordered a dirty martini.

A different bartender was working. He handed her the drink minutes later and she took a sip. She smiled at the man. "Perfect."

He nodded and walked away after she paid for her drink. She sighed and took another sip.

Jazz was running errands concerning the pack and she'd snuck out of his house for a few hours to think.

He was still upset that she wouldn't let him change her over and they'd been going back and forth all week. She understood. Growing up around weres, she really did. It was like telling a devout Catholic boy he couldn't get married to a woman he was having sex with, lived with, and loved. It wasn't going down easy one bit with Jazz. While she understood, she couldn't change it.

It might be programmed into him that he needed to change her into a werewolf, to mate her so his scent was hers...but she couldn't become a were.

It wasn't safe for either of them.

Her phone buzzed in her jean's pocket. She sighed. Jazz must have gotten home earlier than expected and found her gone. He'd probably be worried. She eyed the incoming number. It wasn't familiar.

She answered with a frown. "Yeah?"

"Shawna?" The voice was male and husky.

"Who's this?"

The man chuckled. "Damn. Break my heart. You married me and you don't recognize my voice?"

She was stunned. "Hi, Allen. I'm sorry. I'm distracted and surprised to hear from you is all. Did you get a new phone?"

"Yeah. And I get it. I bet you're surprised. You're usually the one who calls me when you want something. Now I need a favor."

"Okay. What do you need?"

"Tell me where you are. I know you're somewhere near Hollow Mountain. And I'm using a burner number for a reason. We need to talk. I'm in town."

"How did you know where I was?"

"That's what I want to talk to you about. I think you're in trouble, sweetheart. Where are you? I'll come to you."

She gave him the name of the bar, and he said he was only five minutes away. She hung up and chewed on her lower lip. She didn't like Allen being in werewolf territory.

She'd never told Ron *or* Allen about her past. She'd kept them away from her adopted family because it would have put them in danger.

She sipped her drink and then ordered a soda. Seeing movement in her peripheral minutes later. She turned. Allen grinned at her as he crossed the bar.

She took him in. At six foot-one, Allen was imposing. He had wide shoulders and was still incredibly fit. He had an exercise group on the police force that he worked out with several times a week so they could all keep in shape. Five years before, he'd switched from car patrol to motorcycle.

Truth was, he looked great. He was tan, fit, and his age only showed in the graying hair at his temples. He was forty-one now, if she did her math correctly. He looked ten years younger except for those touches of gray.

"Damn, sweetheart. You look good," he chuckled.

She stood up and was embraced in a hug. Her feet left the floor and she laughed. Allen was a bear hugger. He held her for almost a minute before easing her down to her feet. His brown eyes sparkled with amusement as he touched her hair.

"Red looks good on you. It brings out your eyes."

She smiled. "Thanks. I wanted a change and I really like it."

"So do I. Let's get out of here. We need to talk." His smile died. "You're in trouble."

"I'm always in trouble." She blinked up at him. "What kind are you talking about, specifically?"

"Not here. I've got a motel room. Let's go talk privately." He looked at the bar. "Nice place."

His sarcastic tone wasn't lost. "I have my reasons."

He nodded. "Let's go."

He gripped her hand, and she let him lead her outside. He glanced around the parking lot until he spotted her Jeep. "Let's take my bike."

"I'll just follow you."

"Let's take the bike," he repeated with an intense look. "Trust me."

She sighed. "You're being all mysterious and it's getting annoying."

"I know. Come on, Shawna." He grabbed her hand and tugged her forward.

"Wow." She raised her eyebrows when they walked up to his Harley. "Very nice. When did you pick this up?"

He grinned. "It was my Christmas present to myself. Like it?"

"I love it."

He laughed. "Wait until you feel her between your thighs."

"Yeah, yeah. Always the charmer." She climbed on the back. "I'm in love though. It's pretty sexy."

"I wasn't lying. Helmet."

She nodded and took it. She tugged the helmet on her head as Allen put on his. He started up the bike and Shawna grinned as she wrapped her arms around Allen's leather jacket. He released the kickstand and pulled into traffic.

She really did love his bike. She'd always been partial to them, but she didn't like them in big cities. Too many idiot drivers in a hurry. Hollow Mountain was a small town and traffic was light. She was relieved when Allen turned into the Hollow Inn. She didn't want to run into Were Dan at the River Motel again. She climbed off the bike and handed Allen his helmet back.

He fastened both helmets to the bike and led her to his room. The motel seemed decent enough. Shawna stepped in, and spied Allen's saddlebags for his bike lying across the bed. While Allen locked the door, she grabbed a chair at the table, and spun it around. She straddled it, folded her arms across the back, and rested her chin on them.

"So, what's up?"

He sat down across the table from Shawna and gave her a long look. "Someone has been checking into you hard, sweetheart. Full background checks. The works. I have you flagged, so when they started to dig, I was alerted."

She rolled her eyes. "That's so sweet of you to flag me."

"You know I worry about you. What are you into now? I'm not kidding about the hard part. I did some digging of my own. Someone has pulled everything on you, including court records."

She frowned. "What court records? I've never been arrested."

"Our divorce records, for one. They got copies of all the paperwork that Ron's lawyer filed with the court for his will when he died. They even ran Ron's medical history. I found out they pulled his death certificate and got a copy of his autopsy."

She softly cursed. "Did you find out who?"

He shook his head. "They're covering their tracks. I traced some of it back to a private dick from this area though. And your Jeep is being tracked."

Shock hit her. "No shit?"

"No shit. I did a little inspection on it before I walked into the bar. It's hidden behind your spare tire at the bottom by the bumper. I left it there. You don't want to let on that you know you're being tracked before we get a chance to question them."

"How did *you* know about it?"

"Lucky guess."

She shut her eyes in frustration, took a deep breath, and then opened them. "Thanks for the heads up."

"What in the hell are you into?"

"The regular shit." She shrugged. "Nothing special."

"You still tracking bad guys?"

She gave him a look. "We aren't supposed to talk about that. No questions, remember?"

"I remember. You remind me every time you ask me to pull up info on some rapist in some small town—but you're in deep this time, Shawna. Someone really has it out for you. They know where you are and have followed your movements for a few days, according to the file I saw. They had notes on Merl Perkons, the guy you had me check up on."

She frowned. "What did it say?"

"Just his name. That's all. I wouldn't have noticed it if I hadn't pulled the information on him for you."

Shawna swallowed hard. Someone knew she had killed him. *Great. Fucking great.* She kept going over everything in her head. Merl's body would never be found. She knew that. The Nightwind pack would have quietly disposed of him.

"Sweetheart, talk to me. You know I'll cover your ass."

She met his concerned gaze. "I know. Thanks, Allen."

"Just because our marriage didn't last, doesn't mean I don't love you."

She nodded.

"You're in trouble. Someone has it out for you and they're covering their tracks. My next step is paying the private dick a little visit."

"Don't. I'll handle it. What was his name?"

"John Reynolds. He's got a place on Ninth Street in town here."

"It's a small town. That means whoever hired him probably came from here."

"Whoever was running you through the police system did it from here too." Allen arched an eyebrow at her. "That's how I knew where you were. I figured someone here in law enforcement or someone who knows someone in law enforcement called in a favor. That's where the information was requested from, but there was no name on the request. That tells me it was a favor called in from one police station to another. Know any cops who have it out for you or someone with ties to the police department here?"

She shook her head. "I'll find out though. I've been here longer than usual, and I haven't made too many friends. It's probably one of them."

"If you're hiding anything, like I'm sure you have been, let me help you. I don't want you to go down for something bad."

Shawna took off her coat and dropped it on the table. She was getting hot. Her heart was racing. She glanced back to her ex-husband. "I keep telling you to not ask questions. I'm all right, okay?"

His frown deepened. "Damn it, Shawna! Let me help you. I know you're never coming back to me, and I accept it, but at least let me help you out. You're all alone."

She gave him a pointed look, and said, "I am not alone."

His face reddened a little. "Oh."

Shawna shrugged, studying him. She knew he still had feelings for her. He'd actually tried to win her back after Ron died. She'd told him the truth, that she would always love him, but more like a friend than the way a woman should love a man.

"His name is Jazz. I really love him."

"Jazz? God. Don't tell me you're dating a guitarist in a damn band."

"No." She laughed. "He's not in a band. He sings in the shower some-times though. That's about as close to it as it gets with him."

"You're happy with him?"

"I've never been happier."

"He takes care of you?"

"Yeah. He's very protective."

"Then tell him someone's on your ass. Or is he some kinda snowflake who's going to flip?"

"Jazz is anything but a snowflake."

"You need someone tough, Shawna. Whatever you've been into is dark. I've known that for a while. And I know you can take care of yourself, but if you need help, I want you to call me. I'm going to hang here for a day or two before I head back home, but I can be back in hours. I'll keep my phone on me at all times. Use the number I called you from. Save it."

"I will." She nodded. "Thanks for the heads up."

Allen studied her. "This guy isn't like Ron was, is he? Because Ron had money, but in a fight, he wouldn't have done so good. He was a good man...but he was soft."

"He's not like Ron. He's a badass, I swear."

"How bad?"

"Not anything to be worried about. He'd never hurt me."

"Okay." He sounded reluctant. "I guess I'll take your word for it. Do you want me to run him? I'd sleep better at night knowing you haven't hooked up with some ex-con."

"I grew up with him." She tucked a stand of hair behind her ear and met Allen's gaze with a smile. "I know everything about him."

"Oh." Allen sighed. "I guess that's good then."

"Yeah. He's a great guy. He—"

The motel room door burst open, the lock breaking easily, leaving behind twisted metal and splintered wood.

Jazz stormed in. His shoulders were tight with anger as he quickly glanced at Shawna before his narrowed gaze landed on Allen.

"Ten seconds to explain." Jazz's mouth was set in a firm, angry line. His fists were clenched at his sides. "Then I'm going to tear this asshole apart, babe."

Shawna jumped up and moved between the two men. Allen was inching toward his jacket. She knew he had a gun. He always carried a concealed weapon.

"Jazz, relax! This is Allen. He's my ex-husband."

Jazz's blue eyes narrowed even further. "You're in a motel room with your ex-husband?"

"This is Jazz?" Allen grunted as he looked Jazz up and down one time. "Well, at least he's not a snowflake."

Shawna almost laughed, and would have if she wasn't worried about Jazz at the moment. It was obvious he was furious, and dealing with an angry, full-grown alpha werewolf was a very dangerous situation —even if he was the love of her life.

She ran her tongue over her lips and explained, "Allen is a cop. Someone has been running me in the system and digging into my past. He drove up here to warn me and let me know what's going on. We were just talking. He's helping me out—that's it."

Jazz took a deep breath. To anyone else it would have seemed like he was just trying to calm himself down, but she knew he was inhaling the room.

"What? You didn't believe that nothing's going on? Where's the trust, babe?"

"You're in a motel room with your *ex-husband*." Jazz's voice was a little too gravelly to be normal. "I've been having you followed so I know you're safe."

She frowned. "'Cause that's not creepy."

"You think you're tough, but I worry with everything else we have going on right now." He looked meaningfully to Allen, leaving it unsaid that the Nightwind pack was on the verge of a full-fledge territory war. "And then I get a call saying you hooked up with a biker in a bar and took off to a motel on his bike."

"So you assumed I was cheating? Give me a break. I saw a woman *expose* herself to you in your own kitchen, and I still trust you. I'm sitting at a table fully dressed with a man, and you can't do the same?"

"Wait just a second." Allen sounded pissed. "A woman exposed herself to him—in front of you?"

"When I moved in with him, one of his ex-girlfriends showed up, not knowing Jazz and I were together. He's not a cheater, but—oh hell, never mind." She glanced back to Jazz. "I'd never cheat on you."

"What was I supposed to think?" Jazz grit his teeth. "I was told you let him maul you in public and then left the bar with him. You let him drive you to a motel!"

"Maul? He gave me a hug. *A hug.* I hug people. *You* hug people."

Jazz still looked furious. "Fine, I trust you, but you can't blame me for going a little nuts."

"A little? You kicked in another motel room door."

"Another one?" Allen repeated.

"The last one was mine. It's a long story." She turned back to Jazz. "Since you're here, would you like to be introduced or would you just prefer to go all *alpha*?"

Jazz took another breath before he glanced back to Allen with a glare. "She's mine now. So don't even think about it."

Shawna sighed and glanced at Allen. "I told you he's protective. I'm sorry."

"Don't apologize for me to him," Jazz snarled.

Shawna tensed. She studied Jazz carefully—and saw his eyes.

Shit. She put her hands on his chest. She needed to calm him down before he lost it and sprouted fur in front of Allen.

Allen would freak out, and he was armed. She didn't want her ex-husband to shoot Jazz if he lost his skin in exchange for fur. It likely wouldn't kill Jazz...but still.

"Babe? Look at me." Her voice was soft.

Jazz lowered his gaze. He instantly reached down and gripped her hips as Shawna maintained eye contact.

"I love you. I'm yours. Allen and I are friends now. Listen to me and calm down. You need to get control of yourself. The stress is starting to show in your eyes." She knew he'd understand. "And Allen doesn't need to see that." Code for he doesn't know about werewolves. "All right? I'll explain everything. Just calm down for me, babe."

Jazz nodded and took several deep breaths. She knew her scent would help him. Touching her would help too. Weres were ultra-territorial, and right now, Jazz was feeling jealous. He needed to establish his claim or he'd lose control.

Several heartbeats later, she felt his body relax against hers, and finally explained the situation.

"Allen found out a local private detective has been digging into my life. He also realized that I have a GPS tracker on my Jeep. Someone has been following my every move."

Jazz looked stunned. "What's the guy's name?"

"John Reynolds."

Jazz's eyes narrowed. "I know him."

Shawna studied him, seeing the rage on his face again, after she just got him calmed down. "I see. He's a local?"

"Yup. *Very* local."

Shit. She understood perfectly what Jazz was saying. Someone from the Nightwind pack was digging into her past.

"Do you think maybe Des just wanted to check me out?" She almost felt hopeful.

Jazz shook his head. "No, he wouldn't do that."

"You're sure?"

"Positive. He also doesn't work that way. And you're practically family to him. He'd never feel the need to hire someone to check into you. He'd just ask you directly if there was something he wanted to know."

Shawna believed him, which was a nice feeling. She rubbed his chest through his shirt. "I guess you'll be talking to this John Reynolds."

Jazz just clenched his jaw rather than say anything.

"That's what I thought." She turned and eyed Allen. "Thanks for the heads up."

Allen was frowning. "Can we talk for a minute, sweetheart?"

Every muscle in Jazz tensed. Shawna's did too. She wanted to curse. Allen did that on purpose, calling her the endearment just to dig at Jazz, and she knew it.

Allen obviously didn't like Jazz, and it was clear the feeling was mutual. Shawna could almost taste the tension between the two men.

"No, anything you need to say you can do it here." Shawna frowned at Allen. "I love Jazz. I appreciate the warning, but we're going to leave now. It was good seeing you. Thank you again." She turned back to Jazz. "Let's go."

"Why don't you head outside?" Jazz released her. "I'll be there in a minute."

"No way in hell am I letting you two be alone."

Jazz looked down at her. "I let you have your way with Krystal. Now it's your turn to let go. I'll behave. I swear. Trust goes both ways."

She scowled. "Fine, but he came a long way to warn me and he was looking out for me. Remember that." She turned and shot Allen a warning glare of his own. "I love him, so keep your gun in your jacket. We're getting married and I won't be left a widow again."

Allen nodded. "We're just going to talk."

Shawna rolled her eyes and released Jazz. She grabbed her coat, shot each man another warning glance, and headed outside. She nearly smacked straight into a grim-looking Jason standing outside the motel room door.

"Tattletale," she muttered to him.

"Just doing my job." Jason sniffed at her curiously. "Good thing it was innocent. He probably would've killed the guy."

Shawna flipped Jason off. "I don't cheat."

"Another good thing," Jason said softly. "Jazz went insane when I told him you left with a biker and were pulling into a motel."

"He's my ex and we're just friends. He—"

"I heard," Jason cut her off. "Seriously though, please don't ever cheat on Jazz. He wouldn't handle it well."

"I already said cheating's not my style," she assured him.

Shawna let Jason lead her to his SUV. She saw Jazz's sports car parked illegally. The engine was still running. She shook her head and changed directions. She climbed into Jazz's car and smiled at Jason.

"He's wants to be the big bad wolf. That's fine, but now you're Jazz's ride. Tell him I'll be at home—and to cool down before he gets there."

She slammed the car door as Jason stormed after her. She knew he meant to stop her. She threw it in reverse before he could. Shawna waved before pulling away. When she was down the street, and stopped at a light, she finally put on her seat belt, and properly adjusted the seat. She eyed her rearview mirror and laughed. Jason was standing on the street corner looking pissed off.

He couldn't follow her. He'd leave Jazz stranded if he did.

JAZZ STUDIED THE HUMAN AND TOOK A DEEP BREATH, TRYING TO REMAIN calm. A part of him wanted to kill the guy. This man had been married to Shawna once upon a time. He'd gotten to call Shawna his wife...while their marriage lasted.

Allen glared at Jazz with the same intensity. "Do you love her? 'Cause I'm not kidding, if you jerk her chain and break her heart, I'll make you pay for it. She's been through enough without that kinda bullshit going down."

"I love her more than my own life." Jazz clenched his fists at the insult. "I'd rather die than hurt her."

"Fine. We'll see." Allen studied Jazz with a dark glare. "You have a temper. Make sure you never turn it on Shawna. I might be a cop, but I swear to God, I'll take off my badge if you hurt her. They'll never find your body."

"The same to you."

Allen finally sighed and his shoulders dropped with some sort of defeat.

"Shawna loves you. She's *nuts* about you. She said she's never been happier in her life. She looks really good too. I never thought I'd see that happy look in her eyes again, but when she spoke about you, she lit up like Christmas morning. I'll always love her. Letting her go was the worst mistake I ever made. I was young and stupid. She's got some issues, and I didn't know how to deal with them. Be smarter than I was. If you aren't, I can guarantee you that I'll be there to catch her if you dump her."

"Don't hold your breath." Jazz relaxed a little. "She's my other half, and I'm not letting her go...*ever*."

"I hope so for her, sake since she's in love with you." Allen hesitated for a moment. "She has nightmares and wakes up screaming sometimes. Ron, her second husband who died, he and I became friends. He didn't know how to handle it. He came to me for advice. When she wakes up screaming, well...don't touch her. She freaks. You just need to talk to her softly and she'll calm down."

Jazz frowned. "She's lived with me for over a week and never woken up screaming."

"She will. She always does. She comes across as a hard-ass...tough as nails and a real little hellion, but wait until she wakes up from her nightmares. She cries and shakes. Puts herself in a corner and balls up tight. If you try to touch her, she really *will* freak out. She never says why. I thought maybe her folks abused her. Or maybe one of her ex-boyfriends beat on her. She won't say...but it breaks your heart to see her like that. She recovers in about five minutes, but she'll go sleep on the couch. She can't stand to be touched after one of those nightmares."

Jazz shut his eyes, knowing what those nightmares were about. He nodded after he had a chance to catch his breath and looked back to Allen. "Thanks. I'll remember."

"And watch her back." Allen reached into his jacket and held out his card. "Someone has it out for her. If you can't handle it, call me. She's the important factor in all this. Don't let your pride get her killed. Get in touch if you need help. My cell is on there. Use it. I'm not going to be on duty for a few days. I'm sticking around here until at least tomorrow."

"Thanks." Jazz took the card. "But I can tell you that I have it handled. I have someone watching and protecting Shawna around the clock. That's how I ended up here. If you'd been an attacker, you would have had her guard on you in a heartbeat, but because she went with you willingly, he just followed."

Allen cursed under his breath. "Don't tell me you're a drug dealer."

"No, I'm in land development. But there are some people Shawna has rubbed the wrong way, so I was worried. I'd rather her get annoyed at me for sending a babysitter, as she calls it, than let her roam free without backup when things are dangerous."

Allen nodded. "Okay. Good."

"She's mine now," he warned once more. "Don't forget it. She's my life." Jazz reached behind him and pulled out his wallet. He removed two hundred dollars. "For the door. Sorry."

He handed it over and then left without another word.

13

---

*S*hawna was in the kitchen when she heard Jazz storm in. The front door slammed hard. She waited, knowing he would use his nose to find her. In seconds he stormed into the kitchen a little too fast to be considered normal. His handsome face was etched with anger as he stopped in the doorway and pinned her with an intense blue gaze.

"Don't ever do that again," he growled. "I could have killed him, Shawna."

"Still not calmed down, huh?" she responded.

"Don't ever go with some guy to his motel room. Maybe my human mind understands it, but my other side doesn't!"

"Yeah. It's so much better when women come into your house and start flashing you. He was fully dressed, and so was I."

He growled again. "Shawna."

She pulled her shirt over her head and dropped it, giving him a naughty smile. "Want to reassert your claim?"

He moved so fast, she grunted as he grabbed her, and Shawna found herself laid out flat on the island. Jazz reached for her jeans, and she heard the zipper go down. In seconds, he'd yanked them off her legs.

She smiled to herself as she watched him tear off his shirt, because he looked incredibly sexy when he was pissed off and his eyes were a little wild. She wasn't afraid of him. She knew he wouldn't hurt her. He tore open his jeans and kicked off his boots. He just shoved his jeans down and tugged her hips to the edge of the island. He was between her thighs in a heartbeat.

He reached for her bra, and she moved to help him get it off. Once she dropped it to the floor, his gaze ran hungrily over her body and he growled softly. "You drive me nuts."

She grinned and sat up to run her hands slowly from the hard lines of his abs to his broad chest. "You're really hot when you're jealous. I love you, babe. Were you really expecting to kick in the door and find me in bed with another man? After missing you and loving you all this time? Come on, Jazz. Give me a break."

He grabbed her ass, forcing her tight against his body. "I need you now."

She reached up and cupped his face. "I knew you would. I'm all yours, Jazz. Always. Forever. Just yours."

His mouth came down on hers, and she opened to him, moaning against his lips when he kissed her. He ran his hands up her bare back and then around. He cupped her breasts with a low growl before he broke the kiss and his gaze locked with hers.

"I'm still angry." He didn't sound it though, and the look in his eyes was anything but angry. Desire burned like blue fire, making her ache more.

She was already breathless as she asked, "Take me in the family room."

Jazz kicked out of his jeans and lifted her. She wrapped her legs around his waist and wound her arms around his neck. He brushed kisses on her neck and shoulder as he walked them into the family room. He stopped at the doorway and gave her a questioning look.

"The couch," she decided. "I want to be on top."

He let out another soft growl and walked to the couch. Shawna unhooked her legs and he sat back against the cushions. She smiled and lifted up, shifting her hips until the thick head of his cock was pressing against her, and then sliding down. It felt so good. She threw her head back with a soft moan as she sank down on him slowly.

"I love you," she whispered. "I love you so much."

Jazz groaned and thrust up into her. "God, babe. I love you too."

Shawna lowered her head and studied him, enjoying the look of raw, untamed pleasure reflected in his gaze. She moved slowly at first, up and down. The friction made the pleasure electric. She played with his nipples, tracing them with her fingers. Jazz leaned his head back against the couch, watching her with hooded eyes. He bit his lip; his teeth were long, and she saw blood a minute later. She kept moving on him and lowered her face. She kissed him, tasting his blood on her tongue.

"More," she whispered against his lips. "Mating heat, Jazz. Let's do it."

He groaned and turned his head. He bit his finger and held it out to her. She sucked it into her mouth, holding onto his hand.

"You turn me on so damn bad," Jazz moaned, watching her hungrily. "God, you have a gorgeous mouth."

She moved on him, riding him leisurely, as she sucked on his bleeding finger. She felt the change start pretty quickly. Her desire kicked up a notch and she lost the ability to move leisurely. She rocked her hips faster, releasing his finger and throwing back her head.

"Jazz!"

He snarled, his hold on her tightened, and they ended up down on the carpet next to the couch. On top of her now, but still buried deep, he braced his arms so he didn't crush Shawna with his weight and then he was pounding into her. She wrapped her arms around him and held on. The sensations were too much, and she shuddered from the tidal wave of pleasure. She shouted his name too soon for her liking, but she couldn't stop it.

Jazz followed her a minute later, burying his face in the crook of her neck. He groaned loudly as he shot deeply inside her. His body shook, but she just held on tighter, riding it out with him.

They were both breathless in the aftermath, chests rising and falling as they tried to recover.

After a moment, she smiled and asked, "Better?"

He chuckled, his breath warm against the curve of her neck. "Much."

"Jazz?"

"Yeah, Babe?"

"I ache." She moved her hips. "More. Again. Show me I'm all yours."

He lifted his head. Shawna saw his eyes changing, becoming more wolflike than human. She stared into his face and he smiled, showing off deadly canine teeth that were still sharp. She gripped his face curiously. She didn't feel him going furry at all, but his eyes were definitely wolfy.

"How are you doing that? Only parts of you are changed."

"I'm learning more control with you."

"That's amazing. I can kiss you."

He moved, driving his hips into hers, and she moaned.

"Watch the teeth," he groaned. "I so want to bite you."

"I know. I love you, Jazz."

"I love you too, Babe. Now let's stop talking."

She laughed, and then that laugh turned into a loud moan. Jazz kept moving in her, driving her to another climax.

Jazz placed Shawna on the bed. She was passed out cold. He kissed her cheek and covered her with the sheet. She smiled in her sleep and turned on her side, snuggling deeper under the covers.

Jazz sat on the edge of the bed and brushed his fingers through her hair, adoring her so much it hurt. She was only human. He had to keep reminding himself of that. He'd worn her out, and he felt more than a little guilty about it now that the bloodlust had faded.

He stood up, still naked, and grabbed the semi-automatic handgun she'd left on his dresser. He set it on the nightstand next to her. Then, he dressed quickly and left the room before he forgot his mission and crawled back into bed with his mate.

Downstairs, he called Desmon.

"Make a run with me, and please send Jason over here to watch Shawna. She's sleeping in my bed and should be out for a while."

Desmon paused. "You know Jason has a mate too. She might start missing him at some point. Miles could—"

"No," Jazz growled before he could stop himself. "Miles isn't mated. Jason's the only one I trust, and I have a fucking issue. Are you running with me or not?"

"Okay, I'll bite. Where are we running?"

"John Reynolds has been checking up on Shawna. There's a tracking device on her Jeep. It's parked in town. I want to know what in the hell is going on."

"Jason and I are on our way." Desmon hung up.

Jazz eyed the ceiling and listened. It was quiet in the house. He shut his eyes and listened harder. He could hear Shawna breathing slowly and deeply from upstairs.

He took a cooling breath and forced the wolf under his skin to stay calm.

His mate was safe.

And Jazz was going to make sure it stayed that way.

He walked to his office and put on the boots he kept in there, an older pair he could toss away if he got blood on them. He opened his gun vault in the corner and grabbed a harness and two semi-automatics of his own. He strapped them on and put on his jacket.

Then, he went to the front door and waited for reinforcements to arrive.

JAZZ ROLLED DOWN THE WINDOW OF HIS PARKED CAR AND SNIFFED THE air as he studied the small one-story building in front of them.

He glanced to Desmon sitting next to him. "He's in there."

"Yup." Desmon nodded. "Do you want me to go in as alpha or am I backup?"

"His ass is all mine." Jazz couldn't hide the growl in his voice. "He's screwing with my mate."

"Fair enough," Desmon agreed. "So, let's do this."

Jazz climbed out of his car as Desmon got out of the other side. They walked quietly to the door of the private investigator's office. Jazz inhaled again.

John was alone. His human receptionist wasn't there.

Jazz opened the door and stepped inside. As he expected, the front area was empty, but he could hear John on the phone in the back.

John Reynolds looked up when Jazz stepped into the open doorway of his private office, Desmon right behind him.

John paled.

At sixty-two, he only had a little gray in his otherwise thick, shiny brown hair. As a werewolf of their pack, he was fit, but John was more an office guy than a fighter. He hung up the phone without a word, keeping all his attention on Jazz and Desmon.

"To what do I owe the honor of a visit from you both?" John kept his tone cool.

Jazz stalked over to the desk and glared down at the man, which had to be intimidating. John wasn't big for a werewolf. He was only five-foot-eight with a slight build.

"Talk." Jazz made sure his tone brooked no argument. "Who hired you to follow Shawna or are you doing this yourself? What are you after? Talk fast."

John flinched. "Is this job a problem?"

"Yes, why is there a tracking device on my mate's Jeep and why are you snooping into her life?" He growled the words.

"Mate?" John choked out. "I thought she was someone you were fucking. No one said anything about you mating her."

"*Talk*," Jazz repeated, as he partially shifted right there in the office. His teeth grew long, and he made sure his eyes became primal and wolflike.

"I was hired by Leroy Goodwin a few days ago," John confessed in a rush. "He heard about a were-hunter in town and he wanted to hire her to take care of some issues. That's the thing now. You hire a hunter when you need help solving a problem the Alliance could come down on a pack for. He wanted me to check her out and learn everything about her to make sure she was good before he has me offer the job. I had a description and hit up motels right away. That's how I figured out her name, since she's staying in town. Then I dug for information that could link her to any other reports of a were-hunter sighting. I hit paydirt. This wasn't a onetime deal for her."

"What have you told him?" Jazz snarled.

John blinked. "Everything I found out. She's been doing this for years and years. She's killed well over twenty weres that I've found. No bodies. *Ever*. Just missing persons. You know how that works. She only goes after the bad ones. Real bad sometimes.

"She was hurt four years ago and spent three days in the hospital. Her injuries were serious, but hospital records say two men came in and helped her break out early. I got the impression they were shifters. They likely busted her out, gave her blood and let her heal up naturally. So, she knows how to take care of herself. She has connections. Overall, not a bad track record as far as I'm concerned. I recommended her to Leroy. I told him she's impressively good. I was supposed to approach her this weekend."

"What's the job exactly?"

"I don't know. He wouldn't tell me who he wanted taken out and I didn't ask. I was supposed to offer her the job yesterday but he kind of freaked out when I told him that she'd been spending time with you, Jazz."

"I bet he did," Desmon grunted with a look at Jazz, before he turned back to the private detective. "We're heading into a turf war with them, John. You should lose pack protection for this."

John's gaze shot to Desmon. "*What?*"

"You keep to yourself and don't come to most of the pack meetings. You don't live on pack land, and that's fine...but you know they're not friendly neighbors." Jazz took a deep breath to calm his wolf raging under the surface. "The Goodwin pack has expanded, and they want us to give up some of our territory that borders theirs. We've refused. And now, unfortunately, it sounds kind of like you're helping the Goodwins take over your own fucking pack."

"He never said anything like that. I assumed the problems were his." John was shaking his head. The scent of his fear flooded the office. "Shit. You think he wants to hire that crazy bitch to cut some of ours? She's scary."

"She's not a bitch," Jazz clarified softly, before a low growl rumbled in his chest. "And she's definitely not crazy."

"Sorry. I didn't mean it that way. She's a female hunter and she lives in our world and I just—" He swallowed hard. "I meant no insult. Desmon, I promise, I'd never go against Nightwind. I didn't know. I swear!"

Desmon sat calmly in a chair. There was a dark edge to his voice as he demanded, "Tell us everything."

"He wanted to pay her a hundred grand to kill three wolves. That's a hell of a lot of money. I figured she'd jump at the job. I've spoken to some of the people she's helped. She only took a grand from the Andersons. They have a daughter, and their neighbor was a shifter. They're a human family, but they know the truth. They've lived in werewolf territory for generations. Some of the family married into a pack, but this male was sniffing hard at the daughter. Terrorizing her. He was a shit. You know? Got off on threatening to rape and terrorize her.

"They went to the alpha, but it was the guy's nephew, and he doesn't give a shit about a human. Your mate," he eyed Jazz, "took care of the problem. That asshole disappeared and the girl's safe. The Andersons offered her twenty grand to make this kid stop. They were going to take a loan out on their place, but your mate only took a grand. Said that was plenty. She even offered to do it for free, but they wanted to pay her something."

"That's my Shawna." Jazz found himself smiling in spite of everything. "All heart."

"Yeah. She's all heart." Desmon grinned and said dryly, "She's the nicest were-hunter we know."

Jazz shot him a look, then asked John, "Was he only hunting for info or was he looking for dirt on her?"

"Dirt too," John sighed. "He said if she wouldn't agree to work for him that he wanted something on her. To tell you the truth, she's pretty clean. Her first husband's a cop, so he probably taught her well. The only real secret I found on her was shit he couldn't use. She's rich. She doesn't look it or live like it. Her Jeep is twelve years old. She lives in a mobile home in Danton. It's not even new. It's an older one. She shops at discount stores.

"The bitch—I mean *woman*, has major bucks. Her second husband was loaded. He died of cancer. I checked him out too, at Leroy's request. He thought maybe the money was dirty, but her husband was wealthy at birth and did even better investing it. He raked in the dough. I got copies of the records when his will was filed with the courts. We're talking millions. She sold the house months after he died. I don't know why. She bought the mobile home, and she owns the land it sits on. A lot of it—over a hundred acres.

"The worst thing I had on her was she's a hunter, but Leroy could never use that against her. Then he'd be exposing her *and* our kind."

"Anything else?"

John hesitated. "He had me send someone out to her home and look to see if I could find anything there. It's an older mobile home but she's made it pretty nice. Comfortable. Looks normal, but she has an arsenal under it. There's a hidden door in the floor of her walk-in closet. She dug out a room under the mobile home. It's got weapons up the ass. If she's ever attacked there, she could hold off a small army for days. She also practices a lot. She has hay bales piled up on her property with targets. Tons of casings on the ground. She must go out there almost daily to shoot. From what I hear, she's a good shot. She's also good with throwing knives. All the trees around her home are marked with knife grooves."

Jazz frowned. "What about men?"

"You want to know her sexual history?" John asked hesitantly. "She's your mate. Don't you want to ask her?"

"*What about men?*" Jazz repeated with a growl. "Tell me about the guys who broke her out of the hospital."

John took a deep breath. "I had my guy talk to her neighbors. Not much going on, but sometimes four men show up. It was probably a couple of those guys, but there was no description in the hospital records. They drive an old Bronco. You know, those big lifted jobs? No names or license plate number available. From the descriptions, they're all tall, wide, and look similar. They stay at her place once in a while for a week or two. I got the impression they were shifters, but who knows for sure?

"A few times there were a couple of women with them. A neighbor remembers seeing a baby one of the men had with him in town. A cute little girl. Maybe two years old.

"Before all of that, I couldn't find anything except that she was married twice. The address I had on her before she married her second husband came up with nothing. No one remembered her. That's all I have."

Jazz scowled. "I'll find out."

"Jealous?" Desmon arched an eyebrow at him. "Man, she's yours now. And a wolf with as many marks on his bedpost as you have probably shouldn't be throwing stones."

Jazz growled. "It wasn't that many."

"I just wouldn't be digging up the past. That's asking for trouble," Desmon turned back to John. "You quit. Do you understand? Destroy everything you found on her and get rid of that tracker on her Jeep. It got left where it was because of the tracker. Next time you get a job like this, you inform me when it comes to that pack. Are we clear? The Goodwins are bad news, and anyone loyal to Nightwind has to tread lightly where they're concerned. Unless you'd rather answer to Leroy Goodwin and have him as your alpha. You just let me know."

"Fuck no." John shook his head quickly. "I'm Nightwind all the way. I swear. If I'd known he was causing trouble for us, I'd have sent him packing. As it was, I figured a few less Goodwins in the world wasn't necessarily a bad thing."

He smelled honest.

"I believe you." Desmon nodded. "Just avoid Goodwins. Got it?"

"Yeah. Sorry. The money was too good. I should have known."

"I know this is your business, but things are tense. We have to stick close to home right now." Desmon sighed. "Just keep your ears open."

"I will." John stood and let his gaze drop to the floor until they left.

Jazz looked to Desmon once they got back into his car. "You think Goodwin wanted to hire Shawna to take us out?"

"Yup, I'd bet half the pack land on it. I bet he shit when he heard she was spending time with you." Desmon laughed. "He probably wanted to wait a week, figuring she might end up killing your ass anyway."

Jazz growled and flipped Desmon off. "Very funny."

"You know I'm not wrong." he shrugged. "I figure if he wanted three of us down, it's me, you, and Jason—or Miles. Either way, you're on the hitlist for sure, and he might try to hire someone else. You know what that means?"

"Fuck."

Desmon chuckled again. "Pack house, buddy."

"What are *you* laughing about? Your mate calls it the college dorm from hell. She'll demand you have the guys clean it up."

"We're close enough that I don't have to move my family in."

"Bastard."

"I told you we could tear out the tennis courts since no one uses them and you could build your house there. But no, you wanted woods around your place."

Jazz sighed. "I don't suppose I could take one of your guestrooms?"

"Pass." Desmon laughed. "I don't want you hearing me and Amber at night...or during the morning...or the afternoon."

"It would be hard to hear you over me and Shawna." Jazz grinned. "You have a pup now. You should be keeping that shit down."

"He's too young to know what's keeping his mom up at night." Desmon gave him another smile before he sighed. "Joking aside, we probably shouldn't both be sleeping in the same house. As my mate says, you don't put all your eggs in one basket. For the good of the pack, just in case, I think we should split up. I'm going to bring a few of the guys over to my place for backup."

"You're getting Amber's sisters there, right?"

"Just Katie, even though she loves living alone now that we fixed up their old house. Luckily, Bea went back to the college last month, and I don't see a reason to bring her home for this shitshow. We'll set up schedules, sleep at different times, and make sure we're on guard around the clock, not just on the borders, but at home too."

"Fuck. Shawna is so not going to be happy."

"I don't know who's going to be more miserable. Your hunter mate or all the guys who are going to be living with her."

Jazz softly cursed, and grunted, "Great."

14

---

*S*hawna felt lips brush her shoulder and smiled as she opened her eyes. It was dark outside now, but the room was coated in a distant gray glow. She figured the hall light was on and turned her head to find Jazz sitting on the edge of the bed fully dressed, bent over her.

"Wake up, babe." He brushed his lips across her forehead. "We need to go."

She blinked and tried to push back the fog of sleep. "Go where?"

He hesitated. "The threat of the Goodwin pack has been moved up. Des and I found out that the reason you were being investigated is because Leroy Goodwin wanted to hire you to kill three werewolves in this area. I'm not a betting man, but if I was, I'd say Des and I were on the top of that list."

Shawna twisted and sat up. "Who do you think the third was?"

"Could be Jason, they know he's a loyal enforcer, and he's a strong beta wolf. Or it could be Miles. He can't shift, but he's still Miles. A wolf would have to be insane not to fear him—and he's our best scenter. Either way, it doesn't matter. The Goodwins likely want to eliminate the top structure of the Nightwind pack and Leroy probably figures it would be easy to take the entire pack and our territory if we're all gone."

"I'd never do that," she promised. "If he had me investigated, he should have known I only take out the assholes...the really bad ones. I'd never go after you guys."

"He was trying to dig up dirt to blackmail you with and he was going to offer you a hundred grand."

"You know I would never have taken the job, right?" Her gaze locked with Jazz's. "I'm not a mercenary. I take out problem shifters who are causing pain and terror to helpless victims."

"I know that. Des knows too. We can't stay here though. We need to move closer to the pack to be safe."

"Okay." She wasn't going to argue if it meant keeping Jazz safe.

Jazz let out a sigh of relief. "Let's shower. We both still smell like sex."

"You carried me to bed." She shoved off the sheet and grinned at him. "That's sweet."

He smiled back. "I wasn't going to leave you on the carpet in the living room. I had Jason come over to protect you while Des and I went to talk to John Reynolds."

"I would have liked to have gone with you."

"I know." He led her toward the bathroom, his rough palm casually touching the small of her back. "That's why I waited until you were asleep."

"Doesn't Jason have a mate?" She turned to glare. "How does he feel about playing watchdog over your mate instead of his own?"

"Jason understands. You had someone after you." Jazz sounded completely unapologetic about it as he opened the bathroom door for her. "Your car was being tracked."

She headed toward the shower still naked but stopped when she heard a low growl.

Shawna turned to see Jazz staring at her bare body, his light gaze becoming wolflike before her eyes. Now clearly sidetracked from their debate, he took a deep breath and followed her.

When she bent over to turn on the shower, he ran his finger up her spine. "Does that hurt?"

Shawna frowned at the slight sting his touch caused, and reached around, feeling the rough patch on her lower back. "What in the hell is that?"

"Carpet burn." He lightly slapped her ass, and a smile sounded in his voice. "Next time, let me be on bottom."

"Let you?" she huffed though she couldn't hide her amusement as she stepped into the now steaming shower. "You're the one who took us to the floor, Jazz."

He was laughing as he pulled off his t-shirt. A minute later, he stepped into the shower behind her and set a clean washcloth next to the soap on the ledge. Shawna worked on adjusting the temperature, making it just a little hotter because this house could get cool. Werewolves weren't as sensitive about temperatures as humans.

He wrapped an arm around her waist, holding her close like he couldn't resist. Not surprisingly, the warmth of the water didn't seem to matter to Jazz one way or the other as he stood there, holding her, the hard outline of his thick cock pressing against her back.

"I thought we were in a hurry," she observed, but reached back to pull him closer anyway. "You're going to distract us both."

"Nah, I won't let us get distracted. I just like to feel you. Having my mate here, showering with me. I enjoy it." He moved his hips to prove his point. "But I'm an adult. I can control myself."

"Okay," she agreed. "'Cause if a territory war is really coming, we're going to wash, get out and head to where we're supposed to be. I don't plan to be the reason we lose."

"Yes, ma'am." He leaned down and kissed her neck, his breath warm against her ear. "I'll be good."

A smile tugged at her lips as she grabbed the soap to make quick work of washing up.

"Where are we going to hide out?" Shawna asked as she tried to ignore the sensual slide of his hard chest against her bare back because he refused to let go. "Tell me before I'm the one to lose control."

He chuckled, but then explained, "We're heading to the pack house. We'll be staying in my bedroom there. It'll be safer. All the wolves will be coming in who're fighters. We're sure Goodwin will leave the families alone."

"Why so sure?" she asked cynically.

"It's pretty standard werewolf behavior. If they kill all the fighters loyal to the alpha, it's easier to take over a pack. Families protecting young will usually go along with a power change to stay safe. You saw what happened when Desmon's father died. My dad killed off all his enforcers but let Des and Miles live because they were still pups. They try to convert the younger ones, but that doesn't always work out."

Jazz took the washcloth from her and started soaping up her back. "If we're being honest about it, Des and I are guilty of the same thing. My father didn't have that many fighters to take down, because he wasn't worth being loyal too, but it still happened."

"Did Desmon contact any of the people on my list?" Shawna turned around in Jazz's arms, letting the water wash the soap away as she looked up at him. "If we beef up the pack, we won't be such a desirable target for the Goodwin pack. They'll think twice."

"He did, actually. Several of them are already on their way." Jazz washed himself quickly. He was quiet for a moment before he asked, "When you were in the hospital a few years ago, who were the two men who showed up to take you out of there?"

"Wow." She couldn't hide her shock. "Your detective guy in the pack is really thorough, isn't he?"

"Who were they?"

"The Riley brothers. They were off helping someone and didn't get my message for a while. The second they did, two of them came to get me. I was scared that my target was going to find me again after he'd ambushed me. I managed to get away, but I was too hurt to leave on my own once I got to the hospital. Even though the doctors kept me pretty drugged up, I managed to call the Rileys. They came, got me back home, gave me a little blood, and watched over me until I was back on my feet. Then they took care of my target to make sure he wouldn't come after me down the road."

"And the four men who stay at your mobile home sometimes for a week or two? Four big men who drive a large Bronco?"

"The Riley brothers," she confirmed again. "I have some acreage and I have a good training area on it. They camp out there from time to time. Sometimes we spend holidays together."

Jazz was frowning. "Have you ever had sex with any of them?"

"Damn it, Jazz. I told you. You're the only shifter I've ever slept with willingly."

"I believe you." He sounded honest. "Did any of them *want* to bed you?"

She gave him a look. "What do you think?"

"All four of them have hit on you?" he asked with a growl.

She smiled. "They're good guys and we're friends. Okay? You'll like them. I've never even kissed one of them. I swear."

"Okay." He relaxed. "I can't blame them for being attracted to you." His gaze raked up and down her body. "They have damn good taste."

She laughed. "Let's finish this shower and get out of here before we lose the battle and end up very distracted."

SHAWNA WAS TOO UNCOMFORTABLE TO EAT MUCH.

She could practically feel the keen gazes of every werewolf in that room directed right at her. She moved a little closer to Jazz at the long table they both sat at for dinner, even though they were already squeezed in tight with the others. There were technically twelve seats, but four extra chairs were pushed in to make room, and still there wasn't enough space. Two small tables had been set up in the corners to provide extra seating.

Twenty-two men, including Jazz, were squeezed into the large dining room of the pack house. Shawna and one other woman were the only females there. Janie was a brunette with a pretty face, bright green eyes and a cheerful smile. Apparently, she was a young unmated female who had no other family to protect her. Desmon had asked Janie to move into the pack house while they were under threat, and she'd gladly agreed.

Jazz reached under the table and rubbed Shawna's thigh reassuringly. She looked to him, and he gave her an encouraging smile.

"It's fine. You're scenting nervous. You're safe."

"I know," she whispered back, though she knew most could hear her if they decided to pay attention. "I just don't like being stared at. Do I have food on my face?"

Jazz lifted his head and glared down the table. He growled low in his throat, and Shawna saw men's gazes drop fast. She turned to Jazz and winked at him.

"Thanks."

He nodded. "Eat your dinner, babe."

She dug into her fried chicken and mashed potatoes with gravy and did her best not to look at the men around her. She felt watched, but she knew she was safe and tried to ignore the fact that she was pretty much the center of attention.

The food was awesome, but she was grateful when dinner was over. Desperate for something to do, Shawna jumped up and started to help Janie and a younger man clear the table.

Jazz gripped her arm. "They have it."

"I can help." She gave him a pointed look. "Am I in danger?"

He shook his head.

"Then let me go."

He released her arm and held up his hands. "Okay, clean up if you want."

She moved into the kitchen with dishes. She smiled at Janie, and Janie grinned back in obvious solidarity.

"No one else is volunteering, huh? Just us girls." Shawna rolled her eyes. "I guess Nightwind isn't as modern as they say. I'm shocked we weren't asked to cook dinner too."

"Hey, don't be taking my job from me." The younger man came in behind them carrying stacks of dirty plates. He smiled at Shawna, and then dumped everything in the large sink. "I'm Tim."

She smiled back. "Great cooking, Tim. That was the best fried chicken I've ever had—no kidding."

"Thank you." He blushed. "My mom taught me. I want to be a professional chef. Desmon said that he'll be willing to pay for me to go to culinary school if I really want to do it."

"I think it would be a great investment. You're an excellent cook."

"I have the summer to decide. My older brother went to human school for accounting. He says it's easy to blend. So, I'm leaning toward it."

"Lean harder," Shawna encouraged, because that fried chicken was no joke. "It's obviously something you do well. You'll blend just fine."

She and Janie walked back into the dining room. The men were gone.

"They know there's work to be done, so they must've got to it," Janie observed. "See why all the unmated males live together for the most part?"

"Don't tell me you have to clean this mess of a house."

She shook her head. "The guys tried like hell to sweet talk me into cleaning up before you got here for dinner, but Alpha Desmon told them to get off their lazy asses and have it clean by morning, since they have all this extra company. That'll be fun. If they try to talk you into it, ignore them. Alpha told me to just laugh at them."

Shawna walked to the doorway and grinned. She gestured Janie over and silently pointed. Janie approached quietly and looked toward the living room. Five of the men were grumbling and holding trash bags as they cleared out their empty beer cans and trash.

"I love it." Janie laughed. "Alpha should make them clean more."

"No kidding," Shawna agreed.

Janie turned and studied her for a long moment. "I know you're the human Alpha Jazz has been missing all this time."

"Oh." Shawna felt her cheeks heat, because she hadn't realized it was starting to become common knowledge. "Yeah, I guess I am."

"He really loves you. You know that, right?"

"I do," Shawna admitted. "I love him just as much."

"It's good to see him happy. That's how I knew it was you." Janie sounded like she meant it. "He was never really happy before you showed up."

Shawna nodded, feeling more emotional than she was comfortable with, being in a house full of werewolves, and went back to clearing the table rather than say more.

"Okay, stop spying."

"What the hell?" Jazz jumped at the low whisper in his ear, and turned to Desmon, who was standing behind him in the hallway around the corner from the dining room, looking amused. "How'd you sneak up on me?"

"'Cause I'm stealthy." Desmon gave him a cocky grin. "And you were too busy spying on Shawna to hear me coming."

"They were talking about me," Jazz admitted, feeling exposed. "It's hard not to listen."

"As a mated man, take my word for it, there are some things you don't need to hear," Desmon assured him.

"She was saying nice things, actually." Jazz rubbed at the back of his neck. "I don't want to let her down. I hate that this Goodwin thing is happening now. What shitty luck we seem to have with that."

"Speaking of Goodwin." Desmon gestured silently to his office where they would have some privacy.

Jazz caught the hint and followed him down the hallway to his office in the pack house.

Once they stepped inside, Desmon closed the door. "Reynolds has been checking his sources since we left his office, and he has new information. He thinks the Goodwins are going to be moving on us soon."

"It's not hard to believe," Jazz admitted. "He smelled honest when we confronted him. He was shocked they were planning to take us out. I don't think he's playing both sides."

"True. We leave John alone for the most part, and he likes it that way. That would all change for him if Goodwin took over." Desmon sat behind his desk, looking pissed. "And he was told that Leroy wants it *all*. He's probably been paying off someone on the Alliance to look the other way if the pack changes hands—you know they don't pay attention to the politics of rural pack wolves. We're too unpredictable. There's talk of him launching a full-out attack on our land. That could bring in a lot of wolves, but we have three alpha fighters, including Miles. That'll help. Plus, we got help coming from Shawna's friends."

"You think they'll get here in time?"

"Some should. The Riley brothers will be here in a few minutes. They're bringing themselves, nine women, and two children. I wanted your impression of them when they arrive. The others won't be here until tomorrow at the earliest. Either way, we need fighters, and Shawna's people that I spoke to seem like our kind of wolves.

The next week is going to be hectic. I know you'd rather be locked up with Shawna somewhere, but I'm going to need your help."

"I understand."

Desmon grinned. "I'm sure you'll have a chance to make up for lost time later though."

"I better. Where are we going to put all these new wolves?"

"The motel. I called Dan. The River is almost empty. It's temporary quarters. I'm going to need Shawna's help if she was serious about supporting us financially. We have funds, but we're looking at adding about fifty more members to our pack."

"Wow." Jazz couldn't hide his shock. "That many?"

"Over thirty of those are males, fighters, and we need them."

"Yeah." Jazz nodded, wanting peace for Nightwind now more than ever. "We do."

"My next step after I get them in place is to inform the Goodwin pack that we've added to our numbers. Let them know we've evened the odds. Maybe the threat will go away without a war."

"I just hope this works out."

Desmon sighed. "Me too. Anyway...I spoke to all the wolves I invited at length. I liked them, and I was very clear about what I wanted. They all agreed. I'm going to have them come here, get introduced, before putting them up at the River Motel. And I called Casey. His distant cousin works for a company that sells manufactured homes. He thinks we can have some put in quickly on pack land until we can have more homes built. I was going to try buying something on the edge of town for a few of the bigger families. There's nothing worse than living in a damn motel. We can put up a few of the single men here at the house."

"Good. It all sounds good. Should I get Shawna? I think she was planning on helping Tim with the dishes."

"Maybe." Desmon shrugged. "But let's meet these Riley brothers and see what we think. I'm sure they'll want to see her. When I told them it was Shawna who gave me their number, they asked if she was going to be here. I assured them she was. I also mentioned *you*, so they aren't surprised by your romantic involvement. They sounded protective of her. Is this going to be a problem? I need you coolheaded."

"Shawna swears they're like brothers to her. She says they're all just friends, and I believe her. It shouldn't be a problem. I'm jealous as hell of anyone who has been a part of her life while I wasn't, but I'll keep a lid on it. It's my private issue."

"Good." Desmon stood up. "Let's go outside. They should be pulling up at any time."

Jazz grinned. "I smell like Shawna, don't I? Even after the shower?"

"Yup. Everyone at dinner could smell it." Desmon nodded. "I hope they don't have a problem with you, because they're definitely going to know you're the guy she's with. No doubt about that."

"I'm glad." Jazz grinned. "Yeah, let's get out there. I'm dying to meet these guys. Shawna said they're tough as nails. Real badasses. I want to see what her version of a badass is."

15

Jazz and Desmon walked into the pack house living room while Shawna was still doing dishes in the kitchen. Desmon quickly told the men gathered there to be on their best behavior, and they all nodded without complaint. Some of them looked pretty excited. Desmon cast a warning glare around the room.

"Do *not* approach the women with them. I mean it. From what I was told, most of them are afraid of men. Unless you want to go outside with me for a dominance fight, you keep it in your pants."

"We'll behave. This is so damn cool," Brandon said excitedly. "One of us could find a mate."

"Don't get ahead of yourselves." Jazz did a little glaring of his own. "Treat these women with respect—like they're your sisters."

"I'll be a gentleman." Dante grinned. "I swear."

Desmon narrowed his eyes at him. "No playboy antics, Dante. You're the biggest flirt we have. Behave. I mean it. Without these new wolves, we're looking at a fight from hell with the Goodwin pack. Keep that in mind."

"I got it," Dante swore, turning solemn. "I don't mind a fight, but I don't want to lose anyone I care about."

"None of us do," Jazz agreed, and cocked his head toward the door. "I hear vehicles."

Desmon and Jazz walked outside. They watched an older black Bronco pull in the circular driveway. Behind it was a RV, and following that, a red SUV. The vehicles came to a stop in front of the pack house and two large men climbed out of the Bronco first.

Jazz studied the men and could clearly tell they were brothers. They were big bastards too. The two of them were almost identical in body size. Six-foot-four, probably weighing around two-fifty, showing off broad shoulders and thickly muscled arms, since they were both dressed casual in blue jeans and tank tops. They had shoulder-length black hair, and their piercing blue eyes were narrowed, as though attempting to sum up Jazz and Desmon as the brothers climbed the porch steps.

"I'm Jordon Riley. This is my brother Cord. Our other brothers, Kade and Cage, are with the women." Jordon's gaze went to Desmon. "We appreciate the invitation. It's hell not having a home and always living on the move."

"I can imagine it would be." Desmon smiled. "We're glad you're here. I'm Desmon Nightwind and this is my best friend, Jazz Zendell. He's also Shawna's future mate."

Jazz nodded at them. "Welcome."

"Yeah, we noticed that." Cord Riley inhaled, and then a smile tugged at his lips. "The shower you took didn't cover up what you were doing before we got here. I never thought I'd see the day our girl would hook up with a shifter. That was a plot twist none of us expected."

.on wasn't as easygoing about it. "Be good to her. Shawna's special. ʋe think of her like family, and there's nothing we won't do to protect family. Keep that in mind."

"I understand." Jazz nodded. "She's my life, and I'm pretty damn protective of her as well."

"Then we won't have any problems." Cord nodded. "Just watch my brother Kade. He tried like hell to talk her into dating a shifter, but she was dead set on account of her first love."

"Bad experience," Jordon explained. "It almost cost Shawna her life. She dreams about some guy. She calls out for him in her sleep."

"Screams, more like." Cord sighed. "The first time we were camping out at her place, all four of us busted through both of her doors when she started screaming his name. We didn't know she was asleep and having a nightmare about some ass named Jeremiah."

Jazz felt sick. The knot in his stomach stole his voice completely. The wolf under his skin nearly howled out loud in pain.

Rather than risk losing control and shifting in front of the Riley brothers, he turned and stormed into the house, intent on finding his mate. Though her ex had mentioned her nightmares, he didn't know Shawna had screamed for him personally—desperate for help—even in her dreams.

The guilt was too much.

Jordon Riley frowned at Desmon. "What was that about?"

"We know all about Shawna's past. Jazz was supposed to mate with her sixteen years ago. His real name is Jeremiah."

Jordon looked at him in horror. "*What?*"

"Jazz's father was the lead alpha of our pack." Desmon took a deep breath. "He sent Jazz and I off tracking so he could get us out of the way." He grit his teeth. "Jazz's father and three of his enforcers attacked Shawna. We could smell her blood on them when they got back. Jazz and I killed those men *and* his father for it.

"Jazz searched for her for years, refusing to take a mate. He eventually believed she was dead, but still wouldn't take a mate. We didn't even know she was alive until recently. She's the only woman he's ever loved. They're true mates. He's probably with her right now. I know I would be, in his shoes."

"Shit." Jordon sighed. "I'm sorry. We didn't mean to hurt him."

"We didn't know. We'll explain it to Kade and Cord. Fuck. That's messed up." There was a low growl to Cord's voice. "They're *all* dead? The ones who hurt her?"

Desmon nodded. "Jazz killed his father's three enforcers the moment he smelled her blood. And he made them suffer. He's spent a fortune over the years trying to find her. He didn't know that she'd been found alive after the attack. Her family moved her to another state. She'd changed her name and had been lost to all of us until recently, when she blew into town to take out one of our pack members. She didn't call to let us know what he'd done because she assumed the alpha who attacked her was still in charge. If she had called me, I would have killed him myself and saved her a trip."

"And that's why you're so protective of women," Cord guessed.

Desmon nodded. "My mother was abused badly by that same pack leader after he killed my father. Jazz and I share a sister because of it. We were too young to fight then, but once we could take him down, we did."

"We?" Jordon eyed Desmon.

"Jazz and I are best friends. I'm pack leader, but Jazz is my second. He's not my enforcer. We lead this pack together. We always have. We were sixteen when we took the pack. We held it then, and we've had nearly every alpha within five hundred miles try to take the pack from us since—we're still here."

Cord softly cursed. "That's amazing. I've never heard of anything like it before."

Desmon nodded. "We had good reasons, and we were determined. We had a hell of a lot of rage, and we're never letting something like that happen again."

"We'd love to become a part of your pack," Jordon decided for all the brothers. "It would be an honor."

"We went over the rules and what I expect." Desmon looked from Jordon to Cord. "Do you and yours agree?"

"We do." Jordon nodded. "We give you our oath, Alpha. There's just one thing you should know before you accept us."

"What's that?"

Jordon swallowed and looked to his brother for one long moment before he admitted, "We're not full werewolves."

Desmon was stunned, because he could sense the power coming off both the brothers. "Wow, it doesn't smell like the human side has affected you, but sometimes it works like that. Our top enforcer had a human mother, but he still shifts, and he's a mean fighter when he's protecting someone."

"No, you misunderstood. Both our parents were shifters...but we're different than you're used to."

Desmon studied both men closely. "Then what in the hell are you?"

Jordon took a deep breath. "Our father was a wolf. Our mother was a shifter too. She just didn't turn into a werewolf."

Desmon frowned.

Jordon sighed. "May we?"

Desmon shrugged. "Sure."

He watched both men remove their clothing. Naked, the brothers backed down the porch. Jordon eyed Desmon.

"We're both different. I take after my mother. Cord takes after our father. Kade and Cage are twins but not identical. They also take after our mother."

Desmon motioned with his hand. "Go ahead. I can't wait to see this. Shawna knows, doesn't she? She asked me if I was prejudiced. I'm not, by the way."

"Yeah, she knows." Cord nodded. "Here it goes."

Desmon watched the men ease to the ground. They shifted fast. He was both impressed—and completely shocked as he stood there staring down at the brothers now in their animal forms.

Desmon glanced briefly at the massive dark wolf...then just stared opened-mouthed at the black panther standing casually in front of the porch. Desmon swallowed and walked down the steps.

He paced around the big panther. He'd never seen one in person. Jazz ran into a were-tiger once in Arizona, and Miles worked with all sorts of shifters when he was with the Alliance, but as a general rule, wolves avoided enormous cats.

And were-cats weren't known for being social. Their territories rarely, if ever, crossed.

The panther watched him warily but stayed still.

Even knowing how nervous Jordon Riley was, Desmon couldn't help but smile. "Amazing. I've never met a panther in person." He held out his hand. "May I?"

The panther nodded his head, and Desmon moved closer, touching the panther's side. The fur was thick and soft. He backed away, letting his hand drop, and moved in front of the large cat. He studied his enormous paws, the claws beyond deadly.

"I accept you into the pack." Then a laugh burst out of Desmon. "We have three panthers in our pack. That's pretty badass. The Goodwins are going to shit when they get a look at you."

The men shifted back and dressed quickly. Desmon continued grinning, and Jordon and Cord smiled back.

Cord was the first to speak. "Thank you. I'm glad you seem so happy. We were afraid we'd show you and you'd send us packing. Most wolves get a little nervous when they see my brothers shift."

"Are you kidding?" Desmon shook his head. "I didn't even know were-panthers existed. I thought it was only lions and tigers. Maybe a few cheetahs here and there."

"Yeah. We get that a lot. There aren't that many. My mom's people kind of stay hidden and not many of them like the States. Panthers draw too much attention if they're spotted. We're not native...not that lions and tigers are either, but they've learned to blend more with humans. Most of them are city cats. They don't shift as much. That's not our style." Jordon eyed him. "So...it's not a problem? You can understand why we have a hard time finding a place to land, but us Riley brothers stick together. We're all about loyalty and family."

"You're welcomed into our pack," Desmon repeated. "I accept you with pride and honor. I've found temporary lodging for you and yours. The River Motel in town is expecting you. I booked you ten rooms. I hope that's enough. We're working on securing more permanent housing. Would you like to come in and have a late dinner? We have leftovers."

The front door opened, and Janie stepped out. She smiled shyly at the two brothers and moved to Desmon's side. "Jazz told me you might need my help?"

"I do, actually." Desmon smiled down at Janie, letting his excitement show. "This is Jordon and Cord Riley. This is my assistant, Janie. She's here to greet the women in your group and help them feel welcome."

"Hi, Janie." Jordon smiled back at her. "Let me go get everyone and tell them we have a home. They've all been pretty worried."

Desmon nodded. "Are the women wolves? It doesn't matter. I'm just curious."

"All of them are but one. She's a panther. Patina is a cousin of ours. She didn't have any family left after our uncle died, so she looked us up." Cord chuckled. "She's adjusted to wolves well now."

"But not so much in the beginning." Jordon grinned. "We had to coax her out of a tree often."

16

---

*S*hawna jumped when Jazz came up behind her. He was so fast, she barely had time to register him in the kitchen before his arms were wrapped tightly around her waist.

She grunted from the impact and stopped her work of wiping down the stove. "You're squeezing me to death, Jazz."

He eased his hold on her but didn't let go as he buried his face in her hair and took a deep breath. "I'm so sorry."

Shawna turned in his arms, her smile dying. The look on Jazz's face scared her and his blue eyes were swimming with tears.

"Jazz? What's wrong?"

He stared down at her, and then looked to Janie, who paused in her work drying a plate. Next to Janie, Tim put a handful of soapy silverware into a tub full of water resting in the bottom of the sink.

"Should we leave?" Tim asked him.

"No, sorry, we'll leave." Jazz pulled away and took the spray bottle out of Shawna's hand to set it on the counter.

"Are they here?" Janie asked him curiously. "'Cause Alpha said I could help welcome them."

Like most unmated wolves, Jazz knew Janie was looking for a partner, and same as the others, she was excited to meet the newcomers.

He nodded. "Yeah, they're here. I'm sure Des would appreciate the help."

"Oh yay!" She set the plate down "Sorry, Tim."

"It's okay." Tim shrugged. "I clean this kitchen all the time by myself."

Jazz pulled Shawna into the hallway, and the look on his face had her heart beating hard and fast inside her chest. She let him lead her upstairs to his room, wondering what on earth could have happened with the Rileys to upset Jazz like this.

"What is it?" she questioned when he pulled her into his bedroom and locked the door behind him. "What did they tell you?"

He stood there for a long moment, his breathing ragged as he shook his head. "When you were attacked by my father...you screamed for me. You were begging me to help you, and I wasn't there."

She opened her mouth, temporarily stunned, because she didn't remember telling the Riley brothers that little bit of information. Even if she had, she couldn't imagine why they would decide to share that with Jazz five minutes after meeting him. They didn't even know Jazz was the first love she'd lost—or so she'd thought.

Then it occurred to her.

"They told you about my nightmares. Thought they were being helpful." She shook her head. "Dumb bastards."

"Your ex-husband did too, but he didn't say you called out to me. I don't know...it just got to me when they said it. They didn't know I was Jeremiah." He nearly choked on the name. "God, babe, I'm sorry."

She reached up and cupped his face. "It's all right. I know if you'd been there, you would have tried to save me. I know that."

He buried his face in her hair, causing her hands to fall from his face. He breathed into her skin. He held her tightly in his arms. Shawna held him back. She touched him and brushed kisses against his neck.

"Hey, it's over. It was a long time ago. I haven't had any nightmares since we've been together," she whispered against his ear. "Maybe you chased them all away. I love you, Jazz."

He nodded against the curve of her neck and inhaled. Then softly growled. "You're going into heat."

"You mean I'm ovulating?"

He nodded. "You're about to."

"That's bad timing with us being stuck in the pack house, since I imagine that's going to make you horny," she guessed.

Jazz pulled away and looked at her. "Would I scare you if I made love to you during that time?"

"I'd scare *you* if you didn't," she teased. "But maybe you should find condoms. In the middle of a war is not a great time to get pregnant. If you say I'm ovulating, I believe it. I know you wolves can smell it from a mile away."

Jazz stared into her eyes. It was clear the wolf side of him wanted to argue, but he just said, "Okay."

He smiled and brushed her lips with his. Shawna shut her eyes and opened her mouth to his exploring tongue. She groaned, molding her body to his, knowing she could argue with him about condoms in a few minutes.

And then someone pounded on the door.

"Sorry," a male shouted out. "Desmon wants you both downstairs."

Jazz pulled his mouth from hers with a curse and gave Shawna a pointed look. "I'm going to beat him."

"I'll hold him down." She nodded. "You hit him."

Jazz laughed and called out to the man behind the door, "Tell Desmon he can wait. Give us a few minutes."

Shawna looked up at Jazz as the male grumbled away. She cupped his face with both hands and whispered, "I love you."

"Ditto." He smiled down at her. "You're amazing. I'd do anything for you."

She leaned up and gave him a quick kiss. "So, let's go be grown-ups and deal with this impending war. Your scent is all over me, I'm sure everyone knows I'm yours, even if I'm ovulating."

Jazz let out a low growl.

"Play your cards right and you'll get lucky later—I promise."

Jazz growled once more in complaint but opened the door anyway.

JAZZ GRIPPED HER HAND AND TUGGED HER DOWN THE STAIRS. SHAWNA was giggling. She turned on the step, jerked her hand out of his, and tried to run back to the top. She got about two steps up before Jazz grabbed her around her waist. She squealed in laughter as she found herself thrown over his wide shoulder. Jazz couldn't seem to resist and smacked her ass hard. She hit his ass back, since she was hanging so close to it.

"That's not fair, Jazz," Shawna whined with amusement. "Put me down. I want to slide down the banister. It was made for it. Look at that curve."

"The only curve I like looking at is your ass." Jazz laughed. "And you're not going to break my beautiful, fine ass when you hit the floor at the bottom."

"Your ass? It's my ass."

He smacked her again, lighter this time. "I'm the one who sees it. I don't want you bruised up or broken."

"You're no fun."

"You weren't saying that earlier today. Now stop wiggling around. Desmon is probably waiting for us in his office."

"Actually..." Desmon laughed from below. "We all wanted you in the living room. The Rileys asked to see Shawna. I just don't know if they wanted see her at *that* angle."

Shawna tensed. She lifted up, using Jazz's back to brace herself, and stared down the stairs to the bottom foyer. She saw all four Riley brothers, Desmon, Jason, and a few of the other pack members. They were all grinning but one.

She felt her face flush, but still lifted a hand and waved. "Hi, guys."

Jordon Riley snorted. "I see she's still trouble."

"And mouthy," Cord added.

Cage laughed. "And has found someone to keep her in line."

Kade growled softly, but Cord turned and glared at his brother.

Jazz took Shawna down the stairs before she could see the rest of the exchange. When he reached the bottom, he put her back on her feet, setting her to the side of him.

That's when Kade turned his dark gaze on Jazz.

The two of them stared at each other.

Shawna cursed softly. Kade had feelings for her. No matter how often she'd told him she could never return them, he was always trying to change her mind. She moved slowly and stood in front of Jazz.

She bit her lip. "Hello, Kade. Stop staring down Jazz."

Kade's gaze lowered, and he looked to Shawna instead, studying her from head to foot. Jazz growled and tensed. Shawna reached back and grabbed hold of him to keep him in place. Jazz moved closer, pressing against her back, and gripped her hips with both hands. She just held him tighter. She knew his instinct was to push her behind him and protect her.

Kade's gaze met hers once more.

"Kade Riley, don't make me kick your ass again." Shawna frowned at the man because he was being a jerk, and they both knew it.

He suddenly smiled. "Again? I let you win."

"Right." She sighed as the tension drained out of her. "I made you eat mud. Now behave yourself and tell us you're happy for us."

His gaze lightened as his grin spread. "He looks all right. I'm happy for you."

"Thank you." Shawna grinned back. "I'm glad you guys are here."

Kade nodded. "So are we. Thanks for hooking us up, Shawna."

"You're welcome. How many women do you have this time?"

"Just nine," Jordon answered. "We found homes for the rest of them."

Shawna studied him. "Really?"

"There's a pack in Illinois that's mostly females. They weeded out their assholes, and they wanted as many women as we had, but nine of them wanted to stay with us. They're still a little man shy."

"How is it working out with your cousin?"

"She's staying out of trees these days."

Shawna turned to Desmon with a smile. "So you accepted them?"

Desmon nodded. "Yeah. Panthers are cool."

Jazz cleared his throat. "Panthers?"

Shawna laughed and tilted her head, looking over her shoulder since he was still molded to her back. "Their father was a wolf. Their mother was a panther. That's why their smell is hard to detect. Kade, Jordon, and Cage are cats when they shift. Cord is the only wolf."

Jazz looked stunned. "No shit? I didn't know cats and wolves could get along well enough to mate. That's pretty amazing."

Shawna grinned. "You should see them fight. I've seen them outnumbered six to one and they *still* kicked ass."

"Only to save your ass." Jordon arched an eyebrow at her. "Shawna here walked into a were biker bar and decided to get drunk while she was ovulating. We warned her it wasn't a good time, but she was pissed off about a job, so we followed her. Some of the men thought she smelled too good to resist. We made them rethink it."

Jazz frowned down at her. "You should know better, babe."

"I knew they were following me." She shrugged. "And they were pissed off about that job too. We all needed to blow off some steam. It's amazing what a good bar fight will do to make everyone feel better."

Kade chuckled. "True. She picked a bar that was well known for breeding assholes, so it needed to be cleaned up some anyway." His gaze slid to Jazz. "You have your hands full with that one. Good luck. You'll need it."

Jazz wagged his eyebrows. "I look forward to it."

Kade nodded. "Speaking of...you should mate her. I can see that you two belong together. Why are you dragging your paws?"

"She won't let me," Jazz said, "and I won't force her."

Kade arched an eyebrow and looked to Shawna. "What's your problem? He seems to love you. He's an alpha and he looks like he can kick ass, so he's tough enough to keep up with you. Why are you holding out?"

"I have my reasons."

Kade frowned. "Spill now."

"You know I was attacked." She eyed him. "They marked me, Kade."

He blinked. "I know that. I took care of you after the hospital when you got beaten up and saw the scars. You were so zoned out on medication, who in the hell do you think dunked your ass in a tub? What's the problem?"

"You don't live with wolves enough to know what the marks mean. I can't ever strip naked and change in front of the pack."

Kade frowned at Desmon. "Why not?"

Desmon sighed. "It's a horrible old tradition. When a mate is unfaithful or a bitch is deemed—for lack of a better word—useless, alphas would claw them. It marks them as a pack whore. We don't tolerate those traditions, but the previous alpha did. He marked Shawna thinking Jazz wouldn't mate her. The first time another pack saw her at a multipack run, and she stripped down to change, there could be a major problem. The men who follow the old rules would feel it was their right to mount her."

Kade looked furious. "Are you saying she's not safe in your pack?"

"She's safe in our pack," Desmon assured him. "It's *other* packs she's not safe around. Jazz and I have personally spoken to every male in Nightwind. They know if they even look at her wrong, they'll die. Jazz has damn near begged her to let him mate her. She still refuses."

"We've dealt with a lot of abused women and we might have a solution." Jordan turned to Jazz and Shawna. "It would be difficult for you...but there's a way to fix the situation."

Jazz eyed him. "What are you talking about?"

"Yeah...what?" Shawna agreed.

Jordan looked to his brother, and Cord sighed and explained, "We had a woman whose werewolf boyfriend, asshole that he was, dug his name into her back with one of his claws. She was human. She had a shifter child by him. She wanted to be a shifter too, to protect her child, so I changed her over...and I used my claw to slash open the scars he put on her.

"You know when humans are first changed, that's when the healing ability is at its fullest, to ease the transition. After you're changed, if the wounds were bad enough, the scars remains. But changing from human to were the first time, the body goes into overdrive during the change. If the scars are reopened beforehand... Well, it damn near completely healed about ninety-five percent of her scars. His name is gone from her back, and all that remains is a few grooves."

Jordan nodded. "I don't envy you the task if you try it. The primal side of you would likely rebel. But if you could control yourself, reopen her skin where the scars are, then change her, she'll heal without them. It would be painful for you both. Her physically, you emotionally...but those scars would be gone. You'd just have to be careful to go over the exact scars with your claws. And the cuts would have to be deep."

Shawna was shocked. "Really?"

Jordan nodded.

Shawna bit her lip and gazed up at Jazz hopefully.

He looked grim. "I couldn't hurt you like that, babe. Even if my mind understands, the wolf in me could never cut into you. The scars don't matter. We'll never take you to a multipack run. We'll run in my woods together. I can't tear your skin apart. I love you too damn much. Just let me mate you."

Cord cleared his throat. "I would be willing."

Jazz growled.

"I meant, I could slice her skin—if that's what she truly wants. I wasn't offering to change her over," Cord corrected. "I would never do that for another man's mate."

Shawna turned in Jazz's arms. "I want to be your mate, but I won't ever agree if it means that you'll have to fight and die to defend me just because of some scars. Do you understand?" She grabbed both his hands and squeezed them. "I want to do this! I *want* to be your mate. Cord knows what he's talking about." She searched his gaze. "One painful day is nothing compared to the lifetime we'd have ahead of us. Will you do this for me, Jazz? Please?"

He stared into her eyes and nodded reluctantly. "I would do anything for you, babe. *Anything.* I just can't slice you open with my claws." He looked to Cord. "Are you damn good with yours?"

"I'd be a hell of a surgeon," Cord promised. "I swear."

Jazz sighed. "You slice her skin, and I'll handle the changeover part."

"We could ask the doctor to do it," Desmon cut in. "We have one for things like that. Modern pack here, remember?"

"She can't have pain medication—even local anesthesia," Cord reminded them. "As I'm sure you know, any medications can mess with the change. It's too much of a risk. Maybe your doctor knows what he's doing in theory, but I've actually done this before, more than once. Besides, the thickness of our claws works better than a scalpel at removing the scars."

Before anyone could respond, the ring of a phone cut through the sudden tension in the room. Desmon reached into his pocket, pulled out his phone and stared at the screen for one long moment before he said, "It's Leroy Goodwin."

"Well, answer it," Jazz barked at him.

Desmon pushed accept and held the phone to his ear, looking grim. "What do you want?"

He listened for a long minute before rage crossed his face. "Let me remind you, Leroy, the last time you tried to fuck with us, you lost a brother and a lot of other strong fighters. I'm tired of this territory war, you're hungry for something that will never be yours. And you're not the only one who's been recruiting. If you want a fight, you'll be biting off more than you can handle. It'll make your last attempt look like puppy play, I swear."

Desmon listened, then growled, "We'll keep the humans out of this. We'll meet at the border of Hollow Mountain at eight o'clock. No weapons."

He hung up seconds later—then Desmon threw the phone, smashing it into a wall.

No one said anything for a long moment.

Since Shawna hadn't heard the other half of the conversation like the shifters in the room probably had, she whispered, "So, I guess that didn't go well."

Desmon turned to her. "The stupid son of a bitch wants a numbers fight. He won't listen to reason. Said we either turn over the pack by noon tomorrow, or he's going to come and kill every shifter he comes across. *In town*. In front of humans," he snarled. "I told him we'll take this to the mountain tonight. He agreed."

Jazz took a deep breath. "We've had worse odds."

"And we've always won," Desmon added.

"Barely," Jazz huffed under his breath. "And we're lucky you didn't get put down by the Alliance for killing Gary the last time."

Jordon cleared his throat. "Don't forget us. You said no weapons. No one said anything about not having panthers, right? We're members of the Nightwind pack now. That means your fight is our fight, and..." He grinned. "We're good at evening out bad odds."

Shawna nodded and looked from Desmon to Jazz. "They can kick serious ass. Six on one was a breeze for them."

"We owe you." Desmon eyed the men. "I didn't want to make you fight so soon after getting here."

The four brothers shrugged.

"We're defending our home now too," Cord answered. "And we could use a good fight, couldn't we, boys?"

The other Riley brothers smiled.

"Count me in," Shawna added.

Jazz growled. "No weapons are allowed on the Mountain, Shawna. That leaves you here. You aren't going out there with us."

She cursed. "That's not fair. This is my pack too."

Jazz hugged her. "You can defend our women and cubs. You can use guns off the mountain. We're going to have fighters guarding the house, but we need all the protection we can get. We'll call in all the females to come here with their pups. Goodwin is a bastard, he might send some of his people here to screw with our families, regardless of the terms. They'd assume most of our fighters had to leave for the battle. We need you here. They don't play by the rules."

"I believe that." She nodded grimly. "I'll defend the house. That's not a problem. Protecting women and kids is my specialty."

"We'll arm our women, too," Kade added. "We've trained them. They're good fighters. We've been surviving on our own for a long time, so we made sure they know how to protect themselves. Between Shawna and the women we've brought, it would take a small army to breach this house."

Desmon turned to a few of the pack males. "Make the calls. I want all the women and cubs brought to the pack house. Attacking families in the middle of pack land would bring the Alliance down on him in a dangerous way and ruin the pristine reputation he's lied so hard to get, but he wants our territory badly enough to do it. We'll all meet here and go together. Have Jason call Miles, tell him he has to leave his weapons at home. He's not going to be happy about that."

The men nodded and headed off in different directions. Some of them were already on their cell phones.

"Maybe we should have Miles stay here and help Shawna protect everyone in the pack house," Jazz suggested.

"I think we're going to need Miles at the border. He's still an alpha wolf. No matter what form the others are in, they'll have a hard time beating him, even if he's trapped in skin. He doesn't need weapons to fight. If anything, we'll have the element of surprise on our side with him," Desmon argued. "If we lose the border, we lose everything."

"He's an alpha too?" Jordon asked.

Desmon nodded. "We're cousins. His father and mine were brothers."

"A full-out territory war is always a numbers game." Cord looked quizzically at Jazz. "Another alpha would help, but why does he have to stay in skin?"

"He was severely injured years ago," Jazz shared. "He's heavily scarred and he can't shift anymore."

"Shit," Kade muttered. "He can't shift at all?"

"Even alpha form is too difficult for him," Desmon admitted. "He's lucky to be alive. He *can* shift, but it's really painful and he gets stuck."

Shawna frowned. "Stuck how?"

Jazz sighed. "When he first tried to shift after he got out of the hospital, he'd get stuck halfway between changing. He was trapped that way for days. It was agonizing for him. He kept trying. He was finally able to shift fully but then he was stuck that way for almost a month. He finally gave up trying and remains in skin now."

"That's horrible." Cord shivered. "That poor bastard."

"He's tough, and he has ways to fight without weapons." Desmon sounded confident. "We'll take him with us and arm everyone here to the teeth. If we lose at the border, everyone's in danger. We need Miles where the fighting is."

"He'll be glad to go. Miles is always ready for a fight." Jazz was grim. "He's a wolf trapped in skin. That's not easy."

Shawna frowned. "Is he dangerous?"

Desmon shook his head. "Just grouchy as hell. He's a hermit. Jazz and I go check on him often. Jason and Brandi live next to him on the north end. They get along okay. He's not rogue or dangerous to others unless they're shifters who trespass on his property with bad intentions."

Jazz turned to Shawna. "I want you to swear to me that you won't leave this house. Our families really do need your protection. The Goodwins would be breaking massive laws by attacking our women and pups, but I don't put it past them."

Shawna stared up at him. "I swear. I'm not an idiot. I'm not going to go running out into the middle of a turf war with just my guns... unless someone has a machine gun handy for me to borrow?"

Jazz chuckled. "I'm fresh out, babe."

She smiled. "Oh well, I'll just hang out here, I guess."

Jazz suddenly grabbed her, lifting her into his arms. He looked at Desmon. "I need a little time with my mate."

Desmon nodded. "Don't get too worn out. We need you in fighting form and she needs to be awake when we leave. No shifting."

Jazz nodded. "Not a problem."

Shawna wrapped her arms around Jazz's neck. He carried her upstairs to their bedroom and kicked the door shut. He turned and bent a little, letting her reach the doorknob.

"Lock that damn door."

She locked it, and Jazz walked to the bed and stood her next to it. "Strip fast. We don't have much time."

Shawna stared at Jazz as she started to strip. "Come back to me, Jazz. If it gets too hot, run, damn it. I mean it. Don't you dare die on me after we've found each other again. Retreat, regroup, and then attack. It works. I've had to do it often."

Jazz nodded. "You said yourself, your people are good fighters. Combined with ours, how can we lose?"

"I'm going to be worried sick about you."

He was stripped naked and very aroused. He gripped her face in his hands. "I'll be worried about you. I'm a good fighter, babe. You remember me from my teens. I'm ten times better and stronger now. Des and I have had to take on some really scary packs over the years. I'm coming back to you. Just be on alert, all right? Leroy Goodwin can't be trusted. I'm afraid he'll send some of his men to attack our families, to pull as many of us off the mountain as he can. We'd be divided."

Naked, Shawna inched closer to Jazz, her body touching his along their fronts. "I can hold them off, and the Riley women really *are* great fighters. I helped train some of them myself. They have lots of weapons hidden in the RV. I can hold off an army with those women."

"All our teenage pups will be here, and they can fight better than most full-grown wolves. We've made sure of it. If you need to rely on them, do it. And we'll have fighters stationed outside the house too." Jazz still sounded concerned. "You won't be all alone."

"Don't worry about us," Shawna assured him. "Promise me that if you do hear about an attack on the house, you'll trust that I can defend it. I *can*, Jazz. I'm not the teenager you remember either. You hold the mountain and don't worry about anything else but getting back to me. Promise me you won't freak out and get distracted, or worse, leave to come rush to my rescue. I can hold this house."

He smiled. "I promise."

"Now make love to me."

He lifted her up his body and his mouth took possession of hers. Shawna moaned against his lips, her arms and legs wrapping around Jazz. He climbed on the bed on his knees and gently lay Shawna down under him one last time...before the battle that could possibly steal her away.

17

Shawna studied the women and young cubs assembled in the living room. There were so many of them, werewolves spilled into the dining room. Little ones were underfoot everywhere. Teenage girls giggled from the corners, while the young men showed off and did a good job of ignoring the occasional scolding from a stressed-out mother.

A fire marshal would probably fine them for how many people they had in one house, but that was the least of their problems.

The women who came with the Riley brothers sat on a couch and stood in the corner, looking slightly uncomfortable, but determined. Janie sat with them, as though she took her job as official welcomer very seriously.

Shawna wore her jacket, body armor, and had all her favorite weapons strapped to all the right places.

She smiled at Amber, Desmon's wife, and lowered her gaze. Amber was the official head bitch in charge, and it was customary be respective of her.

"With your permission, Alpha."

Amber Nightwind was a petite blonde woman holding a dark-haired baby, bouncing him on her hip to keep him from fussing. "You go right ahead. Desmon trusts you. That means I do too."

There was a huff of anger from Amber's sister, Katie, who was small in stature like Amber, and just as blonde. Though Katie's hair was shorter, cut in a stylish bob that showed off her light eyes...currently dilated in obvious wolf fury.

In front of everyone, Katie stormed toward the kitchen, leaving Shawna standing there feeling awkward.

Amber just groaned and looked toward to ceiling as though she too was trying to control her temper. For one long moment, Shawna was worried she had screwed up and offended the head female in charge.

Amber shook her head and whispered, "I am so sorry, Shawna. Katie's a new werewolf. Desmon changed her a few months ago because that's what she wanted, and it's safer that way. She doesn't go out in the human world like our other sister, Bea. She's happy on pack land, but she's having a hard time controlling her temper since the change."

"Hey, don't blame the change. She's always been like that," Janie cut in. "I've worked with Katie in the pack office. She's the kind of girl who always speaks her mind. We all know she's mad about Merl. She dated him for a long time. She's allowed to be upset, right? Those are her true feelings."

"Right, that too. Thanks so much, Janie, for bringing that up." Amber rolled her eyes, looking irritated again. "It's perfect timing."

"Wow. So...that's an unfortunate development someone should've probably mentioned before now." Shawna winced at Amber. "You let your sister date Merl?"

Amber shook her head. "It's a long story. I was not a Merl fan, and I'm not sorry he's gone, but she did date him. I'll give you the rundown later, after this is over and we have chance to sit down to dinner and actually get to know each other."

"Yeah, okay." Shawna nodded. "He killed my brother. You know that, right?"

"Yes, I fully understand. Like I said, I was never a fan of Merl," Amber assured her. "What do you think we should do?"

Everyone fell silent after that, following their alpha's lead and looking to Shawna expectantly, which sort of surprised her.

"We need weapons. We need to be able to fight," one of the young men called out from the corner, before Shawna could speak.

Girls giggled until a woman who was clearly his mother called out, "Jeremy Taylor. You shut your mouth!" Then she rounded on Shawna. "My son is thirteen. He's not fighting. He's still a cub."

"I completely agree with you." Shawna gave the woman a serious look. "I think all cubs need to hide in the basement. We're not losing any teenagers today. The house should be safe, but just in case, we need all the cubs hidden."

"Jazz said we could fight," one of the older teens called out. "We can defend the pack as good as the other males at the border. We train all the damn time. What are we doing it for, if not to fight?"

"If you're not a full-grown werewolf, you're not fighting today, buddy. Not on my watch," she assured him. "I've got enough on my conscience, and I don't care what Jazz has to say about it. You can tell on me later and see how it goes down."

There was a lot of grumbling, but no more arguing. Shawna didn't make any fans amongst the teenage boy population of the Nightwind pack, but she did earn quite a few, "That's right!" from the mothers.

"I always knew Jazz had good taste." This from the woman who smacked her son in the head.

"I second that. Jazz obviously does have good taste," Amber agreed with a smile at Shawna. "Let's start heading to the basement, and I'll stay up here with Shawna to sort out the responsibilities for anyone over eighteen who doesn't have cubs to protect, and would like to help guard the house on the off chance some of the Goodwins make it past our wolves patrolling outside."

It took a while, there was more posturing from the young male werewolves, but their mothers all did an excellent job of not putting up with their shit and herding them into the basement.

Luckily, the basement was massive and unbelievably secure. The Nightwinds had built a real-life bunker underground, equipped with tons of extra supplies, several bathrooms and more than enough space to house everyone.

There were about twenty wolves left, all of them women, except for Tim, who had just recently turned eighteen. The rest of the adult men were either guarding outside or fighting at the border.

Shawna walked around slowly, checking their weapons and making sure they knew how to use them. One by one, she assigned them positions around the house. She ended with the Riley brothers' panther cousin.

"Hello, Patina. Nice to see you again."

Patina nodded her head. Her eyes were an amazing green and shaped like a cat's, even in human form, which wasn't typical...and meant she was probably nervous and trying to hide it.

Being in strange surroundings was extra hard on cat-shifters.

"I'm giving you lookout duty because, let's face it, you're fast and you have great balance regardless of your form. You'll need to stay in skin for that—"

"I prefer fur," she whispered. "Especially when there's danger."

"I understand, but I need you to remain in skin. You can't wear a vest or use weapons as a cat. I know you hate vests, and they restrict you a little, but it's an order. Someone might shoot at you if they spot you on the roof. I'm depending on you to inform me if you see any danger. We have guards in the woods surrounding the house, and we'll be in communication with them, but we need you too."

Patina growled a little, but nodded.

"You keep a sharp look out on all sides. Nothing should be moving. Do you know your directions from where we are currently? North, south, east, and west?"

Patina pointed in each direction, reciting them, and Shawna nodded.

"This is one of the most important jobs." Shawna stared at the pretty were-panther. "Do you understand? You're our eyes and ears to warn us so we can defend the house and each other. I'm trusting you to help us stay safe."

Patina straightened her shoulders and smirked. "You're not just trying to get me out of the way because I can't fight great? I'm getting better."

Shawna took the woman's hand and met her gaze. "I know you can fight well enough, but we need you up on the roof. You have amazing balance and you're fast. Wolves can't do what you can. A good lookout is vital."

Patina grinned. "I won't let you down."

"I know you won't." Shawna tilted her head toward the kitchen. "Go to Tim. Get a vest, a radio and a gun. If you see anything besides the guards outside, contact us immediately and stay down."

Patina saluted and almost ran for the kitchen.

Shawna smiled at Amber. "She'll do an excellent job."

"She's young," Amber whispered. "Are you sure—"

"She's twenty-four. She spent way too much time in fur with her family and she doesn't have a lot of people skills. She's skittish, but she's trying. Plus, she has amazing tracking skills. It's a huge benefit to have a panther on the roof."

"You're good with people."

Shawna shrugged. "I try. Now, you need to respectfully get your ass to the basement with your son."

Amber glanced around and lowered her voice. "I feel like it's my place to be up here defending instead of hiding in the basement behind locked doors. I'm Desmon's mate, and he's alpha. I should be helping to protect our pack."

Shawna bit her lip. "Jazz and Des unofficially share the title, right?"

Amber nodded. "Yes."

"Well, you have a nursing baby." Shawna kept her gaze locked with Amber's. "Your job is to protect your son and stay safe. My job is to protect the house, the women and the cubs. It's Jazz's mate's job to hold up this end, all right? And I *am* his mate, even though we haven't completed the bond.

"Right now, I'm a fighter. You're a mother. Please go to safety, Amber. Let me do this job." She smiled. "Maybe one day, if I'm lucky, I'll have little ones to protect too."

Amber blinked back tears. "We'll be like Des and Jazz. We can share the job as lead bitches, all right?"

Shawna laughed and suddenly hugged the woman. "Deal."

"I'm so happy Jazz found you." Amber squeezed her tightly. "Be careful and don't get killed."

"I'll protect the house no matter what. I swear."

Amber pulled back and met Shawn's gaze. "Protect yourself too. Jazz needs you. We all do."

"Go now and lock everyone in." Shawna's tone became dead serious. "Don't open that door for anyone but me or your mate. Do you understand me? If we're captured, the enemy could torture one of us to get you to open that door. I don't see it happening, but just in case, I need to say the words."

Amber shuddered, but she nodded. "Thank you." She turned to everyone still present. "Shawna is pack bitch in my absence. You obey her."

Amber took her son from Brandi, Jason's mate, and grabbed the woman's hand. "Come on, you're staying down there with me. I need the support."

"Yeah, it has nothing to do with me being a fragile human without a lifetime of combat training like Shawna," Brandi mused with a small smile.

"That too," Amber agreed. "But I do need a friend right now."

The two women went down the stairs to the basement without complaint, which was a blessing.

Afterwards, Shawna found Tim in the kitchen, still handing out weapons. "Tim, you protect those stairs to the basement. Do you understand me? No one goes down those stairs that doesn't belong there. Take weapons and a radio, and go defend that space."

"But I wanted to help up here."

"You heard what Amber said, I'm acting pack bitch. Now listen to me and do what you've been ordered to do."

Tim nodded reluctantly, gathering up the weapons and ammunition he would need before heading down the stairs.

She faced the women. "Those who aren't already armed, do it now and get into positions. Keep those radios on and do *not* fire until you have a clear shot. If they get past the guards, they'll try to make us run out of ammunition. Don't waste bullets." She took a deep breath. "Move."

Shawna was left with three women besides herself. "We're floaters. Do you know what your job is?"

Maria, who came with the Riley brothers, answered, "We go where needed, if anyone calls out for help."

"We got this, Shawna," Susan, another one of the Riley women, added confidently. "We're protecting this house."

"Okay." Shawna nodded as she heard another woman approach, probably searching for an assignment. Trying not to let her nerves show, she turned.

Katie stared back at her, her eyes a normal blue now, and she seemed somewhat embarrassed. "I can help, too, you know."

"Maybe you should go down with your sister?" Shawna wasn't sure she could trust her.

"No, I want to protect the pack. They're my family." Katie sounded like she meant it. "I'm sorry I lost my temper earlier."

"It's okay. Like Janie said, those are your feelings. You were just being honest," Shawna admitted.

"He was an asshole...Merl," Katie whispered after a moment. "I know that more than anyone. I tried to help him, but—"

"That wasn't your job," Shawna assured her. "You deserve someone a lot better than Merl."

"Maybe one day." Katie shrugged. "Now tell me what you need me to do. I'm sorry I don't know how to fire a gun."

"We'll correct that after this is over. Right now, I need you to be prepared to run ammo where it's needed if we're attacked." Shawna gave her a smile. She liked the woman when she wasn't growling at her. "That's an important job. If we run out of ammo, we're screwed."

Katie nodded. "I got it. I won't let anyone down."

Shawna's phone rang. She yanked it out of her pocket and answered. "Hello?"

"Hi, babe," Jazz said softly.

She smiled. "Hey, sexy."

"I just wanted to tell you we're here. How are things there?"

"Good so far."

"It should stay that way. Noah says they have the outside protected. Don't forget to reach out to him. Make sure all the communications work."

"I will. We're ready and waiting. Don't worry about us. I have this place covered. Tell Des I talked Amber into going below to the bunker. She's locked in safe and sound with his son."

He sighed. "Thank you. He was worried that she'd stay to fight in case there was danger."

"We came to an agreement."

"Thanks." Jazz sounded relieved. "I'll tell Des. It'll help him focus more. He's been going out of his mind. I love you, babe."

"I love you too, Jazz. Come home and mate me."

"It's a promise. I have to go."

"I'll be waiting." She hung up.

Shawna checked her weapons. She tested the volume on her radio and used it to check in with Noah, who was in charge of guarding the perimeter of the pack house. Next, she called out to the floors inside and made sure everyone was alert.

She sat down with the other three floaters and told them the sad truth.

"This is the hard part. The waiting."

JAZZ SHIFTED NEXT TO DESMON, SWITCHING TO SKIN AS THEY CAME back from scouting. He walked over to where the majority of the Nightwind fighters were stationed at the border. He eyed the Riley brothers and all the other men hiding in the woods, waiting. Some of them were in skin, others in fur, all of them ready, with a tense sort of excitement that hung heavy in the air.

Everyone was dead silent. They could all smell the Goodwin pack closing in around them. Jazz clearly heard them shuffling in the woods. They weren't even that good at keeping their steps silent.

So, screw it, Jazz didn't bother with keeping quiet, either.

He winked. "I hate these fuckers. Do they think they're sneaking up on us?"

Desmon gave him a dark smile, flashing sharp canine teeth. "They don't realize they're doing us a favor by keeping us together."

Jazz eyed the panthers already shifted. He couldn't help but be impressed by the three Riley brothers. Even Cord, the only wolf brother, was a big, mean-looking bastard in fur.

He spotted the panthers starting to move out. One of them scaled a nearby tree and disappeared like a ghost in the darkness.

He looked to Desmon in question.

Desmon lowered his voice. "They're going to stay hidden and hit from behind. They promised to stay together. They can use the trees to travel. I almost wish I could see the Goodwins' faces when those panthers come down on them."

Jazz grinned. "Me too."

"My mate is safe, right?" Desmon whispered. "I know it would break all kinds of laws for the Goodwins to attack our families, but—"

"Shawna will protect her." Jazz felt sure of it. "But let's get this over with and go home."

He heard a howl to the left, too close, and tensed in anticipation of the fight. "Game on."

Desmon growled. "Game on."

Jazz sniffed the air and saw the shadows moving between the trees. The Goodwin pack had arrived. It seemed like there should be more of them, but it was hard to judge when they all came out of the woods at once.

Before they could reach the clearing, one was grabbed mid-leap and thrown against a tree so hard, it likely killed him.

Then another met the same fate a blink of an eye later, causing others to scatter in fear.

Jazz caught only a flash of Miles in the darkness, eyes bright as he worked at creating confusion before their enemy could reach where the Nightwinds fighters were hiding.

He wasn't surprised it was Miles who'd decided to start the war.

Jazz stayed in alpha form, half-man, half wolf. He growled and slashed at the first furry body that made it past Miles's chaos. A scream of pain tore from the wolf that was sliced open and thrown aside.

Desmon growled and went for Leroy Goodwin, who was in alpha form as well. Jazz backed him up, staying close to Desmon. He was determined to keep the Goodwin wolves from blindsiding his friend while he fought the other alpha. Maybe Desmon would kill the bastard, and they'd be done with this territory war once and for all.

Screams of pain, snarls, and growls surrounded them.

The smell of blood and fear saturated the forest.

In the back of his mind, Jazz still thought there should be more of them.

18

The waiting didn't last long.

It felt like five hours, but according to Shawna's phone, which she was mindlessly thumbing through to keep herself distracted from the pounding fear, it took about ten minutes after she'd hung up with Jazz for things to go south.

"Fuck, Shawna," Patina hissed over the radio. Her voice was low, but she sounded terrified. "There's incoming on all sides. I don't think these are the Nightwind fighters."

Shawna was on her feet in an instant, grabbing her radio. "What do you see?"

"I see men coming up on all sides. I hear fighting farther out, where the patrols are, and now they're sneaking toward the house. Some are in fur but mostly they're in skin. They have guns. I see some rifles."

"And you're sure they aren't Nightwind wolves? We have a lot of guards out there," Shawna reminded her.

"No, I think they're Goodwin. They must've done something to our protectors. They definitely look like they're planning to attack."

"Hold on." Shawna switched channels and said, "Noah, come in. Noah?" Panicking a little, she yelled. "Noah!"

When she heard nothing, she took a deep breath, and looked at the other women in the room. She could tell they knew without Shawna telling them what was going to happen.

Rather than repeat herself twice, she turned back to the channel they used in the house and spoke into the radio.

"Okay, this is it. I think Patina is right. We're under attack. There's no response from Noah outside. That tells me to fear the worst. Everyone take calm, deep breaths. Only fire when you have a clean shot. Go for chest shots. That's the easiest target. We have limited silver bullets so make them count. When we run out, switch to traditional ammo, because it'll still slow them down. Remember to keep low to make yourself a harder target. Patina says they have guns. It's likely they're going to be firing back."

Shawna took the stairs two at a time. She was breathing heavily as she made it to the second floor. She ran to the window above the front door and peeked out. The sun was down, but there was great exterior lighting. She saw movement in several spots and pulled out one of her guns. She studied them, trying to make sure they weren't Nightwind, but she could tell these wolves closing in were on the offense.

She took calming breaths and gripped the radio in her left hand.

"They're close enough. We want them to stay back. Aim for any targets you can see and get ready. We're going to open fire at once. On my countdown." She took one more deep breath. "Three, two, one —FIRE!"

~

JAZZ EYED THE GROUND, SADNESS FILLING HIM. THEY'D LOST A FEW good men. He met Desmon's gaze fifteen feet away as they walked through the bodies lying on the ground. Desmon looked grim.

Leroy got away.

He fled when the panthers caught his attention.

Jazz couldn't blame the other alpha. After seeing the Riley brothers in action, he was nothing but grateful they were in Nightwind. An alpha wolf could hold their own if they stayed in alpha form, but regular werewolves were no match for a panther. They had to fight them in groups to even have a chance at winning, and when they were already fighting a war—panthers were a game changer.

"The doctor will be here soon," Desmon sighed. "Whoever can be saved, no matter whose pack, we'll help."

Jazz nodded. "I'm calling the house to let them know it's over and we've won."

He dialed. Shawna's phone rang and rang. It went to voice mail.

He frowned, hung up and dialed Tim's number.

The kid answered on the third ring, and Jazz barked at him, "Why the hell isn't Shawna answering her phone?"

"We're under attack!" Tim almost sobbed over the popping sound of gunfire. "Shawna ordered me below to guard the stairs to the bunker. All I can hear up there is gunfire. It sounds like the end of the world! They brought guns!"

"We're on our way," Jazz growled, turning to Desmon. "The house is under heavy attack and they're using weapons. *That's* why Goodwin ran!"

"Fuck!" Desmon roared. He threw back his head and howled out to all within hearing distance for help.

Jazz grabbed Jason. "Get someone to clean up this mess and meet us. We're going to the house. Find your clothes and your cell phone *now*. Keep it on!"

Jason wiped blood from his face, his eyes still dilated and wolflike. "My mate is at the pack house. I'm not staying here to clean up," he reminded him, his voice more wolf than human. "I'm right behind you."

The clearing filled with shifting men fast. Desmon was jerking on his clothes, which he had tied to a tree nearby. "They're attacking our families with guns! Dress and let's go!"

Jazz didn't bother looking for his clothes, he turned and sprinted for the road where they'd parked their cars. He knew Desmon and the other men were rushing behind him. He reached Desmon's truck first and jumped in the driver's seat. The keys were in the ignition.

Desmon jumped in the passenger side. Jazz already had his foot on the gas before Desmon could pull the door closed.

SHAWNA SQUEEZED OFF ANOTHER SHOT. SHE GRIPPED HER RADIO. "HOW is everyone?"

"It's Maria. We're holding them back from the house. Tina got hit, but it's just her shoulder."

"Ronda here," another female said. "We've cleared the back. We're good over here."

Janie didn't respond. Shawna waited a few seconds. "Janie?"

Silence.

"Shit." Shawna pushed down on the button again. "Patina?"

"Here," a soft voice whispered.

"Cover the front. Do you have ammo?"

"Barely."

"Katie? Get her ammo."

"On it," Katie panted into the radio. "I'm coming, Patina. Meet me on the upstairs balcony facing the front yard."

Shawna rushed for the stairs and gripped the banister. She hooked her leg over it and went sliding down. She passed Katie rushing up the stairs with a bag full of magazines for Patina's handgun.

Shawna hit the landing hard on her feet and stumbled a little. She ran toward the game room, where Janie had been stationed to guard that side of the house, staying alert as she ran.

She heard glass breaking and growls. She pressed down on her radio. "Intruders on the north side, first floor. They've breached the house."

"I talked to Jazz. They're on their way here," Tim's shouted into the radio. "I'm coming up!"

"Hold the stairs," Shawna snarled at him. "Don't move. Protect the mates and cubs, Tim!"

Shawna shoved the radio down the front of her vest and grabbed a second gun. She slowed, hearing the sound of wood breaking and then a whimper. *Fuck*, she swore internally.

She reached the game room and saw that a window was broken out. Two men—one in skin, one in fur—were standing over Janie's form, sprawled on the floor. Shawna saw blood on the floor and on Janie's clothes. She was alive but hurt badly from her brief glimpse.

The man in skin pulled back his foot to kick Janie in the ribs.

"Hey, assholes," Shawna yelled, drawing their attention. "Leave her alone. If you want to play with someone, I'm game."

She aimed at the man and opened fire.

The man went down but the wolf was too quick, ducking behind the pool table. Another man jumped through the broken glass. Shawna saw the gun gripped in his hands and emptied both mags into him. He fell with a groan.

The wolf came at her. Shawna dropped the empty guns, no time to reload. She went for the gun at her ankle but her peripheral told her she wouldn't be able to retrieve it in time to shoot. The wolf was in the air already.

She twisted hard, gripping the knife strapped to her thigh as she yanked the gun free. Something heavy and hairy hit her back. The impact was enough steal the air from her lungs and she felt the gun slip from her fingers.

The wolf's sharp jaws and teeth barely missed her. She stabbed out blindly with the knife she'd managed to keep hold of, going on instinct as she was knocked down.

The wolf hit the floor beside her. Shawna landed on her back after rolling and brought her booted feet up to her chest. The wolf lunged as she kicked out hard.

Her feet made contact with his face and it knocked him back. The werewolf had to weigh two hundred pounds in fur. He shook his head, ears up, and snarled. She saw sharp, vicious teeth and instinctively gripped the knife. If he landed on her when she was flat, she was done for.

Another wolf jumped through the window. Shawna backed up, crawling away from the snarling wolf by her feet. She briefly glanced at the newcomer, hoping he was part of the rescue crew.

He snarled at her, his mouth opening.

Clearly the new werewolf wasn't a Nightwind pack member.

Shawna knew she could be dead in mere moments. She frantically glanced around for the gun she'd lost but didn't spot it immediately. The newcomer lunged for her, launching himself at her chest.

Shawna cursed and rolled under a table. The wolf hit the table instead of her. She crawled out and found herself literally cornered. She was sitting on her ass with one knife and with two wolves snarling at her. They were just feet away.

She swallowed hard.

"Nice wolves." She smiled at them. "Inhale, boys. Instead of tearing out my throat, wouldn't you rather change? I'm ovulating. Don't I smell good?" She inched her way more into the corner and pressed her back to the wall. "I'm not mated."

Shawna saw and heard them sniffing the air.

"I'll do whatever you want. I just want to live," she said softly. "I'm going to stand up and strip. I won't fight," she lied. "We can have a good time."

Stalling for time, she used the wall and her feet to push herself upright. She really wanted them to change back to skin. As wolves, they'd just tear her apart in seconds. She had a chance if they were in their human forms.

Shawna reached for her chest slowly. They weren't attacking. That was good, at least. She slowly removed her coat, still buying time, and then worked on the bulletproof vest. She let it and the radio fall away from her to the side.

Please let Jazz and Des get here soon!

She tore open her shirt so they could see her breasts straining in her push-up bra. She unbuttoned her jeans and slid the zipper down slowly.

One of the wolves started to change. She looked to the other. He sniffed again and started to change as well.

She took a deep breath. Her hand slipped inside her jeans to her hip, and she gripped the second knife hiding there. The first werewolf was totally naked and in his human form, with shaggy brown hair and a hard-on. He growled and tried to grab her.

Shawna yanked out the knife and shoved it hard into his chest. Fear made her adrenaline surge, and with it, her strength. The knife embedded deep.

The man gasped in shock and stumbled back. He gripped the handle of the knife with both hands and yanked it free. He cursed loud and long, lowering his head to stare at the blood running down his chest.

The second wolf, now changed to a dirty-blond, seemed younger, maybe his mid-twenties, but it was hard to guess. He was aroused too...but was staring in shock at Shawna. When he spoke, his voice low and inhuman. "This is the were-hunter."

Shit.

Shawna knew she was in trouble. The knife had missed his heart.

He lunged, and she had nowhere to go. The bleeding werewolf grabbed her by the front of her jeans and shoulder. His grip was brutal, and she screamed when he threw her against the wall. She landed hard, and the pain was instant. She groaned and forced herself to move, even though her body was telling her to just lie there and hurt.

"You fucking bitch," she heard one of them snarl.

"On the pool table," the other added.

Shawna was able to crawl about three feet before a hand gripped her hair and an arm went around her waist. She was pulled from her knees and forced into the air. Her back hit a bared and bloody chest. He was storming to the pool table, with Shawna crushed against him. She felt the hot wetness of his blood soaking through her shirt and touching her back.

She kicked and clawed, but she couldn't pry the steel grip of his arm away from her waist. He shoved her hard against the pool table. Pain shot through her hips as they slammed into the unforgiving wood. The man was heavy as he leaned into her, crushing her between two hard surfaces.

They were going to rape and then kill her, right in the Nightwinds game room, where she was sure Jazz had played plenty of pool games. Her open shirt was yanked off, leaving her in nothing but her bra and unbuttoned jeans.

She heard one of them gasp. "She's a pack whore."

They saw her scarred lower back. It was like her worst nightmare coming to life. She took a deep breath, trying not to feel the terror. *She needed to think.* She forced herself to ignore the pain of her hipbones being ground mercilessly into the wood of the pool table.

She saw some balls on the table, left there by the last player. She fisted one tight and punched upward and back over her shoulder, aiming for the man holding her down, scoring a direct hit to his nose. He screamed, stumbling back and grabbing his gushing nose.

"Feisty bitch," the other one growled. "I'm going to make you bleed."

He lunged at her, pushing her against the unforgiving wood again, and she used the second ball to smash the hand he'd put on the table to get his balance. He swore in rage and pain, jerking back enough to free her.

Shawna twisted, screamed, and clawed at his face. She felt her nails dig into skin, and he threw himself away from her, still cursing.

Shawna didn't think. She reacted. She yanked her legs up and stood on the pool table.

She pulled her jeans higher on her hips but couldn't fasten them. She didn't have time. Both men were bleeding, but they'd recovered enough to come at her. She turned to jump off the table.

Two more men were in the room who'd obviously just changed from fur to skin, since they were naked. They'd also come in the window. They snarled at her.

She was surrounded.

Shawna glanced around, feeling like a trapped animal, and spotted Janie, injured, bloody, but now on her feet by the door. Their gazes met. The males were so focused on Shawna, they didn't seem to see the other woman. Janie took a step forward.

She was planning on fighting to try to save her. Shawna knew Janie would die if she tried.

"Run!" she yelled.

Shawna wanted one of them to survive.

Janie turned and ran out of the room, obeying her acting bitch leader. Someone lunged and grabbed Shawna's booted ankle. She hissed out a curse as she fell. She slammed to her back on the pool table. Another man grabbed her arms, wrenching them above her head.

Howls tore through the night from outside. She heard glass breaking.

The weres tried to hold down her legs, but she kicked and fought with everything in her.

Fuck!

One of the men climbed up on the pool table. Shawna yanked one knee to her breast and kicked out at the son of a bitch. Her boot hit him in the throat. He went flying off the pool table, and then she heard him choking.

A second later, the blast of gunfire echoed in the room and the werewolf holding her arms stumbled back and grabbed his chest. Too desperate to survive, Shawna didn't look to see who was doing the shooting. She rolled and almost hit the floor.

More shots deafened her, and another of the werewolves growled with obvious injury, but then came the hallow click of a gun without bullets. Scared for her rescuer, Shawna turned just in time to see Janie run out of the room.

The wolf Janie shot gave chase, but Shawna couldn't save her.

She was against the wall now, with three very pissed-off werewolves who were naked and bleeding or in pain, both from the fight with her and the bullets Janie managed to fire into them. They obviously weren't silver because the injuries didn't seem to do much damage.

Desperate, Shawna grabbed a pool stick from where they were housed behind her. She used it like a baseball bat, and the three attackers jumped away from the handle as she swung hard. Their reflexes were amazing.

Shawna heard snarling from inside the house and all hell breaking loose, furniture and glass being broken. She felt tears threaten. Her women were being attacked, probably raped and killed. Rage poured through her.

"You picked the wrong bitch to fuck with," she snarled.

She knew they were probably expecting her to cower. Shawna attacked instead. She swung and hit one of them in the face. The stick broke on impact. Acting on pure reflex, she turned and used the broken pool stick like a stake, stabbing another attacker in the throat.

She used their momentary shock to her advantage and dove for her lost gun, which she finally spied out of the corner of her eye. She wrapped her fingers around the cool, comforting grip of her semi-automatic and rolled onto her back, opening fire.

She fired it over and over, screaming in rage.

Unlike Janie, Shawna had silver bullets.

She stared in surprise seconds later when at the *click, click, click,* announcing the empty magazine.

All three of them were down. One was moving. Two weren't. She got to her feet, buttoned her jeans, but ignored the fact that she'd lost her shirt. She grabbed her vest off the ground, desperate for the spare mags, and then found her other two empty guns. She replaced the magazines as she ran back down the hallway.

She needed to save her women.

Two wolves were fighting in the hallway. She didn't know which one to shoot because she wasn't familiar with the Nightwind women in fur form. They twisted, rolling together, their teeth locked on each other—and she was pissed to realize both were male, when their stomachs were revealed. Tim had disobeyed her order. *Damn.*

Both wolves were holding their own, so she edged around them and ran for the entryway—and froze.

Shock filled her when she saw Jazz and Desmon fighting by the stairs. They were in half form, and they were battling four wolves who were attempting to gang up on the alphas.

Desmon threw one away from him, and Shawna fired at the other werewolf who swiped at his head, when she was sure it was clear shot.

Then she shot a wolf in the ass who was fighting with Jazz, intent on helping her mate.

Jazz turned his blue gaze on her and lunged so fast, it was almost hard to see. His arm went around her and in the next instant, she found herself slammed into a corner under the stairs. Jazz released her and spun, his back to her.

Protecting her.

"Where the hell is your shirt?" he snarled viciously.

"They're all dead," she said quickly, knowing he was smelling the males who'd attacked her.

"Don't fucking move," he seethed.

She smiled. "I wouldn't dream of it, babe. I know you have me covered."

"If I had clothes on to give you, I'd *really* have you covered. We'll discuss this later," he said with an inhuman growl.

Shawna just breathed a sigh of relief. The calvary had arrived, and she was more than happy to let them finish the fight.

She shut her eyes and leaned against the wall. She was bone tired and every muscle in her body was screaming in pain after the battle she'd survived in the game room.

19

*I*t didn't take long for the fight to end. She heard Jazz curse softly and his voice was back to normal. It wasn't the harsh, raspy growl he had when he was half changed.

She opened her eyes.

Jazz was standing over her, butt-ass naked and furious. "Where's your shirt?"

She grinned. "I could ask you the same thing."

He lunged forward, almost crushing her against the wall with his body, and started to sniff her neck. Then he moved lower.

She grabbed his face with both hands, dropping her guns to do it. "I'm fine. They're dead. This is as stripped as they got me."

Jazz suddenly grabbed Shawna with shaking hands, sweeping her off her feet. "You're done fighting."

"Where are we going?" She pushed at his shoulder. "One of them was chasing Janie and she's hurt. She saved my life, Jazz."

"Forget Janie. Desmon killed the one chasing her, and she's a *wolf*. She's fine. She heals." Jazz's breathing was ragged as he stalked away, carrying her. "I need to wash their scents off you. I can't be around others with you smelling like that. Unmated and injured...you make me dangerous, Shawna. I want to kill any fucking male who sees you —even my own pack."

"Then let's go." She reached up and touched his face, even as he kicked open the front door and walked out into the open air. "I'm safe."

"No. I smell your blood." He stomped over to a truck she recognized as Desmon's. "I failed you."

"You didn't," she argued as he set her on her feet to pull open the passenger-side door. "You saved me. You saved all of us." She caressed his face once more, savoring the fact that they'd both survived the war. "You came back to me."

"Jazz!" Desmon called out from the porch. "Where are you going with her? Janie says Shawna was injured and I smell her blood. She needs the doctor."

"She's *my* mate! Not his! She belongs in my home!" Jazz roared back. "I'll care for her!"

"Or we could just, you know, treat her here—with the *doctor*—that we have for things like this." Desmon strolled out to where his truck was parked. "Jazz, you know you're not okay right now. It's a very bad idea to take her into your territory, alone, after you've been fighting a war. Your instincts are too close to the surface. Trust me on this."

"*She's mine!*" Jazz roared at Desmon so loudly, Shawna jumped.

"It's fine. I won't die. Let him calm down," she assured Desmon. "Take care of the others."

Desmon rounded on her. "He'll turn you, Shawna. He won't be able to help it. He'll mate you and turn you, and I know that's not the plan you had. You'll be stuck with those scars for the rest of your life."

Jazz growled, already half changed, and went after Desmon, who shifted and met his best friend in a vicious clash of claws and fur.

Shawna screamed, unable to believe what she was seeing.

She stepped away from the truck. It was too dangerous to get in the middle of a fight between two alphas. She looked frantically back toward the house.

Knowing what she had to do, she didn't hesitate before running back, hearing Jazz's howl behind her.

"Cord!" she shouted as took the porch steps two at a time.

Instead of Cord, two black panthers came running out before she could get to the door. She could never tell the panther Rileys apart in fur, but then Kade and Cage transformed, standing there naked. Shawna shouted, "Where's your brother? I need him to get rid of the scars right now!"

The twins frowned and glanced at the alphas still fighting in the front yard.

"Seriously? *Now*? Look at him. If you're really his mate, Jazz could kill Cord for hurting you. He isn't an alpha," Cage reminded her.

"No, she's right. It has to be now," Cord said as he reached the porch, the only one dressed, sporting a blue shirt and bloody jeans. "He's wolf. You know we have no patience. He won't be able to resist turning her after all this, especially since she's been attacked."

He met Shawna's gaze. "I can smell your blood, and I see the pain on your face. I know you're injured...but if you're up to it, I can do it."

"I'm up to it," Shawna promised, though her stomach jerked. Everything already hurt. She could barely breathe, not just from the fear, but from the broken ribs she was almost certain she'd earned during the battle. "Do it now before they kill each other out there. He'll hate himself if he seriously injures his best friend while he's out of his mind."

Cord reached out and grabbed her arm. "Keep Jazz out—no matter what."

"What?" one of the brothers choked, sounding very nervous about that assignment. "I thought we were trying to get the Nightwinds to *like* us."

Cord didn't answer, just pulled her inside, running past Jordon, who had somehow managed to get dressed as well. "Help the twins. They're outside."

In the distance, Shawna heard another terrifying howl, and it made a shiver go down her spine. She found an empty guest bathroom downstairs and pulled him inside. "Do it now, Cord. He can't wait!"

"You're really sure?" Cord jerked the door closed and locked it. "This is going to hurt like a bitch, Shawna. I'll have to cut deep."

"I'm sure. I love him more than anything. I can do this. I'll let him turn me right after. It'll heal fast, right?"

"Yeah." Cord nodded. "He's an alpha. His blood is extra powerful. You'll start healing almost instantly once you're changed."

She unbuttoned her jeans and pushed them down her hips, then she grabbed the sink for support. Somehow, bracing for the pain made it worse—but Cord struck fast.

Shawna didn't want to scream. She certainly didn't want to make Jazz more violent than he already was by hearing her—but the agony was white-hot. She couldn't help her cry of shock. Every muscle in her exhausted body tightened, making her hurt from head to toe.

"You have to be quiet!" Cord stopped. "We'll have Nigthwinds bursting in here from all over the place. I don't want to have to explain this, do you?"

Shawna was panting. Sweat coated her body. "I need something to bite down on. It's been a really fucking long day."

Cord pulled his shirt off, and Shawna spotted the blood on his hands that were half-transformed, his claws long and dangerous.

"This sucks." Cord's voice sounded more wolflike than human. "I really hate doing this."

"I know." Shawna nodded and took the shirt from him. "Do it as fast as you can."

Shawna stuffed the shirt in her mouth and buried her face against her arm. She grabbed the sink with her other hand, and still her entire body lurched when Cord sliced into her back again. She screamed, but it was muffled this time, and she ended up biting down on the shirt so hard, her jaw hurt.

Cord didn't let her down.

He was incredibly fast. Even if it felt like a thousand years while he ripped away the scars of her youth, cutting her deeper than Jazz's father had when he'd caused them.

The trauma of those memories rose, nearly choking her, and she was a shaking, sobbing mess by the time Cord stopped. She sank to the floor in front of him once it was over, hating the weakness, but she couldn't help it. She pulled the shirt out of her mouth and struggled to catch her breath past the pain.

"Come on." Cord swept her up from where she lay bleeding on the white tile. "You're gonna be fine, Shawna. You're strong."

He burst out of the bathroom, and Janie shouted, "What did you do to her?"

Cord didn't answer, he just ran back to the front door with Shawna in his arms. The night air slapped her in the face, cool on her sweat-drenched body, making Shawna realize she was still in a bra. Her jeans were soaked with blood, warm and sticky at the same time.

"It's done!" Cord shouted over the snarls and growls coming from the front yard. He dashed down the stairs with her. "I have to leave you, Shawna, but I know you'll be okay. It's obvious you're his real mate. He'll take care of you. Nature says so."

"I know he will too." Shawna was certain of it as Cord set her on her feet. Her legs were shaky, but she fought to remain standing. "Thank you."

"Next time I see you, you'll be the alpha bitch I always knew you were." He kissed the top of her head. "I have to run now—literally."

Then, Cord took off and ran full-out, disappearing in the darkness.

She turned around, shaking on her feet, noting it took all three massive black panthers and Desmon in alpha form to hold Jazz back.

As she watched, the three Rileys, still in fur, took off in the same direction as Cord, obviously intent on protecting their brother.

She turned back and saw Jazz roar as he broke away from Desmon's hold. He was so terrifying in alpha form, half man, half beast, covered in white-blond hair that was stained pink with blood. He ran on all fours as he came at her, too big to be a wolf, but definitely nothing like a man.

She should have been scared to death, but she sank to her knees instead, giving up on her old life with a surrendering sob of relief.

"*He's dead!* Cord Riley suffers before he dies!" Jazz growled in a completely inhuman voice as he came up to her. His teeth were long and deadly as he wrapped one strong arm around her and pulled her close to him in a projective gesture. "I smell your blood!" He sounded frantic. "Lots of it!"

Shawna just reached up and caressed his fur-covered face, loving him completely, even if he currently looked like something from a horror film. "Heal me first."

"I'll care for you." Jazz nodded, obviously completely lost to his wolf side. "And kill him after."

"Or not," Shawna suggested, and then grunted in pain when Jazz suddenly swept her up.

She wrapped her arms around his neck and curled into his furry body. Jazz took off running, but he held her so carefully, and everything hurt so badly, she would've barely noticed when they broke into the woods except for the darkness swallowing them completely.

She closed her eyes rather than trying to see. It was almost soothing the way he ran effortlessly through the pitch-black forest, obviously moving around fallen trees and large rocks.

Pain still radiated from her back, but she must have passed out, because the next thing she noticed was the warm, rough feel of Jazz licking her forehead. She blinked, trying and failing to see something, and then reached up, feeling a cut where he licked.

He was trying to heal her.

Jazz was breathing hard, but they were sitting now. He had her resting on his lap, and he seemed to be leaning against something. It was impossible to tell where they were when all she could see was darkness. She could hear the river, the gentle rush of it cutting through the forest, and knew it was close.

It was so pitch black to her human eyes, she jerked when Jazz suddenly held his wrist up to her mouth. The blood ran over her lips and down her chest, making her cough in shock.

"Drink," Jazz growled. "You're safe now."

Knowing how healing shifter blood was, and desperate for strength, Shawna grabbed his wrist and drank, ignoring the urge to gag on the warm, coopery liquid as she swallowed.

After a second, she pulled back, but he growled, "More."

She wanted to argue, but she knew it took a lot of shifter blood to actually change a human permanently. She squeezed her eyes shut and pulled his wrist back to her mouth, drinking again, swallowing mouthfuls of blood until her stomach started to churn with the effort.

She reminded herself why she was doing it, to finally be with Jazz, to be a true mate to him like she'd dreamed of so long ago, but it became too much.

Shawna thought she was going to be sick, and she turned away from him, coughing and gagging on the blood.

An electric pulse of something seemed to tear up her spine, and it was so strong, it scared her.

"I'm dying," she gasped, still choking.

Jazz just caressed her shoulder and whispered, "I'm sorry."

His voice was still low with the wolf in him, but his hand felt smooth. She turned back, sucking in big gasps of air, and noticed that he was in skin again, still very naked and almost glowing in the darkness.

It took several long minutes before she could catch her breath, and she realized she wasn't actually dying—not really. Somewhere far away, she thought she heard Jazz coaching her to breathe, so that's what she did, taking in slower breaths of cool air until she felt calmer.

It took her a little longer to really notice she could see again.

She glanced back to Jazz, studying him. She blinked several times, trying to adjust, because he seemed too...*alive*...too sharply in focus. It looked very weird.

They were in a cave of some sort, though she noticed tree roots and what seemed like mud walls. She reached out, touching it, because everything seemed so vibrant. Even her sense of touch felt more sensitive as she trailed her fingers down the cold dirt-packed walls.

She turned toward the sound of the river and saw the bank wasn't from where they were hidden. "Where are we?"

"It's a den I carved on my land—*our land*," he corrected himself.

The heat came next, a warm rush of pleasure that spiraled through her body and pooled into her limbs. She felt herself get wet, and the ache between her legs hit so hard and fast, she gasped from the power of it and reached out to him, craving the safe feel of her mate.

Jazz held her, wrapping strong arms around Shawna and burying his face in the curve of her neck. He inhaled deeply with a low growl, but for a long time, he just held her while wave after wave of heat washed through her body, making her more and more restless.

The ache was almost unbearable.

Somewhere along the way, she forgot the pain of her wounds completely. It faded like it had never existed to begin with. She kept blinking, looking out toward the river, seeing it sparkle like a million diamonds under the shimmers of moonlight that made its way past the trees.

That's when she realized the darkness hadn't changed...she had.

Shawna had night-vision.

"I'm so hot," she whispered, rather than admit out loud she could see better now, in the pitch black, than she ever had in the daylight.

She hadn't realized werewolves could see this clearly at night.

It would've scared the hell out her as a hunter if she'd known that. Now she just stared in awe at the river, seeing it dance over the rocks, listening to every sound the bugs and animals made as they crawled in the trees and over the forest floor.

Jazz picked her up then, ducking low in the den, since it didn't allow him to stand at his full height. Once outside, he carried her to the river and stood her on the bank.

Shawna wasn't weak anymore, just burning up, aching as she unhooked her bra. She pulled at her jeans and kicked off her boots with little care for where they landed—because the smells hit her next.

The horrible, filthy scents sticking to her skin. Everything in her wanted to get them off. She remembered the werewolves who'd attacked her on the pool table and frantically ripped her jeans off her body in her need to be clean.

Once naked, she walked into the river, expecting the jolt of freezing-cold water, but she found it cooling and nice against her bare skin that was so hot, she felt like she was burning up from the inside out.

She waded out until she was nearly waist deep and then dropped to her knees, letting the river rush past her as she held her breath. It felt like she could hold it forever. She hardly felt the strain of it, and getting clean felt so incredibly good after the long battle.

She was suddenly choking on the shock of fresh air when Jazz pulled her out, forcing her back to her feet with a growl. "What are you doing?"

"I smell them," she gasped, forcing her soaking hair out of her face. "I'm trying to get them off me."

"You want their scent off?" Jazz pulled her close, his bare chest hot against hers. "I'll get them off you." He brushed the wet hair off her neck and dragged his tongue up the curve to her ear.

Shawna gasped out loud, because she'd never felt anything in her life as good as that.

"I'll make you forget, babe."

"Okay." She clung to him, tangling her fingers in his hair and holding him close as he licked and nipped at her sensitive skin. "Yes...that's so good. I like that."

Jazz pulled her tighter against him, sliding one hand lower to grab her ass. She could feel him hard against her stomach, and she reached down to wrap her hand around him, aching to feel the long, thick length of him inside her.

It was Shawna pulling *him* down, forcing him closer, until she stood on her toes and captured his lips with hers. The kiss was hot, wet, opened-mouthed and hungry as Jazz met her passion with each stroke of his tongue.

She clung to him tightly, her nails carving small half-moons into his shoulders as he walked back to the bank with her and lay Shawna on the wet sand. She should be freezing, but instead all she felt was Jazz, and the burning, pulsing need for him.

Shawna tangled her fingers in his wet hair as he kept licking and kissing her skin. He slowly moved down her neck to her breasts, sucking on her nipples that were tight and beaded from the cold.

She gasped with pleasure when he slipped his hand between her thighs. She arched into the feel of it, the need still hot and over-whelming as she wrapped her legs around him.

He moved down, spreading her wide to the warm, wet feel of his mouth. His licked her, sliding his tongue upwards with a low growl. She moaned as he closed his lips over her clit. He sucked, his tongue circled, making her moan louder. The man didn't mess around. He went right for the spot that made her body clench hard with desire.

Other low growls filled the air, and Shawna realized they were coming from her too. She clawed at his back with her fingernails, and bucked her hips against his mouth and tongue. Jazz just sucked harder, making sure she couldn't break free from the beautiful torture he was inflicting on her.

She was going to come.

Her entire body tensed, and she threw her head back.

Jazz's mouth suddenly released her.

She cursed, her eyes flying open. She stared down at him as he moved from between her thighs.

"Where are you going?" She shifted under him impatiently. "Why did you stop?"

He crawled over her, his skin so very warm and wet against hers. "I want you to come with me, and I want my teeth locked into you when we both do it. I want to mate you now, Shawna. It's been too long."

She moaned as his fingers brushed against her. She opened wider to give him full access, and Jazz slipped one thick digit inside.

"You're so damn tasty, babe. So damn hot and wet. All mine. I love when I slide into you. It's like coming home, Shawna. I'm going to love you until the day we die. Even after, I'll love you."

She moaned and pushed her hips up against his probing finger. He withdrew it, and she protested with a whimper. She hurt, ached for him to be inside her, and she couldn't stop moving under him.

Jazz gripped her hip with one hand while he used the other to rub his hard erection against her. She bucked her hips, rolling them, desperate to feel him.

He didn't disappoint. He slid into her, and Shawna felt the thickness of him fighting its way in, stretching her, making the pleasure ripple through her entire being. She threw back her head and cried out loudly.

Jazz froze. "Am I hurting you?"

"No!" she panted. "Faster...again...don't stop."

He snarled, tightened his hold on her, and started to drive in and out, burrowing deeper into her body with every fast thrust. He kept her hips locked in place, totally in control, and picked up the pace when he was as deep inside her as he could get. He moved faster, harder, and Shawna panted, moaned, and whimpered his name in a chant.

Jazz started to jackhammer his hips against her, moving so fast that Shawna couldn't tell if the overriding feeling was pain or pleasure.

It felt so damn good, she didn't give a damn.

She was right there, about to fall over the edge, when Jazz's teeth sank into her shoulder.

She cried out and came hard. Her entire body tensed. Her muscles gripped Jazz's cock, squeezing a snarl from him as he fought those muscles to continue to pound into her. He groaned loudly against her skin where his teeth were imbedded, and then she felt him shooting hot and deep inside her as he came. His hips jerked over and over as he emptied his sperm into her one spurt at a time.

She didn't notice her teeth had grown long until she was biting into his shoulder, tasting him, enjoying the spicy flavor of his blood against her tongue in way she hadn't before. The pleasure was everywhere, hazing the whole experience as she bonded to the man she waited so long for.

Jazz was breathing hard. His teeth in her shoulder started to ache after a few minutes of them recovering from their climaxes. Jazz was still hard, and he started to lazily thrust into her again.

Shawna moaned when she finally released her hold on him.

Jazz slowly slid his hands up her body. He cupped her breasts, teasing her nipples with his fingers, fingernails, and thumbs. Shawna went wild and started to shove her hips back at him as he slid in and out of her slowly.

"You're killing me, damn it," she moaned. "Faster, babe. God, it feels so good when you pound into me."

Jazz didn't need any more encouragement. He moved fast and deep, his hips slamming into her over and over. The desire bloomed again that easily, and the pleasure was even more potent. Shawna and Jazz were moaning, panting, until Shawna screamed out Jazz's name and came so hard the second time, she nearly blacked out.

She felt Jazz carefully withdraw his teeth from her skin. He licked the small wound, taking his time. Their breathing slowed as the minutes passed, and he withdrew from her body.

Shawna shivered. "That feels good too, when you lick my wounds. I wish I could kiss you, but you have sharp teeth, Mr. Wolf."

He chuckled. "I'm so not done with you. I want you to drink more. I want you to be strong, Shawna. My life to yours. My heart to yours."

He bit into the flesh between his wrist and elbow.

Shawna was shaking as she gripped his arm. She locked gazes with Jazz as she pulled his bleeding arm to her lips. The taste of Jazz's blood filled her mouth, no longer unpleasant but compelling and powerful. She moaned softly, sucking on his arm.

"Okay, babe," Jazz whispered. "I think it's enough."

She didn't want to stop, but he forced his arm away from her sucking mouth and she had to let him go. She ran her tongue over her lips, showing off long teeth that grew again without her permission.

Jazz softly growled. "God, you turn me on."

"I feel so much." She pushed at his shoulder until he rolled onto his back, taking her with him until she straddled her mate, just the way she wanted. "God, Jazz."

She moved her hips, feeling him thickening and swelling against her stomach once more. "I think it took," she admitted in a rasped whisper. "I feel stronger."

"It did. I can smell you." Jazz's voice was a low growl of desire. "Your eyes." He groaned and shifted his hips, moving until the long, thick length of him was pushing inside her one more. "You're wolf now. You're safe."

Shawna threw her head back when he entered her again. The pleasure was almost too much, but she couldn't help moving her hips until she was sliding down, taking all of him, savoring the rippling bliss.

She rode him until they were both breathless and gasping from the extasy. She bit him again when she came, shaking as pulse after pulse washed over her, until she was forced to let him go.

She collapsed over him in a sweaty, wet mess of exhaustion, lay her head on his chest and shut her eyes. She knew she was stronger than she had ever been, but all of a sudden, Shawna felt the full force of not only the change her body was going through, but the weariness caused by the long battle before.

She drifted to sleep almost immediately.

20

A few years ago, after a terrible battle, Desmon bonded with Amber high in the mountains on the edge of Nightwind pack land. Her journey from human to werewolf was brutal and traumatic, and hearing about it had always scared Jazz to death.

Though Desmon assured him after the first shock of the change, their bonding had been more than wonderful, the initial loss of humanity had been hard on Amber. During a battle, while injured, was never the best time to change a human, but sometimes circumstance demanded it.

It ended well, but Desmon and Amber suffered for it.

Maybe the powers that be felt Jazz and Shawna had suffered enough.

Her change was much easier than it should've been.

After she passed out on top of him at the edge of the river, he carried her back to their den. He had a bag of supplies hidden for emergencies and laid out a blanket for her comfort, even though he knew, as a werewolf now, she could sleep happily in the dirt if she had to. She never once stirred, the change and the fight before it putting her into a deep sleep while she fully healed from whatever injuries she'd sustained.

He tried not to think too hard about it.

She was wolf now.

She would heal.

He just curled around her, using his bigger body to keep her warm, and fell asleep with her. They slept for a long time, well into the late afternoon hours, since he needed healing too. The fight with the panthers and Desmon after Cord had taken her into the house had stolen a lot of his strength.

So did changing Shawna.

And bonding with her.

When he did wake, it was from the sound of footsteps too close to their den. He turned with a low growl, finding himself in wolf form, which was common when he was sleeping outdoors. Even if he didn't mean to do it, sometimes it just happened.

That's when he noticed the small brown wolf curled into him, looking safe and warm. He rested his head back on top of hers and would've been content to lie there like that all day, if another step in the woods hadn't alerted him.

Jazz heard a twig break and growled once more, showing his teeth as he very carefully got up without waking his mate. He quietly walked to the edge of the den, letting out another low warning growl to the intruder.

His teeth were showing as he peeked his head out and looked toward the river, spying the large black wolf he smelled long before he saw him. Rather than walk closer, Desmon headed down river, moving slowly, his tail wagging.

Jazz just growled once more in annoyance.

He'd had no intention of leaving the toasty comfort of his den and his mate, but Desmon tilted his head, beckoning him. It was only the bone-deep loyalty to Nightwind that had Jazz reluctantly following his best friend down river.

He didn't go far.

There was no way he was leaving Shawna, so he changed right there, and asked impatiently, "What do you want?"

Desmon changed too, standing to ask, "How is she?"

"She's fine." Jazz grunted the words. "She's been sleeping for a long time."

"That's normal." Desmon nodded. "The scars—"

Jazz shook his head. "I don't know yet."

Desmon frowned.

"She's in fur, and I'd have to wake her to check out her back," Jazz admitted with a shrug.

"Oh, then she handled the change well." Desmon raised surprised eyebrows at that. "That's good."

"Yeah." Jazz smiled. "A cute little brown wolf. I can't wait to see if her bark is worse than her bite."

Desmon laughed. "With Shawna, I'm not so sure. I'm willing to bet her bite is pretty damn scary. She saved our asses last night."

Jazz's smile broadened. "Yeah, she did."

"She saved everyone. All the women and cubs lived. Every single one." Desmon let out a relieved sigh. "I owe her a huge debt of gratitude. My mate and son are safe because of her."

Jazz's chest swelled with pride. "I have a powerful mate."

"Yes, you do," Desmon agreed. "I just wanted you to know everyone is okay. Enjoy your honeymoon. The pack knows you're officially off duty for the next week or so. Take your time. Help Shawna get used to her new life. I'm sure she'll take to it well. How was the change?"

"Easier than I thought it would be." Jazz ran a hand through his hair that was tangled from everything the night before. "How are the Rileys? I didn't mean to—"

"They understand." Desmon held up his hands. "Look at how insane I went before Amber was changed. It happens. She's yours now—forever. You're mated."

"Yes, I am." Jazz took a deep breath, savoring the knowledge. "It's really amazing. I never thought I'd get so lucky. It just sucks that everything had to go to shit with the Goodwins."

"Oh, that was the other thing I wanted to tell you. Remember when I invested in all that human security equipment after Amber was kidnapped?"

"Holy shit!" Jazz growled in surprise, having forgotten until right then. "All the cameras on the pack house. Do you have footage of the attack?"

"Yes, I do." Desmon gave him a wide, devious smile. "Miles already turned over copies to his buddies at the Alliance."

"The Goodwins are fucked!" Jazz practically shouted. He couldn't believe their good fortune. "When the Alliance sees them attacking our families with weapons—in the middle of pack land—they could actually put Leroy down for that."

"I don't know what's going to happen, but we're definitely in a good position." Desmon's excitement was palpable. "We could gain sanctuary status after this. The Rileys make it even easier. Miles says any pack who accepts outcasts, especially women and cubs, tends to get preferential treatment."

Jazz smiled. "Desmon, if we get that, we'll be untouchable. We'll have Alliance protection forever. All these territory wars could end."

"Our families would be safe." Desmon nodded. "We could raise our cubs in peace."

Jazz felt so incredibly proud. "And my mate is the reason this is happening."

"Yes, she is," Desmon agreed without hesitation. "As I said, we all owe her a tremendous debt of gratitude."

Jazz looked back to his den, needing to be near Shawna with every fiber of his being. "I have to go now."

"Okay, I understand." Desmon chuckled. "Go enjoy being mated."

Desmon shifted back to fur and took off toward the center of pack land. Jazz followed suit and walked back to his den—and his mate— finding her curled up right where he'd left her, an adorable brown wolf, with a red-tipped tail, he saw now, which was even more endearing.

Jazz was the happiest alpha wolf alive as he lay down, wrapping his bigger body around her small one. He rested his head on top of hers and immediately fell back to sleep.

SHAWNA HAD NEVER FELT SO COMFORTABLE.

Safe and warm, she wanted to stay asleep forever.

But her nose itched.

She reached up but ending jerking back at the harsh feeling of scratching herself way too hard. She blinked, trying to look at her hand, only she found a paw instead.

A slender brown paw.

She whipped her head around, seeing a huge white wolf sleeping next to her.

Shawna freaked.

She jumped up, and promptly tripped on her own feet and fell over.

"Hey, hey, hey," a calm voice called out. "Don't panic." A hand touched her neck, soothingly running down the length of it to her back. "You're okay."

She looked back, finding Jazz naked in skin as he reached out to her.

He was petting her!

She stumbled back again, nearly falling out of his den.

"Hey, it's me. Look at me. I'll teach how to do this," he coaxed. "Just breathe."

Shawna wasn't even sure she could manage that. Even breathing felt different, but she tried to follow his words as he kept telling her to stay calm. To breathe. She lay down and rested her head on her hands—paws—whatever.

"Imagine they're hands," he whispered in her ear, still stroking her fur. "Just close your eyes and envision resting your chin on your hands."

She closed her eyes and did what he said, but when she opened them, everything was the same. She was going to be in fur forever!

She whined and was about to jump up when Jazz crawled over her, still petting her, and buried his face in the curve of her neck, even though he was still in skin. This would probably look weird as hell to any random human who happened to walk by.

So much so, she couldn't help but point out, "You're a freak."

"Look at that," he whispered in amusement. "You did it."

She gasped, realizing she was lying naked on the dirt ground with Jazz draped over her. She was human again! *Thank God.* She did not like losing her voice in fur.

Being a wolf had downsides. All of Shawna's bones cracked just thinking about it—

"And there you go again," Jazz chuckled. "Good thing you're cute as a wolf."

Shawna flailed, struggling under Jazz when she realized she was a wolf again—that fast. She whined and barked, wanting to bitch him out as he laughed.

He petted her, whispering, "It's going to be okay, pretty girl."

That just made it worse.

She growled, and before she could think better of it, she turned around and bit him—hard.

"Oh—ow!" Jazz shouted and jerked his arm back, only she hadn't let go of him. "Fuck!"

Shawna tasted the spicy tang of Jazz's blood in her mouth, letting go to see that blood was seeping past his fingers where he held his wrist. When he pulled his hand away, it spurted everywhere, and she screamed.

"Oh my God, Jazz," she rasped, sitting up quickly. She held a hand to her mouth, only to pull back and stare at her fingers a second later, seeing his blood on them. She could still taste it on her tongue. "I hurt you!"

"You're fine," Jazz whispered, gripping his wrist tightly once more. "I'm the dumbass fucking with a scared wild wolf. I deserved to get bit."

"Are you okay?"

"I'm a werewolf, I'll heal," he reminded her, but then winced as he lifted his fingers to look at the wound. "Goddamn, babe. I guess we figured out what's worse, your bark or your bite. You got some power in that jaw of yours."

She was horrified. "I'm so sorry!"

"No, don't be sorry." He gave her a wide smile. "That's good. You're strong. That's what I want."

She just looked at him uncertainly while he sat there analyzing the wound. Then, he licked it himself. He flipped his arm over a second later and licked the top of it.

"This is the weirdest morning after I've ever had," she mumbled while Jazz sat there giving himself werewolf first-aid.

"I got news for you." Jazz licked his arm once more. "Look outside. You missed morning by a long shot."

Shawna glanced outside the den to the river, and blinked, seeing tiny twinkles of moonlight on the water. It seemed like there shouldn't be any light at all through the trees, yet there it was—she could see it.

"That's so weird. I'm not used to this wolf vision yet," she whispered. "What time is it?"

"About nine-thirty at night." Jazz didn't look at a watch, he just knew. "It's normal to sleep for a long time after the change."

"Oh." Shawna licked her lips and looked back at him, hoping she hadn't made a mistake. "What if I can't do this?"

"You're *already* doing it," he assured her. "It takes some new werewolves weeks to shift the first time. You did it in your sleep. That's awesome! And look at you holding form. Not many new shifters can do that the first day, either."

"Really?" she asked uncertainly.

"Yeah. It helps that you were already a tough bitch." He winked at her. "The alpha blood probably doesn't hurt either."

"Does having an alpha change me make me an alpha too?" she asked curiously.

"No, *you* make you an alpha. You were already one a long time before I changed you." He leaned in and pressed his lips against hers.

She cupped his face and kissed him with purpose, pushing her tongue past his lips with a low moan. Jazz let her, kissing her back with a passion that stole her breath.

They got lost in each other for a while before Shawna pulled back and whispered against his lips, "We're mated."

"I'm so happy." He tangled his fingers in her hair and kissed her again.

And again.

Shawna ended up on her back on a soft blanket Jazz must have laid out at some point after she fell asleep. He was draped over her, his warm, hard chest pressed against her bare breasts. It would've been easy to just give into the desire, but she did have questions.

She pushed at his shoulder until he stopped.

When he lifted his head to look down at her, Shawna asked, "What about everyone at the house? Have you heard anything?"

"Des came by earlier while you were sleeping." Jazz ran a hand through his hair and shook his head like he was trying to clear his thoughts. "Everyone at the house lived. He says he owes you a huge debt of gratitude. You kept everyone safe."

"It was a team effort. I can't believe how well all those women fought under pressure. You have a great pack, Jazz."

"*We* have a great pack," he corrected with a smile. "And guess what?"

"What?" she repeated as she smiled back at him, because his excitement was contagious.

"Des has security footage of the attack. He sent it to the Alliance. The Goodwins are fucked." He sounded positively thrilled. "And Miles thinks, with all the new outcast pack members you brought in, we have a chance at becoming a sanctuary pack."

She raised her eyebrows at him. "I remember Miles mentioning it, but what exactly does that mean for Nightwind?"

"Sanctuary packs have special protection. They're deemed safe places for vulnerable shifters and get all the backing of the Alliance because of it. Wolves don't fuck with sanctuary packs. The penalties are too severe, and they can request help from the Alliance whenever they need it. No one wants to risk a visit from an Alliance enforcer. All shifters are terrified of them."

Shawna was surprised. "I had no idea places like that existed."

"It's pretty new. It's the Alliance's way of modernizing wolves and getting rid of the old ways that were so harmful, especially to women and cubs."

That reminded Shawna, and she reached around to her lower back, feeling for her scars.

When she felt nothing but smooth skin, she jumped up and showed her back to Jazz and stared at him over her shoulder. "Did it work?"

"Yep." Jazz just nodded without looking, making it obvious he already knew. "Even if it hadn't, I would've protected you. There's a reason Miles thinks we can get sanctuary status. No one is getting attacked in Nightwind because of some scars—ever."

"But it *worked*?" Shawna felt her back again, unable to believe it. "They're gone. I'm safe!"

"Either way, you would've been safe," he reminded her again as he wrapped a hand around her and pulled Shawna close. He kissed her stomach reverently. "You have no idea the lengths I'll go to, babe, to make sure you're happy and protected. I love you so much."

"I love you too." She caressed his hair as he licked her hip bone. "You think it'll all work out?"

"I do." Jazz sounded certain as he kissed her other hip bone. He inhaled deeply and looked up at her with a dark, wolfish gaze. "And you're in heat."

She had forgotten about her ovulating. "What if you got me pregnant?"

"I could've," he admitted, but didn't seem upset about it. Still, he winced. "How do *you* feel about that? I wasn't thinking and—"

"I don't hate the idea," she interrupted him a with smile. "Maybe it's the wolf in me."

"It's definitely the wolf in you. It's the wolf in me too." He kissed her stomach one more time. "Des thinks we're going to finally have a safe place to raise our cubs. I do too, and I want them so badly. I want to raise a family with you, Shawna. I can't help it."

She fell to her knees and cupped his face with both hands. This was a blessing she never thought was possible. They were together, forever. She always wanted kids, but she never thought it would happen for her. Shawna's biological clock had been ticking for a while now.

"It's rash, but I want a family too. I really do."

"Okay." Jazz smiled once more and wagged his eyebrows. "Everyone knows we're on our mating honeymoon. We have a least a week, maybe more before they start looking for us. They know you need time to adjust to being a wolf. We could hang out here, practice shifting and see what happens."

She kissed him, still holding his face, and whispered against his lips, "Sounds like a plan to me.

∽

The saga continues.
Up next... Kade

ALSO BY THE AUTHORS

NIGHTWIND PACK

Claimed (Nightwind Pack Book 1)

Shattered (Nightwind Pack Book 2)

Cursed (Nightwind Pack Book 3)

MORE TITLES BY LAURAN DOHNER

NEW SPECIES

Fury (New Species Book 1)

Slade (New Species Book 2)

Valiant (New Species Book 3)

Justice (New Species Book 4)

Brawn (New Species Book 5)

Wrath (New Species Book 6)

Tiger (New Species Book 7)

Obsidian (New Species Book 8)

Shadow (New Species Book 9)

Moon (New Species Book 10)

True (New Species Book 11)

Darkness (New Species Book 12)

Smiley (New Species Book 13)

Numbers (New Species Book 14)

Best Friends (New Species Book 15)

CYBORG SEDUCTION

Burning Up Flint (Cyborg Seduction Book 1)

Kissing Steel (Cyborg Seduction Book 2)

Melting Iron (Cyborg Seduction Book 3)

Touching Ice (Cyborg Seduction Book 4)

Stealing Coal (Cyborg Seduction Book 5)

Redeeming Zorus (Cyborg Seduction Book 6)

Taunting Krell (Cyborg Seduction Book 7)

Haunting Blackie (Cyborg Seduction Book 8)

Loving Deviant (Cyborg Seduction Book 9)

Seducing Stag (Cyborg Seduction Book 10)

Falling for Sky (Cyborg Seduction Book 11)

VLG

Drantos (VLG Series Book 1)

Kraven (VLG Series Book 2)

Lorn (VLG Book 3)

Veso (VLG Series Book 4)

Lavos (VLG Series Book 5)

Wen (VLG Series Book 6)

Aveoth (VLG Series Book 7)

Creed (VLG Series Book 8)

Glacier (VLG Series Book 9)

Redson (VLG Series Book 10)

Trayis (VLG Series Book 11)

ZORN WORRIORS

Ral's Woman (Zorn Warriors Book 1)

Kidnapping Casey (Zorn Warriors Book 2)

Tempting Rever (Zorn Warriors Book 3)

Berrr's Vow (Zorn Warriors Book 4)

Coto's Captive (Zorn Warriors Book 5)

MATING HEAT

Mate Set (Mating Heat Book 1)

His Purrfect Mate (Mating Heat Book 2)

Mating Brand (Mating Heat Book 3)

RIDING THE RAINES

Propositioning Mr. Raine (Riding the Raines Book 1)

Raine on Me (Riding the Raines Book 2)

Claws And Fangs

MORE TITLES BY KELE MOON

BATTERED HEARTS Series M/F

Defying the Odds

Star Crossed

Crossing the Line

UNTAMED HEARTS Series M/F

The Viper

The Slayer

The Enforcer

EDEN Series

Beyond Eden M/M/F

Finding Eden M/M

Claiming Eden M/M

STANDALONE NOVELS
The Queens Consorts M/M/F
Starfish and Coffee M/M
Packing Heat M/M

SHORTS
A Kiss for Luck M/F
Mercy Bound M/F

ABOUT THE AUTHOR

LAURANN DOHNER

NY Times and USA Today Bestselling Author

I'm a full time wife, mother, and author. I've been lucky enough to have spent over two decades with the love of my life and look forward to many, many more years with Mr. Laurann. I'm addicted to iced coffee, the occasional candy bar (or two), and trying to get at least five hours of sleep at night.

I love to write all kinds of stories. I think the best part about writing is the fact that real life is always uncertain, always tossing things at us that we have no control over, but when writing you can make sure there's always a happy ending. I love that about being an author. My favorite part is when I sit down at my computer desk, put on my headphones to listen to loud music to block out everything around me, so I can create worlds in front of me.

http://www.lauranndohner.com

ABOUT THE AUTHOR

KELE MOON

A freckle faced, redhead born and raised in Hawaii, Kele Moon has always been a bit of a sore thumb and has come to enjoy the novelty of it. She thrives off pushing the envelope and finding ways to make the impossible work in her story telling. With a mad passion for romance, she adores the art of falling in love. The only rules she believes in is that, in love there are no rules and true love knows no bounds.

So obsessed is she with the beauty of romance and the novelty of creating it she's lost in her own wonder world most of the time. Thankfully she married her own dark, handsome, brooding hero who had infinite patience for her airy ways and attempts to keep her grounded. When she leaves her keys in the refrigerator or her cell phone in the oven he's usually there to save her from herself. The two of them now reside in Florida with their three beautiful children who make their lives both fun and challenging in equal parts–They wouldn't have it any other way.

http://www.kelemoon.com